MYSTICAL MAYHEM
BOOK I

DiVINATiON

LUNA EVERLY

For those of you who have a hard time putting into words what a certain tether, a certain connection is with someone—yet it feels like everything and nothing at the same time...

This one is for you.

You're not crazy.

... Or delulu.

"I was never really insane except upon occasions when my heart was touched."

— *Edgar Allan Poe*

TRIGGER WARNINGS

This book contains dark elements such as crime, violence, death, grief, abandonment, alcohol, blood, anxiety, assault, attempted murder, attempted rape, skeletons(animal), occult, use of divination, house fires, burning/burn injuries, knife and gun use, and explicit sexual content. Intended for those 18+

CELTIC CROSS
TAROT CARD SPREAD

1. Where you are right now
2. Potential/challenges
3. What to focus on
4. Your past
5. Your strengths
6. Near future

7. Suggested approach
8. What you need to know
9. Hopes and fears
10. Your potential future

SPIRITUAL LINGO

Clairaliance: the ability to smell a scent/source that holds a message or significance from the spiritual realm. It is usually associated with certain spirits. For example: tobacco, coffee, perfume/cologne, fabric softener, etc.

Clairaudience: the ability to hear messages, sounds, lyrics, songs, words, and/or messages from the spiritual realm. Examples would be spirit having a song repeat in your head that holds an important set of lyrics or a message. Full messages or phrases can also be heard, such as "You should leave."

Claircognizance: the ability to have this inner knowing or a "download" which holds a message from the spiritual realm. An example would be knowing a song is about to play on the radio and it does.

Clairsentience: the ability to feel a range of emotions, sensations, and/or physical touch from the spiritual realm. It is usually in the form of intuition or energy rather than a visual of the actual spirit. An example would be feeling your right shoulder tingle as if someone just placed their hand there. Or it can be feeling overwhelming anxiety that you know is not yours.

Clairvoyance: the ability to see symbols, pictures, words, numbers, and/or visions from the spiritual realm. The ability to predict future events. An example of this would be in your mind's eye, you see the same symbol of a dragon over and over again. It can also play out as a scene, such as in a movie.

Divination: the act of using tools and practices to seek information about the future or things unknown.

Examples:

• *Bibliomancy*: using quotes and passages from written work to receive messages.

• *Ceromancy/carromancy:* using a bowl of water to collect wax drippings in order see patterns, shapes, and symbols that can be interpreted as a message.

• *Necromancy:* contacting the dead through divination tools and rituals to seek guidance.

• *Palmistry:* reading the lines of one's palms to predict future outcomes, gain knowledge on one's past and current life, understand personality traits, relationships, career moves, etc.

• *Pendulum:* a weighted object–usually a crystal–that swings on a chain. It can indicate yes or no based on subconscious thought and/or energy. Spirit can channel through the user to give the answers they seek.

• *Pyromancy:* using a flame to receive and interpret messages from spirit.

• *Runes:* pieces of wood or crystals/stones with the runic alphabet on them. They provide messages when selected during a ritual/reading.

• *Shufflemancy:* shuffling music in order to receive a song with lyrics that hold a message from the spiritual realm.

• *Tarot:* a set of cards used to predict outcomes or the path of energy. Usually linked with intuition to guide the reading.

• *Tasseography:* using tea leaves, coffee grounds, or even wine sediments to seek out patterns and symbols in order to interpret messages from spirit.

N.B. There are many more tools for divination. These are just some of the main ones.

Medium: an individual possessing psychic and clairvoyant abilities who communicates with spirits beyond the veil or in the afterlife. They are the bridge between realms—the physical and spiritual. *It is important to note that mediums have clairvoyance, but not all those who have the ability of clairvoyance are mediums.

Natal charts: an astrological map that shows where all the stars and planets were at the exact moment you were born. It is a tool that helps facilitate a better understanding of personality, life paths, one's strengths and challenges, relationships, subconscious, and even karmic patterns, etc.

Past Life Regression: a therapeutic practice usually using hypnosis to access memories, experiences, emotions, and information from a previous incarnation.

CHAPTER I
SAILOR

Present

"Sailor, you have to get up. Sailor! Get the fuck up now. You have to move!" I hear Cameron grit out, desperation lacing his voice in pure agony.

But, where the hell is he?

*My eyes water and sting as I gasp, sucking in the smoke-laden air. I'm in my bedroom...I think...or...*whose *bedroom is this? My heart thunders under my ribcage as it becomes harder and harder to breathe. I clear my eyes with the knuckles of my index fingers and desperately scan the room.* Where are you, Cameron?

Black velvet furniture embellished in rich walnut wood surrounds the massive four-poster bed I am lying in. Beige satin sheets cool the skin of my exposed thighs as I disorientedly sit up. The soothing sensation is so at odds with the climbing temperature of the room. Scrambling to get to my feet, I stand, taking note that the rest of me is only covered by a barely-there lace nightgown.

What the hell? *I sleep in oversized t-shirts—that are usually* stained or decorated in holes. *What the* actual fuck *is going on here?*

A snap *then a* pop *snags my attention to the heavy floor-to-ceiling curtains—which are ablaze. All different shades of orange, red, and yellow lick up the material. Thick black smoke curls in ribbons around them as the ceiling begins to catch. The warm taupe paint easily ignites, followed by the paintings beside the window.*

Like dominoes, and within seconds, the beautiful artwork and tapestry diminish to nothing but char and ash under the force of the beautiful yet deadly element.

My eyes widen in horror as dense smoke and flame obscure my pathway to the door.

I'm trapped.

"You are the flames, Little Ember. They won't hurt you. Come to me," *a deep, gritty voice swirls around me, concealed within the smoke.*

"Don't listen to him, Sai. He's going to get you killed," *Cameron growls in my ear. I whip around in confusion, but entirely thankful Cameron is here. We will get out of this nightmare together.*

Except for one problem. He isn't here.

I inhale sharply through my nose before spinning around in a circle. Instant regret. *My throat and lungs scream from the heavy prickling sensation. Dropping to my knees, I sputter and cough.* That's what they say to do in a fire, right? *This horrific scenario was drilled into us since elementary school.*

Get low, Sailor.

So, I do. The heaviness in my chest only increases as the coughing attack continues, blurring my vision with a fresh wave of tears.

"Cameron!" I wail into the void.

My hands struggle to find their grip on the hardwood floors. The heat in this room is excruciating, the pure power of it singeing my back. I slide my hands down my nightgown in an attempt to wipe the moisture off and continue to crawl on hands and knees towards the door, hoping and praying Cameron is smart enough to do the same. The other voice I heard earlier was probably just a hallucination.

Panic can do that to you. Make things appear that aren't really there. Or even real for that matter.

The bottom of the open door comes into view. Thank God! I am getting the hell out of here—wherever here may be. My pace quickens and my lungs scream out for fresh air. I'm so close.

A slight breeze from the doorway brushes a strand of the caramel highlights framing my face across my nose. I quickly tuck it behind my ear and drag myself closer to the door. Relief floods my veins at the sight of a potential exit from this chaos.

Until a pair of shiny dress shoes steps in front of my exit.

No. No. No. No.

A man in all black, like a dark angel, crouches down before me. The top two buttons of his collar are open, revealing smooth, warm bronze skin. A hint of a tattoo is visible at the crease between his collarbone and neck. Rolled-up black sleeves cuff his forearms at the elbow, which rest casually on his knees. Each inner wrist has ink etched into it, the black script nestled beautifully between highways of bluish veins and thick tendons.

The left: Life.

The right: Death.

Before I have a chance to question anything, or even connect those two words with Cameron's warning, his left hand reaches

3

out and clasps my chin between his thumb and index finger. Tears cascade down my face as my breathing becomes labored.

I'm going to pass out from smoke inhalation before I even make it out of here.

He tilts my head back, shifting his grip to cup my face instead. The pad of his thumb scores across my cheek, wiping away the tears and leaving a chill in its wake. My vision goes in and out, the edges pulsing with grey stars. The only thing anchoring me to this moment, to my consciousness, are the two bright green orbs piercing through the impending doom.

"I wouldn't normally object to seeing you on your knees for me, Little Ember. But right now? I need you to take my hand and walk through those flames with me." He points to the door behind him, which is now fully engulfed in them.

"Don't," Cameron warns, his voice barely a whisper.

The corner of Dark Angel's mouth curves into an amused smile. "He doesn't trust me when it comes to you. But you trust me, don't you, sweetheart?" He stretches out his hand in offering.

I scan the room, searching for Cameron one last time as my vision falters and nearly goes completely black. My hands and knees give out on me as I collapse to the floor in pure exhaustion. In a last-ditch effort, I reach for the man's hand. Fear is quickly replaced by a feeling of...peace? Am I dead?

"Sailor! Come on, get up, Sai," Cameron groans, feeling closer now than before.

But I still can't see him.

I can't see anything but the face of the dark angel. His jade eyes shimmer with what appears to be delight swirled with determination as he collects me in his arms. He pulls me in close and cradles me to his chest as if I were something precious to him.

4

Those intense eyes of his study me for a fleeting moment before he rises to stand to his full height. Damn, the man is tall. He must be over six feet. The heels of his dress shoes hammer against the floor perfectly in sync with my heartbeat as he carries me towards the door.

Towards the overwhelming heat.

It's almost unbearable as we make our approach, but his skin remains cool against mine as he continues towards the flames. Like ice to a sunburn, his body delivers a deliciously relieving chill down my spine. Dark Angel chuckles. I think? His chest vibrates against my shoulder.

The flames grow brighter and hotter as we reach the threshold. He couldn't possibly be thinking of walking through that? Right?

He takes a step forward and I gasp. Oh he is definitely walking through that.

One moment, we are approaching the door; the next, we are both surrounded by flames. They burn him. His clothes catch first, followed by his beautiful black hair. The radiant skin of his face starts to redden and blister, yet my clothes, my body, remain untouched.

"You are the flame, Little Ember. Remember that. That soul of yours is still just as stubborn, I see. Yet, it remains so beautiful, so powerful that even death couldn't take you from me. And even if it did, I would find you. I'll always find you, Sailor."

He places me down in the hallway, which is clear of the fire. Flames twirl and coil around his arms as his hand finds my face. How strange that it is still cold to the touch. As if the flames don't exist.

Yet, they do.

They continue to consume his body. Those striking green eyes on me the entire time...until his hand falls from my face and he perishes into nothing but a pile of ash at my feet.

"No!" I scream out as overwhelming grief settles over me.

CHAPTER 2

RIOT

Past

Sweat pools on my chest as I sit up and slide back, leaning my trembling body against the headboard. I blow out a shaky breath as the bedside lamp clicks on next to me. The back of my hand swipes across my forehead, collecting the moisture speckled across it while I attempt to catch my breath.

"Riot? Are you okay?" The blonde from last night inches closer to me, prompting me to retreat. Damp satin sheets squelch over my legs before my feet hit the floor. I quickly don the pair of boxers I dropped a few hours ago when I had her sprawled out across my bed.

"Fine," I clip, running a trembling hand through my soaked hair.

She raises a microbladed brow, clearly not convinced. The other follows shortly after in a gesture of surprise. "I didn't know you had a wrist tattoo...that's really hot."

I glance down at the life and death ambigram tattoo inked into my left wrist.

"It's new," I grunt while walking over to my bar cart and

pouring myself two fingers of bourbon. I toss it back, the burn in my chest a reminder of how it felt to be in that nightmare.

The recurring one.

With *her.*

And I'm not talking about the blonde in my bed.

Which is why I rarely have sleepovers—unlike my fraternity brothers. This place is practically a brothel by the end of the night.

Pivoting on my heel, I trudge towards my en suite. Being the president has its perks—a private bathroom being one of them. Danielle watches me, her tongue darting out over her lower lip as I pass by. *Ahh.* She thinks I am approaching her for round two... three, is it?

Whatever the fuck number.

At this rate, I really don't care. She simply needs to be out of my space and out of my fucking *bed*. My still trembling hands slide over my face as I mask an annoyed groan.

"I need you to go home, Danielle." I cross my arms over my chest. The annoying organ beneath my sternum begins to hammer like a drum. "I'll have one of the guys drive you. I'm sure someone is still up." My gaze drifts over to the digital alarm clock on my end table.

It's always around 3 AM when these nightmares occur.

And this one was particularly brutal. More so than normal.

She pouts as she slips back into her clothes. In an attempt not to be a total dick, I decide to walk her downstairs. I'll always ensure she gets home safely, but this rendezvous is officially *over*. Three times is beyond my limit when bedding the same woman. It's over the second they get too close or ask too much. I'm shocked I even let her stay this long.

Sadly for her, it appears Danielle's best-by date has just expired.

Nausea churns in my gut, and I feel physically ill. I can't shake that fucking nightmare or the woman in it. She still lingers heavily on my mind as I open the bedroom door. That haunted look on her face when I burned for her has set me on edge.

Danielle and I descend the grand staircase, my pace more hurried than hers. The original wooden banister is smooth against my palm as it winds into a spiral, leading us toward the foyer.

"Can I call you again? Tonight was fun...until it wasn't," Danielle sighs, swaying backward on her heels.

My feet grind into the staircase, and I stop abruptly.

Knowing exactly what needs to be done, I whip back around to face her and snap. "No. Like you said—it was fun. *Until it wasn't.*" Her blue eyes widen a fraction at the ice in my tone.

My shoulders raise and I shrug impassively before turning back around to barrel my way down the stairs. Complete shock registers through me as I slam into another body.

Instinctually, my hands reach out to steady whoever just yelped, preventing them from falling down the remaining flight of stairs. As if working on their own accord, they wrap around the soft curve of a familiar waist. No, not just familiar...*an exact replica* of the woman who haunts my fucking dreams.

9

On a mutually sharp inhale, our eyes collide through the darkness of the foyer.

Two ardent doe eyes, like ramekins of crème brûlée, settle on mine. *They are beautiful.* Wildly unique. Warm vanilla honey with torched specks of sugar.

Stunning. Just like my dream.

Perhaps I'm still dreaming? No, but that can't be. I've only experienced nightmares when she graces them. *And right now?* This feels like *peace.* Definitely not the hell I endure during them.

"Oh my God! I'm so sorry," her sweet voice infiltrates my racing mind. Soft hands grip my forearms, attempting to balance our swaying bodies. Both of us are still reeling from the impact.

If she recognizes me, she doesn't show it. *How could she?* We've never met before. Cam rounds the staircase from the kitchen, placing a hand on her back. A blush creeps up her neck and stains her cheeks pink.

She likes him.

And that's a problem. Because I am finding it incredibly difficult to drag my eyes away from hers, trapped in the depths of their familiarity. I eventually turn to look at my fraternity brother Cameron, then over to his twin, who has now walked up to stand behind him. She's almost an exact replica of him, minus the more feminine and delicate features, of course.

"Sorry. The girls were just heading up to my room to sleep. They've had a little too much to drink," Cameron states, irritation lacing his tone.

Proving his point, Cameron's sister Olivia snorts before holding back a wave of giggles. And for some reason, that puts me on edge. Protective of the woman directly in front of me.

Although I trust the majority of my brothers who live here, not all are part of the *inner circle*. Any asshole can be wandering this house. Especially after a big party like the one we hosted tonight. We've been having them more often, trying to raise money for a club we are opening after I graduate at the end of this year.

"Are you sober?" I ask him, directing my attention back to getting Danielle the hell out of here.

"Yeah. Baby sis and her friend Sailor," he nods toward the woman I still have my hands on, "are visiting from New York and Maine. I wanted to make sure one of us stayed sober."

Sailor. Interesting name for a woman. I wonder why her parents chose that name? And why does it make my heart beat erratically when I say it in my mind? I'm wondering many things right about now, but voicing them would be crazy. Well, maybe not *too* crazy—we are close to The French Quarter after all...New Orleans being the heart of paranormal and mystical things alike.

Olivia smacks her brother on the back. "You are only older than me by two minutes and twenty seconds, Cam. Get over yourself," she huffs.

Sailor bites her lip, holding back a smirk. She glances up at me with curiosity before removing her grip on my arms, forcing me to do the same. I regretfully release her waist and sidestep her to whisper in my brother's ear.

"I'll get them settled in, if you drive Danielle home." The plea is clear in my voice, if not already written in bold letters across my face.

Cam must take pity on me. And I'm grateful for it. "Alright. Danielle, I'll drive you home. Girls, behave yourselves. Our president has offered to get you settled into my room. I'll be back in less than twenty minutes," he warns, extending his arm wide and showing Danielle the way.

Sailor's face falls at the mention of Cameron leaving. An uneasy feeling coils around my gut. The muscles of my forearm start to twitch. Suddenly, the need to reach out and touch her again becomes almost unbearable. I'd do almost anything to soothe the hurt swimming in her eyes.

Before I get the chance to, Sailor's face hardens. A mask slides into place and her bravado kicks in, yielding a strong defense.

"We don't need a babysitter, Cam," she retorts through clenched molars. "And I certainly know how to deal with a few drunk assholes. I'm a bartender. Or did you forget that?" she adds snarkily.

Ahh. This goes beyond *like.* She has a *crush.*

Danielle rises on her toes as she passes me and places a defeated kiss on my cheek. I almost forgot she was still here, completely ensnared by the *little ember* in front of me.

Eyes narrowed.

Teeth practically bared.

All it would take is a little prodding for her to ignite. For that anger simmering under the surface to explode.

And I'm kinda here for it...

Cam's face heats with silent rage, but he remains quiet, further pissing Sailor off. His face isn't the only one turning a shade of red. The apples of her cheeks stain pink. She scrunches her nose, and in the most bratty way, shoots him a dirty look. I hold back a laugh that has risen in the back of my throat.

Damn, she's fucking feisty.

My brother doesn't justify his actions with words, just ignores her completely, and jogs the remaining stairs to catch up with Danielle.

Again, a protectiveness stirs inside of me. This woman, who was somehow in my nightmare less than ten minutes ago, is now, by some miracle, in the flesh next to me. *How?* I have no clue. I need to speak with some of the locals I have become friendly with—they may have the answers.

Once the front door clicks closed, I turn on my heel to lead the ladies to Cameron's room...

Except, they are already gone.

M y knuckles connect with the wooden door three times. Giggles erupt from behind it, reminding me how young they still are.

"May I come in?" I ask through the door.

There is a brief moment of silence followed by a disgraceful attempt at whispered gossip before the door opens wide. Sailor stands at the threshold of the door. Hands cupped over her bare hips, that little crop top she's wearing barely covering her ivory curves. The thin material shows off the swell of her breasts, which rise upon each inhale to greet the low neckline. Those stunning eyes of hers linger on my chest—at eye level for her—before greeting mine once again. Her pupils dilate as she bites the inside of her cheek. *Did she just now recognize me... or am I reading too much into this?*

"Respectfully, *Mr. President*, we don't need a babysitter. As I *just* explained to Cameron...Liv and I are plastered and we are tired. You don't have to worry about us sneaking off and taking advantage of your boys or getting knocked up and derailing their beautiful futures. We just need a bed to sleep in." She fakes a yawn and leans against the door frame.

"That thought never even crossed my mind, sweetheart," I fire back.

Sassy little thing.

I'd kill to know what's going on in that pretty mind of hers. Curiosity has me lingering in her presence instead of heading off to bed. Which, when dealing with a woman with her temper, I normally would.

Mimicking her, I cross my arms over my chest and rest a shoulder against the molding we now share. Unable to help myself, I lower my head and lean in closer. This woman has me by the fucking balls, and she probably doesn't even know it. She would be the first one to ever do so. I inhale my frustration, and her sultry scent slaps me in the face. Heat radiates across my cheek as if I actually had been. So much so, I stagger back a step.

It's fucking potent.

And alluring.

And so *eerily* familiar.

Makes me want to run my nose along her collarbone and press my lips to the delicate skin under it. *Would her heart pump against it just as furiously as mine is right now?*

I release a silent breath as my mind scrambles to figure

out what her perfume consists of. Which is a poor attempt at trying to distract myself, while simultaneously trying to get my shit together, before I scare the girl. *She doesn't know you, asshole.*

Sailor absentmindedly twirls her hair around her finger, once again embracing me in her intoxicating scent. The notes are tropical, yet warm? I'm no perfume connoisseur, but my mom used to love it when my Dad and I gifted her a bottle for her birthday. Every year, I took pride in finding her the most unique ones—which makes me somewhat familiar.

Bergamot, patchouli, and some sort of flower you would find in a tropical place. It is unique, almost reminding me of incense.

I suppose it's fitting for an ethereal creature like herself. Everything about her is so damn hypnotizing. From those unique crème brûlée eyes to the pair of perfectly plump lips, to that attitude she uses to shield her vulnerability.

Perhaps Cameron isn't seeing her clearly, but I see right through that armor she wears like a second skin. A sigh rolls over my lips like some love-drunk fool. She notices, her eyes widening a fraction before settling on my lips.

Symmetrical caramel blonde strands frame her gorgeous face and stand out against the long waves of raven colored hair. The tips of my fingers burn with the desire to tuck them behind her ears. A precursor to tilting her head back and grazing my lips over hers. Permanently fixing that scowl she's wearing.

Sailor's eyes may hold a sadness that resides deep within, but her mouth...*Fuck,* that mouth vocalizes her strength. It is the weapon she wields to keep the fight in her going.

One that I will discover the heart of soon enough.

She leans into me, batting long eyelashes lightly coated in mascara. That might be the only makeup she has on. Her skin is flawless, the reason seeming to go far beyond her youth. Sailor's ivory skin is luminous, glowing like the flesh of an apple dipped in honey. And my God, I'd be lying if I said I wasn't curious how it would feel against my tongue.

Or how sweet she would taste if I got to explore right down to the core of her.

"There is *one* thing you could do for me," she whispers, interrupting my amorous thoughts.

I raise an intrigued eyebrow. "Do tell, *Little Ember.*"

The nickname I've given her in my dreams slides so easily off my tongue. *And damn if it doesn't suit her.* As if on cue, a flicker of fire dances behind her eyes. Maybe even a bit of recognition before they cool again.

"I forgot a sweatshirt. Normally, I run pretty warm. For some reason, I'm fucking freezing. Any chance I could borrow one?" *Odd. But I'll take the bait.*

"I'm sure Cameron has plenty in his drawers. I doubt he'd mind lending you one." I point to the dresser by the bed that Olivia is now passed out on, face-first in the down feather comforter.

"He would, actually," she states, pursing her lips briefly like she ate something sour.

I nod, backing away from her and breaking this spell she has me under. "I'm the room next door." I jab my thumb out to the right before heading that way. "I'll grab you one."

"Thank you," she whispers again, shooting me a dazzling smile that nearly has me tripping over my own feet.

Who the fuck am I becoming? This behavior is *not* me. Far from it. I'm the cold one, the calculated one. *Composed.* Some would even say ruthless when it comes to my objectives in life.

But not soft.

Definitely not fucking giddy. *If that's what this even is.*

I twist the handle of my bedroom door with a little more force than necessary, loosening the old doorknob and making it wobble. *Goddamnit.* I'll have to fix that later. Bolting over to my en suite, I push the tap to cold and splash my face. Water drips off my chin and into the sink as I hang my head and take a steadying breath.

"Wasn't expecting your room to be so cold and gothic. I took you for more of a warm and fuzzy kind of guy," *she* says dryly.

My head snaps up in amazement at the pure audacity she has walking into my personal space. Addictive eyes catch my gaze in the mirror, making the hair on the back of my neck stand up.

"I don't recall asking your opinion," I snide.

There he is. The beast. My natural behavior is coming back, and that sappy shit is swirling down the drain as we speak.

CHAPTER 3

SAILOR

Past

Okay. So his room is a touchy subject—that means he holds secrets. *Big ones,* if you ask me. Even though the man may be sexy as all sin, he is also Cameron's *president*. Which will make finding out what sort of illusion he has Cameron under even more dire.

Since the moment we arrived this evening, Cam has been on edge. Guess I can't really blame him... he and I are sort of a secret ourselves.

If you'd even call us *a thing*.

It's...really fucking complicated between us, okay? Let's just say we've been friends since we were kids, always dancing the stupid line of friends or more.

That all changed recently.

Ever since he joined the fraternity, he's completely cut off our line of communication. I only get updates from Liv. Which is why I was shocked when she invited me to visit him this weekend.

I *will* find out what is going on with him.

Starting with retrieving the sweatshirt I came here for.

My chin raises in defiance as I sniff the air, wanting to see just how far I can push the brooding man before me.

"Smells like sex in here...that blonde was pretty, no? Guess you're also the one-night stand kind of guy. The type that refuses to have any version of commitment because it might lead to all your secrets being exposed..." I taunt.

Angry feet slap against the bathroom tile as he barrels towards me, stopping an inch away. Adrenaline courses through my veins, causing my heart rate to spike. The abused organ flutters like a hummingbird's wings beneath my ribs. *God, this man is tall.* I crane my neck, my gaze climbing him like a tree as I drink him in.

Ladies and gents, it's perfectly okay to look and appreciate a dark angel such as the man all up in my personal space. A walking, talking *red flag*. However, we must manage to find the restraint not to touch. No matter how tempting they may be.

How could I? He can't be trusted.

Clearly, my body doesn't understand or agree with the concept, betraying that fact in an instant. I take an involuntary step into his space, getting real fucking personal.

Too personal.

He is the reason I can't have Cameron. Liv told me about one of the rules they agree to when joining the fraternity: NO RELATIONSHIPS.

Which is complete bullshit, by the way.

The 'Brotherhood' comes first, followed by perfect grades. And then—and *only then*—are they allowed to indulge from time to time in 'extracurricular activities'.

Sounds like a damn cult, if you ask me.

He leans over, leaving only inches between us. Eyes the

color of fresh moss lock in on mine, stopping my world from spinning on its axis. *This is too much.* Too intense. The subtle masculine scent of leather and wood dances with my senses and sends my stupid, irrational hormones into overdrive.

My heart stutters.

My palms grow clammy.

My lips part like they are running the fucking show, anxiously awaiting the moment they will be claimed by this beast. *Probably devoured.*

This man would eat me alive.

Darkness suddenly clouds my vision as more of his scent coils around me, practically suffocating me. His amused features come back into view as my head pops through the opening of his sweatshirt. My arms struggle to push through the sleeves as I am completely taken off guard.

"You can leave now." He twirls his index finger, indicating for me to turn around and walk right back out his door.

Asshole.

I stomp away, flipping him off and doing my best to ignore the heat running through my body.

Dangerous is what he is.

Cameron intercepts me in the hallway. His face has been nothing short of bored this entire night—*up until now.* Baby blue eyes drift over his friend's sweatshirt, which I am swimming in. They hungrily continue their descent down my exposed legs before climbing back up. His heated gaze lands on the hem that sits just above my knees, completely concealing my sleep shorts underneath.

"Why the hell are you wearing *Riot's* sweatshirt?" he

practically growls, tugging me forward by the strings of the hoodie.

Jealousy.

That was the *exact* emotion I was aiming for when I asked Mr. President–*Riot*–for his sweatshirt.

Raising my hands to his face, I run my fingertips over the blonde stubble at his chin. Cam's features soften a fraction, his eyes losing their ire.

"Where is the sweet boy I once fell for?"

Emotions I don't want to sort through right now clog my throat. I clear it as subtly as I can, spotting a quick look of sympathy from him.

He tugs my hand away but keeps it firmly within his grasp before wrapping his other around my waist. He pulls me closer until we are touching. Until there is barely enough space to slide a quarter between us. His forehead rests against mine and our noses touch. Our breathing becomes labored as we stand there in the empty hallway. The tension that's been built up between us coiled tight.

Years. It's been years of this song and dance.

And I'm fucking *done* with it.

I close the gap and kiss him. He groans painfully as if I were hurting him. Maybe he thinks this is a mistake. *That I'm a mistake.* Trembling hands find my face, cupping my cheeks gently as his eyes meet mine. Indecision warring inside them.

"*Fuck*, Sailor." It takes all of two seconds for his self-control to snap like a rubber band.

With newfound confidence, his hands drop from my face to grip my ass as he lifts me off the ground.

Finally.

Fucking *finally*, this man is giving in to *us* again. My arms lift up to rest around his neck as he walks us into his bedroom. Dread fills me the second he spots his sister asleep on top of the comforter. He is going to put a stop to this.

To us.

Damnit, no.

The feeling is quickly replaced with shock as he shuffles us back out and towards another room across the hall. He releases his grip on my ass to open the door before walking us through and slamming it closed with his back. Muscular arms support my weight as he carries me over to the pool table and places me at the edge of it.

I'm tempted to keep my legs wrapped around him for as long as possible. Stupid doubt creeps its way into my mind. *Will he go back to ignoring me again after this?*

For the second time tonight, he shocks me. Acquisitive hands grip my thighs, spreading me wide and pulling me closer. My core heats at the feel of him, all hot and incredibly hard beneath his jeans. Pressing *exactly* where I need him to.

A moan leaves my mouth as he leans forward to claim my lips. When his hand slides into my hair, I arch my back, molding my body to the firm planes of his own.

"You're so fucking beautiful, Sai."

His hand drops to my chest, caressing each of my aching breasts through the thick material of Riot's sweatshirt. Cameron's eyes darken at the mention of his President's name in my mind.

"This sweatshirt needs to be gone. *Now.* You should have worn one of mine," he grunts as he struggles to peel the hoodie off me. Sparks of hope begin to surge through me.

Maybe I was wrong earlier...

I help as best I can in my drunken state. When I'm finally free of the material and Riot's obnoxious scent, I ceremoniously drop the garment to the floor. My crop top is next to go. Quickly followed by my sleep shorts. I'm left bare and spread out across the green felt of this pool table. The soft material tickles my back as the leather of the pocket bites into the back of my thighs.

Cam makes quick work of his clothes, stripping down until he, too, is bare. I bite my lip at how much more he's filled out since he's been away. Now that he doesn't have football dominating his existence, he must be hitting the gym with his buddies.

Or, *maybe*, he's just becoming more of a man and less of the boy I fell in love with.

Trepidation fills me, eating away at my desire.

Cam leans over and plucks a condom packet out of his jeans pocket. His front teeth tear it open, and he promptly rolls it on with expert finesse. That should disgust me, the thought of him doing this with other women. But my stupid, naive brain refuses to feel anything but excitement.

My heart, however... *let's not go there right now.*

I'll deal with the thousands of insecurities and questions I'm sure to have tomorrow. *Or... maybe never.* I'll just bottle them up and compartmentalize them like everything else in my life.

He runs his length up and down, collecting my arousal before easing the crown in. Cam pauses his entry, giving me a moment to adjust. *Or perhaps to reconsider.* The muscles in his arms tremble as they cage my head between them, on the cusp of using up the last of his restraint. He screws his eyes shut and inhales deeply, hiding those baby blue eyes from me.

"One night, Sai. That's all I can give you," he states ruefully.

The rejection stings. *How could it not?* A wave of tears threatens to fall. So I simply nod in response, too choked up to voice anything now.

Pressure consumes me as he slides all the way in, immediately setting a relentless pace. My walls clench around him as my thighs grip his waist. *Fuck.* This feeling is too damn good to worry about the what-ifs that tomorrow will bring.

I'm putty beneath him, melting into the table and coming undone as he hits that sweet spot.

"Christ, you feel amazing," he groans, pistoning his hips and sinking impossibly deeper. "I know I was your first... but am I still your last?" Blue eyes search mine, desperate for the answer.

"Yes. My body has only ever belonged to you," I pant through the euphoria that's threatening to expose the real me. The side that I've hidden so well–*even from him.*

Truth is, I have been in love with Cameron Eden for as long as I can remember. He was a constant in my life, always there for me, always looking out. And I was blessed to call him my best friend.

The day I truly fell was the day he let me cry my eyes out on his shoulder. The first time my dad left for a fishing trip and didn't come back the same night. He didn't call. Didn't text. Just never showed up. Apparently, deeming me old enough to take care of myself.

I was *eight.*

Cam sat with me, watched movies in my room, and

24

cuddled me to sleep when the bad dreams threatened to take hold of me. He woke me up with chocolate chip pancakes and orange juice when Dad still didn't come back the next morning and the anxiety crippled me, gripping me by the throat.

This man holding me close to him will never understand what his presence in my life has done for me. Or how much I appreciate him.

Warm lips claim mine in a possessive kiss before I explode. Stars ignite across my vision as I detonate around him. All my worries shatter right along with it. He follows right after, groaning his release. Before I even catch my breath, he places a gentle kiss on my neck, then slides out of me.

I wince. Tears sting the back of my eyes.

Emptiness is all I can register at the moment. *In more ways than one.* My vision blurs as salty tears distort it. Through the blur, I track his robotic movements as he removes the condom and ties it into a knot. A single tear slips down my cheek when he enters the Jack and Jill bathroom, wraps the latex in a tissue, then tosses it in the wastebasket.

Gone is the boy I love.

A fissure forms in my heart knowing I let this happen— *again.*

Cameron can't be mine.

And it's all because of that *asshole* down the hall.

"**G**ood Morning," Liv chirps as she hovers over me, throws the covers back, and extends a hand with two white pills.

I groan groggily and push her hand away. I am *so* not a morning person. And today, that statement is especially true.

"I need sleep, Liv." I cover my face with the pillow. Memories of last night come flooding back, filling my body with a mixture of anger tinged with a bit of regret.

Regret for allowing myself to mentally return to the same place I had been in all these years. Regret for coming here in the first place with fairytale-like hope that Prince Charming would recognize the princess was right in front of him the whole time and fall madly in love.

Yeah. What a joke.

The room spins as I sit up abruptly. Liv takes a step back, worry etching her beautiful face. Little does she know I fucked her brother last night—and also at a homecoming party during junior year of high school. In typical Cameron fashion, he'll go right back to ignoring me.

I hastily snatch the pills from her hand and toss them into my mouth. Then, like a savage, I swallow them down without water.

The room spins once again as I sway over to my suitcase on the floor in the corner. I shuffle around for an outfit and settle on black leggings and a vintage Spice Girls t-shirt. *Perfect.*

With impressive speed for being hungover and *mildly* pissed—okay, *moderately* pissed— I get dressed before shoving all the clothes surrounding my suitcase back into it and zipping it. My toothbrush sticks out of the front zipper, along with a travel-sized toothpaste. Grabbing both, I dart out of Cameron's room and head down the hall.

One room over.

I knock twice before twisting the knob. The door cracks open as the antique brass hits the hardwood floor with a *thud.*

Oops.

Sauntering in like I own the place, I bypass a bemused Riot. He's shirtless and leaning against his headboard, reading a book on past lives. *Interesting. I didn't take him for a spiritual person.*

There's a bouquet of pretty flowers on his end table. Uncalled-for jealousy sparks in my chest. *He's just a pretty face, Sailor.* Nothing to be jealous over. I bet he's trying to make amends with the blonde from last night. *Dude could have at least taken his date home.*

The heat of his gaze penetrates my back as I ignore him —*and the flowers*—and focus on brushing my teeth.

"There are three other bathrooms in this house," he barks, his voice closer than I was prepared for.

I tilt my head, finding him leaning against the threshold of the door with thick bronzed arms crossed over his chest. An intricate black dragon tattoo wraps around his entire right side. Its head and claws peak over his shoulder. The claws appear extremely realistic as they pierce into his flesh. What's even more striking are the green eyes of the beast. So similar to his own and peering straight into my soul the way he did last night.

The barbed tail of the terrifying creature snakes around his ribcage and curls up and over his collarbone to rest at his neck. Only now do I register that he isn't wearing anything other than black satin boxers—like he's some kind of royalty.

I peel my galvanized gaze away from him to finish the task at hand.

Brush teeth.

Leave on the next flight out.

Thank God I was approved for a credit card with a five-hundred-dollar limit *before* I left for this trip. I'm going to need it to switch my flight last minute.

"Don't worry, *Mr. President,* I'll be out of your hair in a few minutes. I'm going home," I garble, still violently brushing my teeth.

"Leaving so soon? I hear we have a birthday in the house. You're an Aries. Explains where all that fire comes from." The man smirks like he is enjoying himself, all traces of anger gone.

Smirks. What could he possibly be smirking about? I'm so not a morning person, and somehow, irritatingly so, *he is.*

Well, fuck him and his early bird catches the worm bullshit. He is the reason Cameron can't or won't commit.

I rinse my mouth and aggressively toss my travel toothbrush into the wastebasket.

"One, how do you know it's my birthday?" I jab my finger into the smooth bronze skin of his chest, which burns beneath my unusually frigid one. *I wonder if he has a fever? Maybe, I do.* "And two," I jab my finger again, noticing he flexed beneath it this time, "you can go fuck yourself. This little fraternity of yours is more like a cult. I want nothing to do with you or *him.*" I point to the wall that shares the space between Riot's room and Cam's.

For a brief second, his face falls in confusion. He reaches

for me before dropping his hand and regaining his dark, unbothered composure. A rock has more personality than him.

"Olivia mentioned it this morning when I got back from my run. She was asking where the nearest bakery was," he states matter-of-factly.

"Right. Well, as kind as that is of her—I need to leave." I stand my ground, digging my sandal into the hardwood and probably scuffing it with how much pressure I am applying.

"He didn't remember, did he?" he asks with a gentleness I was unprepared for. That carefully crafted mask of his slipping again.

And I guess my own, too.

"No. He didn't," I whisper dejectedly.

I'm not even sure why I admitted that to him. He's a goddamn dictator. What I really should be doing is giving him a piece of my mind. The speech I perfected and prepared to dish out last night. Which was right around the time Cameron had left me alone to get cleaned up in the bathroom of the rec room.

Anger and disappointment flood my system again, bringing with it a fresh wave of tears. I turn away, refusing to give this asshole any ounce of my embarrassment and pain. He's the reason it's about to erupt out of me like a volcano that has been lying dormant for years.

But...if I were to be completely honest—

I'm the *real* reason.

Because I gave my attention to a boy whom I thought deserved it.

"I'll drive you. Would that be alright?" he asks softly, resting a hand on my shoulder. His touch is gentle and warm, temporarily ridding the ice spreading through my veins.

And for a brief, *brief* moment... I don't hate him.

I just want to get the hell out of here.

I nod silently before returning to my room to retrieve my bag and say goodbye to Liv.

CHAPTER 4
SAILOR

Present

Chills zip through my body as I scramble to sit up in bed. *Breathe, Sailor.* It was just a nightmare. Scanning the room, I take a quick inventory of my quaint studio apartment. It's not on fire. Nor am I still in a delicate black nightgown.

My fingers tremble as I swipe at the moisture pooling under my eyes.

That dream felt so real. *He* felt so real.

Taking another soothing breath through my nose, I attempt to calm my racing heart. The emerald-eyed, dark angel in my dream is *not real*. He's just a drudged-up, twisted, conjuring of my fears and anxiety.

Mix in some melatonin supplements to help me sleep, a shit ton of caffeine that got me through packing and my last shift, and you have yourself some wild dreams.

I anxiously tap the screen of my iPhone as I unplug it from the charger on the floor next to my mattress. *3 AM.* I'll still have a few more hours of sleep if I go back to bed.

That's probably damn near impossible now.

The anxiety I've worked so hard at tucking away over the last eight years threatens to make a comeback. And over the slightest challenge, too. *Cough* My current life.

As it is, the morning will already be overwhelming. *To say the least.* Although most of my shit—not that there's much—is packed up in cardboard boxes by the door, I still have two flights of stairs to carry them down and a short walk to the parking lot behind the bar I used to work at. As of midnight, me and the rest of the staff were officially terminated. The bar and the apartment above it will no longer be owned by the same family. Which means I'm out of a place to live, too.

It's a shame, really. Portland, Maine, is a huge tourist destination. Especially in the summer. Most of the restaurants and bars have been passed down from generation to generation. Now suddenly, so many of them are being bought out by larger investors. New and trendy storefronts, restaurants, and bars will take the place of the once charming and nostalgic dives that frequented this place.

At the ripe age of 26, I can despondently say that I've lived here my entire life. With rarely having the money to venture outside of it, minus my visits to New York City to visit Liv, I have come to enjoy my favorite staples of my hometown.

Over the last few years, more and more shops and eateries have closed. Within weeks, a new modish one opened up in its place. The same thing happened to Frank and his wife, Cheryl, who owned the bar I had been employed at since I was eighteen—*The Rickety Fence.*

They tried, truly they did. But extending their happy hour and hosting paint nights only resulted in a few extra patrons. With new businesses opening up all around them, they just couldn't compete.

The nail in the coffin was when the nightclub *Mystical Mayhem* opened up on one of the wharfs in Old Port this past year. That was the moment Frank knew it was time to sell. There is a rumor that the exclusive nightclub has locations all over the United States. The most famous of them all can be found in New Orleans. I never bothered to look them up. What for?

So here we are. And with only a few thousand dollars in my pocket until I find another job. Thankfully, Genevieve, the sweet old lady who owned the house next door to my childhood home, offered up her home for me to stay in while between jobs.

She is what you would describe as the typical snowbird, often traveling to her Florida condo until the summer heat blazes here. The woman is a saint, always doing what she can for the community...*and me.* Genevieve always treated me like a daughter. I have such fond memories of spending time with her in her garden or cuddling up with her cat and a cup of tea she had made for us.

Yesterday, when she offered for me to stay at her home— with the stipulation that I watch the house, take care of her cat Elvis, and water the plants—I readily agreed.

I was getting far more out of this deal than she was.

And I think she knew that.

Tossing my hair into a bun and slapping on some face cream, I hastily make my way downstairs to Genevieve's kitchen. The electric kettle whistles, alerting me that it's time to feed Elvis. This has been our little routine for the last few weeks. While I enjoy a cup of tea and a good book before bed, Elvis enjoys his pricey, warmed-up dinner at my feet. The poor cat is blind and only has a few teeth left.

As strange as it may seem, I couldn't be more grateful for these moments.

They make this awful transition and chaotic life of mine a little less lonely. Of course, I have Liv to call when I need. But since graduating college, she's moved her entire life to New York and rented an apartment with her boyfriend, Ethan. He's been the center of her whole world, and I couldn't be more thrilled for her. When you think sappy rom com... yeah, that's them. That man makes her the happiest woman alive.

The pair met their freshman year at NYU and have been together ever since. Liv's an executive editor at a fancy publishing company, and Ethan works in finance. Don't even get me started on their apartment in Tribeca. It's freaking massive and newly renovated. I've been there a few times now. Yet, every time I visit, my jaw drops at the opulence of it all.

If anyone deserves it though, it's them. They frequently host charity balls and events to raise money for underprivileged youth. Recently, they organized an event to raise money for dog shelters that are in desperate need of resources. The turnout was incredible. So many sweet dogs went home to their 'furever' homes that day.

Including a poodle-mix named Chester.

The chaotic goofball of a dog really is Ethan and Liv's pride and joy. He even has his own Instagram @adventureswithchesternyc. The account has close to one million followers. Celebrity pup status, if you will. Verified blue check mark and all. Just the other day, they launched his own line of merch.

Which reminds me, my sweatshirt should be coming in the mail soon.

I get comfortable, leaning back into the soft leather recliner and bring the steaming mug to my lips. *Ahh.* There's just something about tea that relaxes you. I tug my sleeves down over my hands and snuggle into the only sweatshirt I have that's clean. The one I've been religiously wearing the last few days. Easily, it has become my new favorite. Not only is it extremely comfortable, but it smells good, too.

I'm not even sure where this one came from. To be honest, it's pretty plain. The buttery soft material is all black with the exception of an embroidered animal skull on the sleeve. Beside it is the letter R. *Thanks, R, for donating it!*

Most of my stuff is either from thrift stores or Goodwill. Over the years, I've grown close with some of the owners. They adore me and always keep unique and cool shit to the side for me, knowing my fashion choices aren't exactly traditional. On occasion, I'll get a surprise box from Liv with designer outfits she doesn't want anymore. My style is a weird little mix of vintage and high-end. Her most recent box will definitely get good use when I go for my job interviews.

A draft flutters in, and I shiver. Goosebumps spring up along my arms. No matter how hard I try, I can never get this damn chill out of me. I tug at the colorful crocheted blanket draped over the recliner and wrap it around me.

There. Now I'm a perfect little burrito all ready to read her book. Well... maybe *more like taco because my hands are still sticking out—but you get the picture.*

And to think as a teenager I ran hot all the time. If I could afford to visit a doctor, I would have my thyroid and hormones checked. According to *Doctor Google*, my thyroid levels can be off, my anxiety can be creating the issue, or I have some other autoimmune disease. There is even a slight chance it could be caused by a tumor in my brain—but I'd like to think that's not the case.

So... for the time being, until I get a job with benefits, I'll manage with tea, sweatshirts, and blankets. A large fireplace equipped with a mantle and grate catches my attention from across the room. Potted plants and pictures of places Genevieve's traveled to decorate it. Tall glass votives and pillared candles are scattered among them, further adding to the home's cozy charm.

If my nightmare didn't shake me up so bad the other night, I may have built a nice crackling fire. Maybe even lit some of those vanilla-scented candles.

Fire.

Slamming the lid back down on my nightmare, I take another sip of chamomile tea. My fingers flip through the pages of my current read before retrieving my bookmark. I'm about to dive back into an exciting world of dragons, fae, and werewolves, when Elvis scares the crap out of me. He bolts from the room, his nails scraping along the wooden floor as he goes.

What. The. Hell? I've never seen him so skittish before.

Glancing at the front door to confirm it's locked, and ignoring the uneasy feeling growing in my chest, I start to read the first few words of the chapter.

Elvis comes barreling back down the stairs. He knocks over a vase of fresh flowers Genevieve sent me yesterday and hides under the coffee table.

Shit. Hopefully, that vase wasn't an antique or family heirloom.

Placing my book and tea down on the snack tray, I get up to clean the mess. *We don't need his little paws getting cut up by glass.* My pulse skyrockets, and my skin prickles as I lean down to collect the larger pieces. I whip my body around, but it's too goddamn late.

James Michaels, Genevieve's estranged grandson, holds up a pocket knife to my throat. He looks just as I remember from our few interactions as kids. Half his face and the majority of his neck are left scarred from a terrible house fire at his family home. He lost everything that day.

His home.

His parents.

His self-esteem.

Genevieve was kind enough to take care of him for all those years. She flew him to the best plastic surgeons in the country. Got him the best therapists in the state.

It wasn't enough. Her love for him wasn't enough.

The day he turned sixteen, without any warning, he got emancipated. Just picked up and left. Never to be heard from or seen again—*I guess until now.*

"It just *had* to be you." He clucks his tongue in mock disappointment. "Poor *little* Sailor. Her mom died during childbirth, and her dad abandoned her because he couldn't stand looking at a murderer. At the spitting image of his wife. Well, what about me? My parents died, too. Yet Genevieve leaves her entire house and fortune to you in her will? I think not. You're not *special*, Sailor. No one will even fucking miss you."

"*Will*? Genevieve is dead?" I gape at him, horrified at the possibility.

"She is. I *killed* her," he states proudly with a manic look twinkling in his eyes. "Sweet, sweet Grandma passed away in her bed. Left a candle burning on her end table next to a bouquet of dried flowers... such a tragedy."

I don't even have time to register what he is saying before acting. *It's not like there is a goddamn pocket knife at my throat.* My leg whips out, kicking him straight in the balls. He roars out, dropping the knife. It skitters across the hardwoods and slips under the couch.

Fuck. MOVE, SAILOR.

Making a mad dash for the front door, I skid on the water and shattered glass from the smashed vase. The side of my head cracks against the ground, nearly knocking me unconscious. Stars dance across my vision, and my cheek grows a pulse of its own. I cry out, trying to catch my breath. But I don't have fucking time! I have to remain focused. If I don't get out of here, this man *will* kill me.

There is zero time to question how he may do it.

Blood gushes from the wounds on my hands, and I think there is a piece of glass wedged into my hip. I stumble trying to stand. *If I can just push through the pain, I can get out of here.* James doesn't give me that chance; he tackles me, crushing me beneath him and the shards of glass. His deeply scarred hands wrap around my throat. I scream. *Or try to.* Fear curls around my gut as he cuts off my air supply.

I am going to die if I don't do something.

Anything.

Licking his dry lips, he moans, "I like a fighter. Makes it even more pleasurable as I watch the light leave their eyes."

He rubs his groin against me before moving his hands to the collar of my sweatshirt and tearing it. Blinded by his disgusting moment of lust, I take the opportunity to grip a large shard of glass next to me and slam it into his abdomen. I was aiming for his dick, but it did the job. He falls back on impact, clutching his wound.

Without wasting time, I spring to my feet, grab my keys off the hook next to the door, and run as fast as I ever have in my life.

CHAPTER 5

RIOT

Present

White hot pain ignites in the back of my throat. I clutch it and cough, turning my cigar over in my hand to examine if any pieces have lodged off it.

Fuck. I can't breathe.

My brothers turn their masked faces to look at me, curious as to what's going on. I bring my rock glass filled with bourbon to my lips and take a hefty sip, hoping that will do the trick. When the pressure eases, I relax, knowing whatever it was just passed.

Christ. That would be a first.

Never in my 31 years of life have I choked on a piece of tobacco leaf while indulging in a quality cigar. Not that I was smoking them right out of the womb–*but you get my fucking point.* I spin the Churchill around in the glass ashtray, still not fully convinced that was the cause.

It's perfectly intact.

Pinching it between my thumb and index finger, I snub it out before pushing the ashtray away from me. Heat replaces the irritation still lingering in my throat as I take another sip of bourbon. Cam, my second, looks at me from behind his antelope mask. He tilts his head, and I nod my own, letting him know I'm alright and don't appear to be poisoned.

Because in my line of work, that is always a real possibility.

About twenty minutes later, we wrap up our meeting. This time, without any other interruptions on my end. My men finish off their drinks and whip out the poker set. The *clank* of chips hitting the table signals an end to the formality of tonight.

Our agenda for the month has been discussed in lengthy detail, and assignments have been handed out. Now it's time to relax. As long as they wear their masks in this room, anyone who wishes to stay can do so. For those who wish to enjoy the upstairs festivities, they may remove their cloaks and masks and take the elevator up.

Many of these men I know—I recruited them right out of college. For our other *exclusive* members—who take their privacy to the extreme—we have a private elevator next to the bookshelf in the back of this room that leads directly to a private section of the parking lot where they have a car waiting.

Anonymity is our number one rule.

Without it, we wouldn't be able to achieve what we do. All of my men are vital to the success of this organization. Each of them plays their role well.

As if I were possessed, my body jerks forward, slamming into the table. A searing pain like fire whips across my back and then hip. I rub at the sensitive flesh beneath my cloak, trying to ease the burn before leaning back in my chair at the head of the table.

What the fuck is happening to me tonight?

Realizing I can no longer focus on the poker game, I pull out my phone and start Googling my symptoms. I am halfway convinced I have come down with shingles when the hairs on the back of my neck stand up.

Cameron jumps out of his seat and rushes over to the black velvet curtains that keep this room private.

"Sai? What are you doing here? What the hell happened to you?" he asks, horrified.

"Cameron?" That sweet voice, the one I know so well, overrides the pain I was just in.

Except it quickly morphs into another type of pain having to hear her say his name like he's her savior.

Shock continues to pulse through me as I swivel around in my chair to see what has brought my *little ember* right to my front door. All it took was a quick inventory of her body to have me inhaling sharply.

Her goddamn cheek is bruised. All shades of purple and blue mottle it. And that's not the only place. Her neck has discoloration there, as well—as if someone wrapped their hands around the delicate column of it. My gaze drops lower to her hands that are dripping blood onto the floor.

With each drop of her blood that hits the black marble, my own pounds in my ears.

CHAPTER 6

SAILOR

The piece of glass that was lodged in my hip clatters across the parking lot pavement at *Mystical Mayhem*. Blood oozes from the wound, saturating my shirt. I stand shakily and take a few steps towards the entrance.

Somewhere in my adrenaline-hazed brain, I remembered Liv telling me something important. That if I were ever in trouble, to go to the club I am now standing in front of and demand to see *The Demons*. I thought it was a joke when she told me, but I guess my panicked brain felt it was worth a shot...*so... here we are.*

There is a line of college kids and a group of women who look like millennials waiting to get in. A black velvet rope keeps them in an organized line against the stone wall at the entrance. Candelabras with at least eight massive candles on each flicker above the bouncers' heads. I bypass the line, getting gawked at by a few guests as I pass.

Well, no shit. I look like hell.

"Miss, there is a strict dress code here and..." The bouncer with the knuckle tatts says robotically, clearly uncomfortable. His eyes trace my path here, noticing the trail of blood I left along the grey stones of the wharf. A strange look crosses his features. One that sends a shiver down my spine.

The same spine I straighten when I whisper, "I need to see *The Demons.*" I say it in the manner of telling a secret—it certainly feels like one.

His eyes widen for a second before he pats his peer on the back. "I'll be back. I'm taking her downstairs." The other male bouncer raises his eyebrows in concern before nodding and collecting an ID from a patron in front of him.

The bouncer takes me through the front door—*which is grand as fuck, by the way.* It's a massive structure made of a mixture of wood and wrought iron. Like something straight out of a Van Helsing movie. He has me following him, leading me into a dimly lit room. Candles and warm lighting give it the effect of a place of worship. The room is lightly saturated in smoke, and the air holds a scent of incense or woodiness. *Sandalwood, if I were to guess.*

A round bar that resembles the Sun and Moon kissing sits centrally. It's beautiful. *Unique.* A few people have gathered there, drinking out of antique-looking glasses. My panic starts to ease, replaced by a sense of belonging. The feeling is weird and manifests emotions I'm not really used to. A calmness rushes over me, plucking each strand of anxiety and letting it float away like a feather.

We continue on with him navigating us through a thick crowd of people dancing. Tantric and sexual, the music makes you feel like swaying your hips. A few guests are already tangled up, lost in the music and one another as they gaze into their partner's eyes. It's their version of unspoken communication.

All I can think about is how *beautiful* that is. To find someone who doesn't require words to understand your love language.

The bouncer pulls a black velvet curtain aside, and we step into a hallway lined with black doors on both sides. At the far end is an elevator. The wallpaper is earthy and moody, an evergreen color with delicate painted flowers. Antique sconces light up the hallway in an amber glow. Some of the doors are open, some closed. I take a closer look as we pass them by. Purple neon signs are posted above them describing the services provided.

One says, *Palm Readings.*

Another, *Tarot Readings.*

Reiki Healing.

Meditation Center.

Crystal Shop.

Past life regression.

Astrology & Birth Charts.

And lastly, *Psychic Medium, Vanessa Corbin.*

Her door is open as we pass, her head snapping up at our approach. Deep blue, almost purple eyes latch onto mine. For a second, I think I can hear her speaking to me, but her mouth isn't moving. "*Seek me out when you are ready to discover your truth... and* his."

I shake my head, causing my vision to blur momentarily. When I look back at her, she is writing in a journal at her desk, heeding me no mind.

Weird.

Maybe I have a concussion.

Red illuminates the ring around the elevator button. The bouncer casually laces his hands over his stomach as we wait. It doesn't take long for the elevator to arrive. We step inside and stand in silence as it descends a floor.

On a ding, the bell chimes and the doors open to reveal another candlelit room. Except this time, there is only a small table by the elevator and laundered robes inside a basket beneath it. Another remains empty beside it. I glance over at the intimidating man, wondering if he'll disclose anything. He doesn't even acknowledge me, just continues to walk past them.

His tattooed knuckles clench as he pulls back yet another velvet curtain. What waits beyond it appears to be some sort of gathering. My heart plummets into my stomach as my eyes land on each and every person in attendance. Every single one of them is wearing some sort of animal skull on their face. And from the looks of it, they have to be real.

Nausea coils in my stomach, and I feel like I'm going to be sick.

What the fuck is this place?

The men are clad in black cloaks, the kind a judge wears or a student would have on at graduation. Cigar smoke billows in the air and wafts up my nostrils as the curtain is pulled back further. They are joking with each other and playing poker. Some are sipping on dark amber drinks. Others are enjoying a beer or a martini. One man spots me first. His chair screeches back as he gets to his feet and jogs towards me.

"Sai? What are you doing here? What the hell happened to you?" a familiar voice asks, horror lacing it at what he sees. Baby blue eyes peer at me from the eye sockets of his mask.

"Cameron?" I sigh with so much relief when it should be the opposite. This is the same man who had gutted me and ripped my heart clean out of my chest nearly eight years ago. But I can't find it in me to be angry or upset with him right now. Old feelings of safety and comfort come to the forefront of my mind, taking me right back to when we were kids.

Another man, the one sitting at the head of the table, swivels his head towards me, clearly interested in our interaction. Rage burns in his eyes.

His *green eyes*.

Oh, fuck.

Now I really know I'm in Hell. Because *those* eyes, *his* eyes, have haunted every single one of my nightmares for the last few weeks.

He's out of his seat before I have the chance to blink. I'm so stupidly intoxicated by his intense gaze, I didn't even have the time to look away. I crane my neck to look up at him. His eyes narrow even further. Those emerald orbs land on my face, searching every inch before lowering to my neck. After a beat, they drop to my hands, which are dripping blood all over this fancy black marble floor.

Drip.

Drip.

Drip.

The skeletal remains of his mask end halfway down his face, leaving exposed a strong jawline peppered in dark stubble. Each sound of my blood splattering against the floor has him clenching it harder. The muscle there tics as he inhales a sharp breath.

"Who did this to you, *Little Ember*?" he growls through gritted teeth. "I want a *name*."

Did the ground just shake, or are my knees threatening to give out on me?

Cam catches me before they do, pulling me to his side and making me hiss in pain. There has to be more glass embedded in my back. Each of my movements feels like an electric shock. He gently tugs me out of the room and over to the elevator. There, he discards his cloak into the empty basket and places his mask on the table. Riot follows at our heels, doing the same.

"I've been staying at Genevieve Michaels' house for the last few weeks while she's in Florida," I start, not revealing every detail about how I ended up there. "Her grandson, James, must have broken in while I was reading in the living room and held a knife to my throat... He tried to... tried..." A sob erupts out of me at the vicious memories flooding back.

Cameron wraps a gentle arm around my shoulder as a shudder ripples through me. Riot just stands there with his fists clenched at his sides, his eyes darting all over my injuries again, like he can now piece the story together.

"Tried to or *did*?" he asks, barely containing the venom in his voice.

"Tried, but I kicked him in the balls and stabbed him with a broken shard of glass. He planned on killing me. *Apparently*, Genevieve left everything to me in her will and not him. He killed her, thinking he would be the one to claim it."

Another sob escapes me. I cover my mouth with my bloodied hand as Cameron pulls my head against his shoulder and uses his strong fingers to massage my scalp.

"Shh, Sai. We are going to take care of this. You're safe now," he soothes.

"James Michaels has been on my radar for some time now. Looks like he's finally come home. I'll handle this one, Cam," Riot announces.

"This was personal, Riot. I want to be the one to do it," Cam argues, shaking his head in disagreement.

I clutch his bicep. "No. Don't leave me, Cam. Let's just call the police. You can wait here with me," I plead.

Riot snorts across from me.

Red-hot anger builds in my veins. "Something funny?" I ask incredulously. "I was just *attacked*."

"Very much aware of that," he barks. "Take a look around, sweetheart." He extends his arm out wide, splaying his fingers towards the room the other men are in before jabbing an index finger to his chest. "You came to *us*, The *Demons*, for help. We do things differently around here." A menacing laugh leaves his full lips.

Dress shoes click against the marble as he steps into my space, towering over me. Thick arms, corded in muscle and tendon fold across his chest as he stares me down.

"I knew you ran a cult. I fucking *knew* it," I seethe.

Cameron drops his hand to the back of my neck and gently squeezes before releasing me. "Sai. What we do here is..."

"Enough," Riot booms, holding out a hand to stop Cameron from saying anything further. "It doesn't matter. She came here in need of our help, and we will deliver in any way we deem fit. The decision is out of your hands now. And speaking of hands, we need to get yours cleaned up. You'll be coming home with us."

"Like hell I will. I am not going anywhere with you!" I shout, drawing the attention of a few of the other members.

He ignores my outburst and leans down, gently tossing me over his shoulder. One hand rests under my ass, the other directly on top of it.

Turning towards his friend, he asks, "Cam, you sure you've got this? I'll make sure she gets to her bedroom safely —just like old times, huh? I guess history really does repeat itself."

"Smug. Fucking. Asshole," I internally scream.

When I arrived back in Maine after my stay in New Orleans—two flights later, I might add—I completely shredded, then *burned* every single one of the memories of that trip. It was like they never existed. There was no chance of them ever coming back to the surface because of how deeply I had buried them inside of me.

The recent exception being my crazy dreams the last few weeks, and Riot being the...*hero* in them?

The mental pain is far worse than my physical pain at the moment. My brain spirals, and all the memories I kept so close to me come barreling through my synapses. Each one vividly reminding me of *exactly* what happened that night.

"Put me down *right now*," I scream again. "I came here because I was scared and had nowhere else to go. I can't leave the house unattended. Elvis is there. He needs me."

Hysteria grows inside of me, and my breathing accelerates. I'm going to pass out.

"Who the fuck is *Elvis*?" Riot asks, his hand clenching my backside as he uses the other to jab the elevator button.

"The cat!" I cry out.

Now Cameron is the one to laugh. "Oh, for fucks sake, Sailor. He's probably blind and deaf by now. He'll be fine.

You're going back to the house with Riot, and that's fucking final."

Who does he think he is talking to me like that? Eight years with Riot really turned him into someone I don't even recognize anymore.

Riot steps into the elevator, and I jab him with my knee. He barely reacts in discomfort. Instead, his hand comes down and slaps my ass in response to my violence.

Monster.

He's a fucking monster.

I just ran from one straight into the arms of another.

My voice cracks as I scream bloody murder. The elevator doors close, and he just *laughs. God, I should have gone to the police instead!*

"That cat is the *only* thing left in this world that gives a damn about me. I'm not abandoning him. *He* would *never* abandon me," I weep, my voice hoarse from screaming and nearly being choked to death.

The doors open, and Riot shifts me to his other shoulder. He retrieves his phone and presses it to his ear as he takes me down the hallway. We end up in the back parking lot. The headlights flash to life on a blacked-out Porsche Cayenne. He gently places me in the front passenger seat and leans over to buckle me in.

"Yeah. Do me a favor, will ya? Retrieve the fucking cat," he says into the phone he holds between his ear and shoulder. "And the litter box essentials. I don't need it shitting all over my house."

The device drops towards my lap. With catlike reflexes, he catches it, already finished with snapping my seatbelt in. Vibrant emerald eyes scan over, then linger on my ripped sweatshirt. A hint of a smile curves the corner of his lips as he focuses on the embroidery on the sleeve. Riot raises a dark brow at me.

"Satisfied?" he smirks.

"Don't expect me to say thank you," I sneer.

"Didn't think you would."

CHAPTER 7

RIOT

J esus, this woman brings the best and the worst out of me. That temper of hers still drives me mad. *After all these years.* Unable to help myself, I reach in and tuck the blonde halo pieces of hair behind her ears. *Still her signature look, I see.*

The leather seat groans as she leans back and settles in, a small whimper passing across her lips. My thumb gently traces over the bruise on her cheek.

How I wish I could be the one to end James' life after what he did to her and countless women across the country. But in a way, I am grateful to have had Cameron offer to do it. That means I get to take care of the little pitbull sitting in my passenger seat.

I shut the door and round the front of my car, taking my own seat behind the wheel. My fingers fumble around with the heat settings, making note to turn her seat warmer on as well. For one, it's the dead of winter, and Maine winters are never kind. Two, I don't need her going into shock.

She's already shivering.

Meanwhile, the internal temperature of my body is like a fucking caldron, driving me to lower my side down a few degrees. I roll the sleeves up on my grey sweater and look over my shoulder before pulling out of the parking lot.

Sailor studies me as we speed down Commercial Street towards Casco Bay Ferry Terminal. Her injured hands are tucked into the sleeves of *my* sweatshirt. The one I gave her so many years ago at my frat house. Not going to lie, whether it be irony or the strange connection we share... seeing her wear it today, of all days, has me feeling hopeful. And a bit possessive.

For what? I don't know.

She hates me. Thinking I'm the enemy. The villain in her story. The monster who corrupted her sweet little childhood crush.

It is the farthest thing from the truth. But she isn't ready to hear that yet. At least that is what Vanessa has told me.

The tires screech as I pull into the parking garage. I'm on edge and beyond fucking annoyed that the last ferry taking cars to Peaks Island was at 5:35 PM. For residents like me, it's the biggest pain in the ass.

To be honest, if it wasn't for the beautiful woman sitting next to me, I would have been inclined to head back to my New York home. *The Demons'* stay in Maine is only temporary as we get the club up and running. This location is our newest addition to the dozen I have opened across the country. The next big step will be international.

A quick look at the dashboard clock tells me the next walk-on ferry will be leaving here at 11:30 PM. Which is in ten minutes. *Great.*

They are already boarding.

And it's the last one for the night.

We'll have to take a water taxi if we miss this one. Which

wouldn't be the worst thing in the world, considering there are a lot of people packing into this one. The thought crosses my mind that Sailor might not be comfortable being around so many people after what she just went through...

Damnit. It will take longer to get a water taxi.

I'll make sure to find us a spot where it will just be the two of us. Fuck, I'll even pay people to stay the hell away from us. I'd like to get her home as quickly as possible. Those wounds need tending, and I'm sure she'd like to get something clean to change into. Possibly some food if she is even interested.

"Everything okay over there?" Sailor murmurs next to me.

Snapping out of it, I reach for the door handle. We've been sitting here for the last two minutes while I've been lost in my own mind. Making my way around to her side, I open her door and extend my hand.

"I'm fine. Come on, *Little Ember.* Let's go. We can't miss this ferry. Either you can take my hand and walk with me, or I'll throw you over my shoulder again. Your choice. Decide now."

She gasps. *Maybe that was a little harsh... but we don't have time for games right now.*

"What did you just say?" Her eyebrows are raised, and her eyes are wide.

I sigh loudly. We really don't have time for her rebellion act. *"Decide now?"* I repeat, in case she didn't understand the fucking options I just laid out.

"No, you said 'take my hand,'" she whispers, almost to herself. *Holy shit.* Is she remembering? Vanessa mentioned that when two souls are connected, they often find themselves in the same dream. My heart slams against my sternum with the notion that it could be true. It sure as shit wasn't the last time I saw her in New Orleans. I may have recognized her, but she had no recollection of who I was.

Has that changed since?

When she doesn't move, I tug her hand and pull her to her feet, then slam the door shut with my free hand. With haste, I usher us down the stairs that lead out to the boarding dock. Part of me feels bad for not giving her a chance to slow down. I should have just carried her.

Needless to say, we made it in the nick of time.

The last two to board.

Thank fuck I had my residential boarding pass on me. Now we can go right to our own little corner of the ship. From here, it should only be about fifteen minutes. The engines rumble beneath us, vibrating the cabin.

And we're off.

"Thanks for meeting me so late, man."

I slap Anthony's back in thanks, and he tosses me the spare keys. An insulated golf cart is idling in front of us. Already warmed up, too. Any other night, I'd have just walked. The fresh air always helps cool my too-hot skin. *And my mind.* The house I rented for *The Demons* isn't far from here; the island isn't very big. You could walk the whole thing in about an hour. Everyone who frequents it either walks, rides a bike, or uses a golf cart.

Tonight is different. I have something in my possession that is incredibly precious to me. I needed speed and comfort.

Chancing a look, I swivel my head towards her. Sailor's body sways with exhaustion, and her eyelids have grown heavy. The entire ride here she was quiet. A few groans of displeasure and irritation. A few mumbled words under her breath that I couldn't make out.

It reminded me of our car ride to the airport almost eight years ago. We barely spoke. Yet, somehow that wasn't such a bad thing. I guess you can't really blame her. Her whole world was just turned upside down.

"Your chariot awaits," I say in my best proper gentleman voice—even though she knows I'm not one.

Bending at the hip, I bow, trying to rile her up and get some sort of emotion out of her. As if on cue, she raises a sassy eyebrow, but surprisingly remains quiet. I wonder if what happened in the parking garage has her questioning her whole goddamn life like I have been?

Sure, asshole. She's thinking about your spiritual connection and not what happened to her tonight. Keep trying to convince yourself she wants you, too.

Doubt.

Such an awful feeling. I've lived with the constant questions my whole life. Am I good enough? Am I doing the right thing? Does my line of work make me a monster?

Now I'm the one fucking spiraling. Am I a monster in her dreams? Because she is an angel in mine.

Nervously, I glance over at her as we drive towards my house on the Atlantic side of the island. Thick strands of her hair are falling out of her bun, which rests against the headrest. Beautiful crème brûlée eyes remain hidden from me beneath her fluttering lids. We hit a bump, and the cart roughly jostles back and forth. Her dark brows come together, forming a little V between them.

Shit. She's in pain.

We'll be there soon, sweetheart. I hit the gas a bit harder.

The headlights illuminate the driveway as I pull up, throw it in park, and toss the keys into my pocket. Little snores are coming from the passenger seat. I can barely contain the smile that spreads across my face.

She's fucking adorable when she sleeps.

A sense of awe hits me, knocking me off kilter. Even through the trauma she just went through and all the pain she's probably in, she still managed to trust me. To let me lead her to safety.

Twice now.

That has to mean something, right?

I collect her in my arms as gently as possible and cradle her so that her head rests against my chest. She grips my sweater and curls herself further into me. Blindly, I navigate the few steps leading to my front door and walk us in.

"Welcome home, Sailor," I whisper.

Creative imagination? Wishful thinking? I'm not sure. But I am almost certain she just smiled.

"Sailor."

I run my hands over her onyx hair, gently rousing her from sleep. It's been about half an hour. Enough time for me to shower and change into sweats. I would have let her sleep, but those wounds really do need to be taken care of.

Her lids flutter open, and her warm eyes look up at me. I'm sitting on the edge of my bed next to her. She's lying on my pillow, two hands tucked beneath her head. For a second, I think she may have actually waved the white flag.

How wrong I was...

Narrowing her eyes, she sits up, pulling her knees to her chest and wincing. "Were you watching me sleep? That's fucking creepy, Riot. I'm sure you're just itching to sink your claws into me, waiting for the perfect opportunity to convert me so that I can do your little cult's bidding."

"Mhm. Got me all figured out, don't you?" I bite back at her accusation.

"The fact that Cameron has stayed with you this whole time...and what I saw tonight...is a testament to how you brainwash people."

"Cameron makes his own choices, sweetheart. Never once have I coerced him into my plans or to do my bidding. He is here on his own free will."

"Well, that makes one of us," she seethes.

She isn't wrong. I didn't give her an option, nor did Cameron. It was out of the question.

"A man tried to rape and kill you tonight, Sailor!" I raise my voice at the thought of how close she came to that fate. I lean into her and clasp her face, softly raising her chin so that her attention is back on me. "Hell would have to freeze over before I let you or any other innocent person out of my sight after what happened."

One lone tear rolls down her bruised cheek. I loosen my grip, thinking I'm hurting her, but she covers my hand with her injured one. *God, this woman gives me whiplash.* I don't care. Not one bit. I'll buy a fucking neck brace if it means she opens up and stops hiding behind that false bravado she wears.

I see you, Little Ember. The real you.

Like earlier, the fight in her dies. Asking Cameron to collect her little senile pet was my good-faith deposit. In the moment, she realized she could trust me—even just for the night.

"Thank you," she concedes through a whisper.

Ahh, she said it.

Progress.

CHAPTER 8

SAILOR

Riot lowers his hand from my face and clasps my own, turning it palm up. His skin feels so soothing against mine. Immediate warmth spreads through me, taking away a bit of the chill. My gut screams at me to trust him, but my brain refuses to.

How can he be trusted when he runs a cult? When Cameron changed so drastically? Not once did he reach out to me after I left New Orleans. My best friend. The one who made me chocolate chip pancakes and watched movies with me.

The Cameron I was reacquainted with at that fraternity house and the one I just saw at the club is *not* the Cameron I once knew.

The flashlight on Riot's phone pulls me out of my reverie. He's inspecting my hands for glass. His index finger glides along the lines on my palms, tracing them. A shiver runs up my spine as he pushes more firmly on the line closest to the top. I gasp at the sensation.

He inhales sharply through his nose.

"Am I hurting you?" he asks, his voice deep and raspy like it's been dragged through gravel.

"No," I reassure him.

Riot clears his throat. Jade eyes connect with mine as he repeats the action on my other hand. He's met with the same response. Another delicious shiver glides up my spine. He notices. That muscle in his clenched jaw tics once, twice.

A hint of a smile grows on perfect lips I may have fantasized about a time or two. *What would they feel like pressed against my skin?*

"There isn't any glass left in your hands," he confirms. "After you shower...I'll put on some antibacterial ointment and wrap them for the night. Are there any other places you think you have glass embedded?"

I purse my lips, unsure if I should mention it. I'll just take a peek at it when I use the bathroom.

"No, I think I'm okay." I go to stand, spotting an en suite across the room. "Can I shower now?"

"Don't lie to me, Sailor. You think I didn't see that huge shard of glass in the parking lot?" He points to my hip. "Or the slit on the side of *my* sweatshirt that's stained with your blood?"

His sweatshirt? *Holy crap.* It *is* his sweatshirt. What are the chances of that?

I've been wearing it so often, not even remembering where I got it from. Memories of me unpacking my luggage come to the forefront of my mind. I was doing laundry after my trip to New Orleans when I noticed I had taken Riot's sweatshirt. After the effort he made to ensure I got to the airport safely, I decided to keep it. *A souvenir, if you will.* Didn't even bother washing the damn thing. His smell was still on it—and it was oddly nostalgic.

Kind of like the words he said to me earlier... and then in my dreams. Those eyes... and those tattoos...

I grip his hands in mine and turn them over, prompting him to raise his eyebrows at me. Not identical, but enough to make my insides swarm with butterflies. Instead of two individual wrist tattoos, he has an ambigram tattoo of life and death on his left. Unable to stop myself, my thumb traces over the ink.

Now he's the one shivering.

"Do you want your sweatshirt back?" I smirk at him, pulling it over my head and holding it out for him.

Humor rests in those emerald eyes as they glide from where my thumb traced his tattoo to my white camisole stained with blood.

"It looked better on you. Unfortunately, this one has to go—but I'll get you another one." He removes it from my hand and tosses it onto the bed.

As soon as his hands are free, they are on me, tenderly poking and prodding over the wound at my side. The muscles of his back are on display at this angle through his black T-shirt, and damn if I don't mind the distraction he's giving me from this exam. To make matters worse, his delicious scent wraps around me. My heart takes flight, its wings flapping as fast as a hummingbird's.

He's the enemy, Sailor. Get a hold of yourself.

But...how at odds that statement really is with how gently he's taking care of me. How he always saves me and sacrifices himself in my dreams. How, once upon a time, he drove me to the airport without question.

Marrying the two versions of him could be a huge mistake...

Detrimental to my mental health.

"May I lift your shirt?" he asks, all traces of sarcasm and humor gone.

Manners? Where's the caveman act? I think I liked him better that way. Because it leaves room for me to protect my heart by showing a little teeth.

I lift my shirt for him, silently giving him permission to continue his exploration. When I glance down, I wish I hadn't. The wound is angry and ghastly. Nausea churns in my stomach, and I nearly gag.

"Don't look at it." He lifts my chin. "Breathe, Sailor. It'll pass."

Fresh air mixed with his alluring scent flows through my nose. I grind my molars, holding back another wave of nausea as he uses the flashlight of his phone again to get a better look.

"It doesn't look too deep. I'd recommend butterfly stitches after your shower," he says all methodically.

The light turns off, and he tosses his phone onto the bed by his sweatshirt before standing up. I follow him as he leads the way to the en suite. It's bright and airy–nothing like the man before me. He's currently brooding. Riot's mood instantly soured when he saw my wound.

Pulling open the glass shower door, he turns the faucet knob, and the sound of running water fills the space. He keeps his hand under the spray, adjusting the temperature accordingly. When satisfied, he turns towards me and crosses his arms over his chest. Bronzed fists are clenched against the crook of his elbows, like he's fighting himself. The muscle in his jaw tics as those green eyes land on my neck, where the worst of the bruising is. I got a nice glimpse of it and the one spanning from under my eye to my temple as I walked in.

"Does it hurt?" He looks at me intensely, scrutinizing my every move.

"A little sore. Mostly my throat," I admit, not yet ready to show him my weakness.

"I'll go make you some tea. Will you be alright shower-ing....alone?" His fingers twitch like he's uncomfortable having this conversation.

"It's not like I'd invite you in with me," I scoff, this time with less bite to my tone than before.

"Not *yet*," he says under his breath as he walks towards the door. "Towels are on the rack. Help yourself to any prod-ucts in there." His voice fades as he enters back into the bedroom.

Butterflies pick up flight again in my gut as I close the door and lean my head against it.

I think I sold my soul to the devil by asking for help.

About an hour later, I am all stitched up and in another one of Riot's sweatshirts, along with a pair of sweatpants. The pain relievers are starting to kick in, easing the throbbing and making the pain more manageable. Steam curls around my mug of tea on the coffee table in front of me. Riot's shadow comes into view from beyond it. He is on the phone in the other room.

From the looks of it, he's aggravated.

The man has been pacing for the last half hour. Every few minutes, he looks over here and stops his pacing. I'm assuming he's on the phone with Cameron.

"I want Landon and Carlos on the trail. We can catch up after. My priority is making sure she heals. Should be yours, too, Cam," he whispers that last part—but I have superior hearing.

Some Netflix dating show is on. I act like I'm watching, drawn into the drama, but my attention is fully on him. Eyes still on the screen, I bring the mug to my lips and take a sip. *Ahh, instant relief.* The herbal blend with local honey soothes my scratchy throat.

"I get it, brother. I really do. Can't it wait another night? I think she could use one more day to get adjusted before you..." He cuts himself off like Cameron interrupted him, then sighs loudly before saying, "Fine."

Anger has him growling incoherently under his breath as he tosses his phone onto the kitchen island without care. Covering his face with his hands, he groans, then drags them down before looking up at the ceiling. "Fuck."

I swing my legs over the side of the couch to stand. He's too quick, already moving towards me. "Sit back down. *Now*." His eyes are as sharp as blades of grass, unwavering in his command.

"Anyone ever tell you you're a real dick?" I question. More serious than not.

Reaching over me, he picks up a lighter on the table and lights a small piece of wood that sits in an ashtray by my mug. It briefly stays lit before the ember continues to burn, creating a pleasant smoke that smells just like him... and his

66

sweatshirt, that I may or may not have been sniffing when he wasn't looking.

"All the time," he responds while winking.

The tan leather groans as he sits down and gets comfortable, then pats the space where I was just sitting. That insult *so* didn't land. I mean, *damn*. The man smiled and winked at me... which has me wanting to goad him even more.

My ass hits the couch, grazing his bent knee on the way down. I expect him to move, to give me a little space, but he doesn't. His body remains pressed up against mine. I could move, shift myself so that my back sits against the armrest.

I don't.

For some reason, his proximity has me feeling the way I did when I entered his club. *Calm. Peaceful.* So I explore it further, letting myself linger a little longer. My focus remains solely on where our bodies touch and the immense heat that comes with it. Suddenly, the static and all the racing thoughts that plague my brain become background noise. No longer am I freezing, but at a perfect temperature.

I can't even tell you the last time I felt that.

What the hell is happening to me?

"What is that you're burning?" I ask, needing to know if it's a hallucinogen. Because none of this is making any sense.

"Palo santo. Its uses vary... the main ones are to promote a sense of well-being. The wood and the oils in it also have medicinal properties used to reduce inflammation and pain. It's been known to help sore throats." His eyes flash over to my neck. "It can also cleanse a space and remove negative energy."

"Looks like it's not working," I laugh.

He tilts his head as if to say, *'Really?'*

"You're still here." I shrug.

He rolls his eyes before giving me a full-blown smile. "That's what you got out of all that? Me being The Big Bad Wolf and not the possibility that maybe...perhaps...I'm just trying to make you as comfortable as I can?" He arches a dark eyebrow and chuckles.

So. Freaking. Hot when he isn't wearing a scowl. And I'm in trouble. *Serious* trouble being around this man.

He's the enemy.

He's the enemy.

He's the enemy, I chant over and over and over again. It's no use, though. He's chipped away at the ice surrounding my soul. And with such little interaction...

I'm not sure I stand a chance at repairing it.

CHAPTER 9
SAILOR

Past

"They did it!" Liv and I shout simultaneously, the both of us hugging and jumping up and down on the metal bleachers.

The packed crowd cheers and hollers. Cow bells jingle and horns blare. The marching band starts playing a victory tune as cheerleaders and coaches run out onto the field to congratulate our team.

Liv blows hot air into her cupped palms and rubs them together. "You're freaking crazy, Sai," she reprimands, her focus on my bare shoulders exposed in this tank top.

"I run hot, okay? You know this." I brush her off.

"Doesn't mean you won't get sick, psychopath." She rolls her charcoal-lined eyes at me.

Cameron jogs over to us from beneath the bleachers. A beautiful smile spreads across his face as he runs a hand through his blonde waves. Beads of sweat cling to his neck and hairline. He scales the fence and clears it, landing at our feet.

"*Eden,*" the coach chides.

Turning around, he shouts, "I'll be right there, Coach. Two seconds."

When he faces us again, he drapes his letterman jacket over my shoulders and pulls me in by the collar, placing a chaste kiss on my temple. "Don't let me see you without a jacket on again. It's freezing."

"I told her that," Liv exclaims, throwing her hands in the air, but I barely register it.

Cameron Eden just gave me his football jacket. In front of everyone.

And he kissed me.

Something shifted between us recently, and I'm more than ready to find out what that means.

"Catch you two back at home for the party?" Eyes like the sky light up with excitement and a bit of mischief.

"Duh," Liv says.

"Of course. You scored the winning touchdown. I'd say shots are in order."

"That's my girl." He shoots me a wink before jogging back down the bleachers and across the field to the locker room.

Plastic shot glasses are refilled for the third...fourth time tonight? I've lost count. Liv is off in her room making out with Andrew from chemistry, leaving me to do a shot with a bunch of strangers. A girl with blue-tinted hair hands me the shot of vodka. I toss it back, grimacing at the burn in my throat.

"God, I hate vodka," complains blue-haired girl. I think her name is Elizabeth.

"I need to use the bathroom. I'll catch you guys later," I respond, motioning to the back door. *I won't catch them later. But they don't need to know that.*

I reach for my wine cooler and squirm my way through the group surrounding the beer pong tables on the lawn. My head swivels, and I rise up on my tiptoes to try and find Cameron. Last time I saw him, he was doing a keg stand by the hot tub.

Nausea hits me hard. My gut roils. *Whoops.* The last thing I ate was a hot pretzel at the game. It would be wise to eat something so I don't puke. I work my way through couples making out and waft away the cloud of weed smoke I stepped through before reaching the back sliding door.

Entering the kitchen, I spot Cameron leaning against the island with his back to me. Goosebumps spring up on my arms as I approach him. Maybe I should just tell him how I feel instead of dancing around it. *I should, right?* My feet become glued to the floor as I stop short.

He's with another girl. Stacy from history. I soo should not tell him. *What if he's into her?*

"Hey, Sailor," she says sweetly.

"Oh. Hey, Sai." Cameron turns around, looking delicious in dark blue jeans and a black t-shirt. The material hugs his body in a way I wish I could. A backwards New England Patriots hat rests casually on his head, and a silver chain peeks out from beneath his collar. *Mmm.* Gotta love a man in a backwards hat.

"I'm next on the beer pong table. I'll catch up with you later, Cam," Stacy announces, placing a hand on his shoulder before excusing herself.

That leaves the two of us alone. I sway a bit on my feet, intoxicated *mainly* by him—and those shots.

Cam swivels his body fully to greet me, hooking his index fingers into my black jeans and pulling me forward. My heart nearly bursts from my chest. *I knew something changed.*

"Have I told you how hot you look in my jacket?" He lowers his forehead to rest on mine.

"No. Have I told you how much those words turn me on?" *Bold. But it clearly worked.*

His hands glide across my hips to grip my ass, tugging me closer until my breasts push up against him.

"Fuck, Sailor," he groans, lowering his head against my neck and placing a wet kiss there. "I'm going to marry you one day. Mark my words. You are perfect for me."

My legs turn to Jell-O as my hands come up to wrap around his neck. *I want him.* I want Cameron so fucking bad right now. He continues kissing me, going back and forth between gentle nips and sucking. Desperate hands rake into my hair, and his lips find mine. He tastes like whiskey and mint gum. And those lips...so soft against my own. The man is a religious chapstick user, always keeping one in his pocket.

I moan into his mouth, opening up for him to slide his tongue in. Which he does, using it to explore and dance with my own. When he pulls away, he brings his lips to my ear and whispers, "Are you sleeping over tonight?"

A giggle escapes me at how obvious an answer that is. I practically live here.

"Yeah. It's not like Dad is home. Last time he came back was over two months ago, and it lasted for only a day, just long enough to get the bills in order."

Empathy paints his features, but he corrects them quickly. "Meet me in my room later, after Liv falls asleep. Which shouldn't take too long—you know she's a light-weight." He kisses me once more and then adjusts himself before walking outside to join the party.

I release a shaky breath, trying my best to calm down. *You have to be mature about this, Sailor.* Which is extremely hard to do, by the way. The tingling of my lips brings a giddy smile to my face. *He kissed me.* Unable to contain myself, a squeal of excitement leaves my mouth for what's to come.

My eyes wander over to the bay window by the sink as I watch Cam at the beer pong table. He sinks a ball in a cup, splashing his opponent with beer. Everyone around him lights up, shouting and jumping on him. Rudely, my stomach decides to groan again, prompting me to grab a handful of Cheez-Its and shove them in my mouth like a squirrel. It better sop up the alcohol. The last thing I need is to be puking when I could be getting laid by *Cameron fucking Eden.*

Ohmygod. I'm going to lose my virginity to my best friend.

CHAPTER 10

SAILOR

Present

The front door opens and the screen door slams against the frame, startling me and causing me to lean into Riot. He cups the back of my head and massages my scalp.

"It's just Cam. You're safe, sweetheart."

And just so we're clear... my heart is beating the hell out of my ribs at the mention of Cam and the fright he just gave me—not because of Riot... or his hands on me.

On an aggravated sigh, he releases me and gets up to greet him. Cam places the crate and litter box down by the entrance of the room. A black duffle bag and my purse hit the floor next to it with a *thud*. Tired blue eyes meet mine, but they are cold. Distant.

"Little gremlin got me good," he complains, rubbing a cut on the top of his hand.

Riot squats down to take a look at Elvis in his carrier. He hisses at him, causing Riot to whistle and lean back on his heels. To my surprise, he opens the latch and reaches in to grab him. A string of profanities later, the green-eyed villain in my story places the furball in my lap. Elvis recognizes me instantly, sniffing my hand and nuzzling it before curling up in my lap. I soothingly pet his soft gray fur. The tremors racking his frail body slow and are replaced with content purring.

Riot reclaims his seat next to me and pets Elvis, who opens his eyes and hisses at him again. He holds up his hands in surrender before crossing them over his chest. I bite my lip, stifling a laugh.

"They say cats are the Devil's pet. I'm surprised he doesn't like you... considering you are literally the Devil incarnate."

From the corner of my eye, I see him shake his head and murmur something about preferring the term '*dark angel*'. I nearly break my neck to look at him with eyebrows practically hitting my hairline. *How many times have I called him that in my dreams?*

Cam's boots thud against the wide plank hardwoods as he approaches us, stealing away my attention. He's changed out of the formal outfit he was in earlier into something more relaxed. When he reaches me, he plops down next to me, opposite Riot. His arm comes up to rest over the top of the couch.

"How are you feeling, Sai?" Cameron asks, sounding exhausted.

"I've seen better days." I shrug.

"The house was empty when we got there. He got away, Sailor... I'm so sorry. We are working on picking up his trail now," he sighs defeatedly.

Ice slithers down my spine. *Got away?* He can be anywhere. Having the knowledge that he killed his grandmother makes me a sitting duck. There is no way he will let me live with a confession like that.

"We'll find him. And when we do, he's not getting away again," Riot growls. *Why is he so invested?*

"Will you stay with me tonight?" I ask Cam, shifting my body to look at him.

He sighs again. This time with more force as he lays his head against the back of the couch. Conflicted baby blues stare up at the ceiling. From my peripheral, I spot Riot shake his head in disagreement. *Is this what they were talking about earlier?*

"I can't, Sai." He sits up and hunches over, placing his left hand on my arm. That's when I see it. The glint of his silver wedding band. *How had I not noticed that before?*

It's not like I expected to see him again or that we would eventually get it right... But *fuck*, it hurts all the same. Because somewhere deep down, I had always hoped *my* Cam would come back to me someday. Especially since his twin sister and I are so close. We were bound to run into each other again at some point.

The barely functioning organ in my chest aches. After the day I had—the fucking last few weeks I've had—the dam fucking breaks. *I fucking break.* Tears well in my lower lids. And in my last attempt at resistance, I bite them back, refusing to let them fall. Riot leans in closer, his shoulder barely brushing mine. It's subtle, but it's there. He's letting me know he's here with me.

That just sets me off even more.

I twist his way, startling the poor cat, who runs away to hide under the kitchen stools. "You were going to have him lie to me? I heard you earlier."

He reaches for me, then thinks better of it. "You've been through hell and back today. I was just trying to help," he replies remorsefully, lowering his head to avoid my eyes.

"Stop fucking helping!" I shout, regretting the way he flinches.

I turn back to Cam, my voice eerily calm. "Anyone I know?"

"Stacy White from high school. We reconnected in college, and things sort of took off from there. I got her pregnant my freshman year, and we broke up for a while. I wasn't ready to be a dad. My main focus was on my fraternity and my brothers."

"Wait." I hold up a hand, my head spinning. "Liv told me you had a strict set of rules to follow. No relationships, being one of them. Did *he* fucking force you to break up with her while she was pregnant?"

I direct my anger back at Riot, nearly jumping out of my seat. My fists clench around the fabric covering them. *How fucking dare he.*

Cam grabs me by the bicep. "No, Sai. That was all me. And they were all lies. I only told Liv that because I kept my situation a secret from my family. Ryder was a great president. He's a great leader, too. *I* chose that. Ry wanted me to do the right thing. He told me he'd keep my spot in the plans we were making for the club. That at any time, I would be welcomed back. *I* didn't want that. *I* didn't want to be a dad."

I gasp loudly, those words hitting too close to home. My pulse pounds in my ears, making it hard to hear what else he's saying.

"You're just like him. *My father.*" It's barely a whisper. I don't even know if I actually said it.

He hangs his head in shame, but I can't find it in me right now to offer sympathy.

"Ryder helped me get my head on straight," he continues. "Stacy and I ended up getting back together my sophomore year, the same year we welcomed our firstborn into the world. Her parents were really helpful. They took Stacy and Savannah in, building them an apartment over their garage. Stacy dropped out of college to take care of Sav. She wanted me to continue my studies so that we would be able to bring in money one day and give our daughter the life she deserved. When I graduated, we got married in the small church down the block from her parents' house, and I accepted a job with *The Demons* right after. It's part of the reason we opened a club here. I wanted to be close to my family."

I have so many questions.

"Why do they call you Riot?" I turn towards the man Cam was calling Ryder, assuming that's his real name.

"That's a story for another night," he says softly.

I turn back around, feeling the anxiety creep back in. "Did you fuck me before or after you got another woman pregnant?" He visibly cringes and keeps his head down.

"Stacy and I were broken up. And I just thought...I thought that maybe you and I could—" he stumbles over his words.

"Could what?!" I throw my hands up in the air as the first two teardrops roll over my cheeks. "Could give me one of the best nights of my life and turn it into one of the worst? Could use my body for your own pleasure and ego? To make you feel better while you had another woman supporting a *growing child* in her womb all on her own?" I scoff and get to my feet. "I don't even know you anymore, Cameron. And I don't know if I ever really did."

"*Sai.*" He clasps my hand in his as I walk by him, stopping my escape. His blue eyes plead with me to hear him out. I tilt my head, giving him one more second of my time. "You can't tell Liv. She doesn't know."

That's what he has to say? *My God,* what did I ever see in him?

"You disgust me, Cameron Eden," I sneer, ripping my hand free of his.

I charge out of the room, making a beeline for the staircase. When Riot catches up with me, he tugs me to his chest and cups the back of my neck, resting his chin on my head. His signature scent soothes me, temporarily knocking my anxiety down a peg or two. I encircle my arms around his waist and release a shaky breath. Then my brain catches up, reminding me I don't even know this man, that he's the devil. But once again, my intuition begs me to trust him.

Dark Angel.

"I want to go home—not that I even know where that is anymore," I whimper. Tears flow at a quicker rate now, soaking his sweatshirt.

"You are home, *Little Ember.* You just haven't recognized it yet," he whispers against my hair.

I don't resist when he bends down and scoops me up. His movements are light as he carries me up the stairs. Halfway, he shouts over his shoulder, "Set the code and lock the door on your way out. I'll see you tomorrow." Honestly, he sounds just as pissed as I am.

For the first time since we met, I really look at him. Through a different lens, in different circumstances. As something other than a villain. Because, based on the facts I learned tonight? He is far from it.

Strong arms lower me to the bed I was on earlier and a thick blanket is thrown over me. I roll over onto my side without the stitches, mentally and physically exhausted, and just cry.

And cry.

And cry some more.

Until *finally,* there are no more tears left, and the world goes dark.

CHAPTER II
RIOT

"**N**o. No. Don't leave me. Please, don't leave me!" Sailor screams, her voice raw with sleep and exhaustion.

I startle awake as my nightmare plays out as it always does. Except this time, right before I woke, she said words I've never heard her say. The ending always cuts out with me in a pile of ash, my body disintegrating.

In this version, I was in *her* dream. Viewing my body—well, what was left of it beside her. Seeing Sailor mourn over me had my heart racing to comfort her. To take away any feelings of grief and abandonment she ever had in this life—or that one. But I couldn't do a thing. Not a damn thing. I was nothing more than an energy surrounding her.

The comforter I slept on top of swishes as I turn over to face the woman of my dreams. Sailor's brow is furrowed, and her eyes are closed as tears roll over the apples of her cheeks. Long dark lashes sparkle with the moisture of them as they flutter. Her eyes dart back and forth under the veil of the translucent skin of her lids. Clearly, she's still in a dream state.

Not knowing if I should, but knowing I can't just lie here

and do nothing, I reach out and gently stroke her face. Her skin is ice cold. Even being wrapped up in a thick knit blanket hasn't done much to warm her. A gentle hand comes up to rest on mine. Baby soft fingers entwine with mine before her grip tightens.

"Don't leave me," she whimpers as her eyes open.

Is she awake now? Does this mean her dream is over, and she is telling *me* not to? Or is she telling the man in her dream? *Fuck. I don't know.*

Glassy, red eyes greet mine. For a second, with the way she was looking at me, I thought she was actually talking to me. That what she begged for wasn't for dream me, or 5D me —as Vanessa would put it—but actually the man lying in bed next to her. But then her smile drops, and those perfectly plump lips purse. Her hand shoves mine off her as she sits up abruptly.

"You slept in the bed with me?" she groans in irritation.

"I kept my distance, sweetheart. As you can see." I point to the undisturbed comforter we are lying on. "We didn't even get under the comforter. It was no different than me sitting next to you on the couch last night."

"It *is* different." She side-eyes me while tilting her head in a reprimanding way. "I need to get back to the house. I'm sure the lawyer and perhaps even the cops will be asking for me. I'd also like to arrange something for Genevieve, eventually." Her voice is fucking adorable, all groggy with sleep, and I'm sure exhaustion from what she went through.

Sailor stands and sways a second before heading towards the en suite. I'll let her wake up and get sorted out.

Like hell will she be leaving.

If the lawyer can't reach her, they will send mail. A damn

phone call, even. Genevieve's remains will likely take a while to be recovered, and *Elvis*, the senile cat she calls a *pet*, is here now. There is nothing at Genevieve's house worth going back for. As for Sailor's belongings, they will all be delivered to the island soon.

She is safe here with me. James can be anywhere. Which reminds me...

I grab my iPhone off the end table and head into my walk-in closet to change into fresh clothes. *Damn, ten to twelve already?!* It's been a minute since I slept like the dead. Could it possibly have anything to do with the woman who occupied my bed last night?

At the thought of her, I eye the closed bathroom door. The water is running. It sounds like she is brushing her teeth. I smile at the fond memories of the little spitfire entering my bedroom back in New Orleans and helping herself to my bathroom. A laugh slips through my usually controlled demeanor. Sailor didn't give two shits about savagely brushing her teeth in front of me. She just stared me down through the mirror, daring me to kick her out.

Scanning my shelves, I spot my favorite suit still covered in plastic from the dry cleaners. I pull it from the hanger, knowing I need to stop at the club later and sort a few things out. Carlos' name pops up on my screen as I dial him, placing it on speaker while I dress.

"What's up, boss?"

"Report?" I clip.

"Trail went cold as we got to New York. He stayed at a hotel in Nassau County, close to the border of Queens. Left his car and phone in the parking lot. Checked out around 8 AM. The fucker thought this through, Riot. He picked a location where he can go any direction, take any sort of public transportation. Hell, he could be trying to take us on a wild goose chase."

"Fuck. Contact Liam Kennedy and *The Bone Breaker,* as well. See if they'll be willing to help us out. And I want extra security at the club tonight. I am taking Sailor with me," I demand as I secure my tie around my neck. "The two of you stay at *The Demons'* condo in Chelsea until we get more information on his whereabouts."

"You got it, boss. I'll keep you posted."

My thumb barely jams the red end button before I toss the cell back down. It clacks against the dresser, carving a new crack into my screen protector. *At least it's doing its job.* Anger saturates my body, flaring it with heat.

How could we have lost him? Fuck!

The knuckles in my hands turn white as I clasp the dresser with both hands and release an aggravated sigh. Untamed black hair falls over my eyebrow and brushes my nose as I hang my head. *We need to find him.* That psychopath won't stop until he gets what he wants. And in order for that to happen, he needs Sailor dead. For scum like him, losing his prey has made this an even bigger game to him. He'll stop at nothing to draw Sailor out. To claim the reward he thinks he's owed.

Little does he know, I'll stop at nothing to bury him six feet in the ground—although, I'd prefer for him to be scattered in the Atlantic in little pieces.

With that being said, my crew needs to seek extra caution. All it takes is a few seconds for tragedy to strike. I want eyes on Sailor at all times.

Preferably mine.

"You would have a walk-in closet for all your suits," Sailor taunts, leaning against the threshold of the door with her arms crossed over her chest. She looks a bit more refreshed, although her eyes are still haunted. "Is it a requirement for your cult? All black, perfectly tailored suits? I mean... *The Devil Wears Prada*, right?"

The corner of her lip twitches as her melancholy mood has lifted. That damn shield she coats her skin in is now firmly back in place. Sarcasm being the finest tool in her arsenal.

"I prefer Tom Ford." I wink at her as I adjust my cufflinks.

She rolls her eyes at me and bites down on her full bottom lip, holding back the smile she wanted to share with me.

"What time is the next ferry? I'm going back to Genevive's with Elvis," she states matter-of-factly.

I take a step forward, my chest brushing against her crossed arms. Enchanting, crème brûlée eyes widen as goosebumps spring up across her exposed skin. The arms of the new sweatshirt I gave her are pushed up to the crook of her elbows.

Losing a bit of my patience, I reach down and clasp the back of her neck. She gasps as the rough pads of my fingers press against her pulse point. Which thrums furiously beneath them.

"I don't think you heard me last night," I fume. "You are staying *here*, or you will come with me to the club. If I am unable to be with you, a member of *The Demons* will keep watch over you."

Her jaw clenches and her eyes narrow. "Cameron said

James is gone. After what he did to me, I'm sure he got the hell out of dodge. He's probably worried the cops will be after him. If you're so concerned, just place a few of your valiant lap dogs at my door."

She acts nonchalant. Cool as a fucking cucumber. To anyone else, steady eye contact and a shrug prove she's not bothered. But her racing pulse and staggered breathing say otherwise.

She's fucking scared.

From what Cameron has told me and what information I've gathered on her, she is used to being alone. What she doesn't realize is that she never has to be alone again.

Not if I have a say in it.

"This isn't up for debate. Until we find that motherfucker who tried to kill you—unless you forgot that part," I raise an eyebrow at her, "you *will* be protected at all times. It's why you came to us. You needed help. And I am going to help you, Sailor. Let me do my job."

"I don't have any money. Fuck, I don't even have my phone. I've got nothing to offer you, Riot." She lifts her chin, too proud to let me peel back those layers and get a good look at her vulnerability.

A brilliant idea pops into my head, bringing instant satis-faction along with it. This plan will give Sailor the sense of independence that she craves, all the while keeping her safe.

Win. Win.

"I have plenty of money. And I don't need a dime of yours to protect you. But...it just so happens that I fired a bartender at my club. We have been looking for a replace-ment. The job is yours as long as you agree to stay here."

She'll be staying here no matter if she agrees or not... but she doesn't need to know that...or the lengths I'll go to keep her safe by my side. Now that I have her, I'm not letting her go. Not like I did last time. Or all the times before that...

Her pulse hammers against my fingers as her eyes light with a hint of excitement.

"I'll accept your offer *if* you take me to the house to collect my phone. I went through the bag Cameron brought, and there are only a few outfits and my toothbrush. I didn't see my phone. Maybe he missed it. I'm pretty sure I left it on the snack table before everything happened."

"It looks like we have a deal, *Little Ember*," I smirk, sliding my hand from the back of her neck up to cup her bruised cheek. "We will stop to grab your belongings and then shoot over to *Mayhem* for your training. I have a few business matters I need to attend to."

"Okay."

She steps back out of my embrace and holds her hand out for me to seal the deal. I grip her soft hand in mine. It's far warmer than this morning. *Perhaps she was still in shock.* I give it a firm shake, then slip past her and into my bathroom to finish getting ready.

"Twenty minutes. That's when the next ferry leaves," I announce, smirking at myself in the mirror.

That was the answer to her original question, which I have now spun to my advantage. The plan to keep her here worked out far better than I could have expected. Honestly, I foresaw her throwing a huge fit.

CHAPTER 12

SAILOR

R iot's fancy Porsche purrs as we pull up to Genevieve's. I can't help but glance over at my old childhood house next door. It's abandoned now, looking as haunted as I feel. A forboding sense of uneasiness rolls around in my gut, making me queasy. I swallow down the lump in my throat, hoping the bagels and coffee we had before we left won't threaten to come back up.

Genevieve is dead.

I can't wrap my mind around that. Or the fact that I almost ended up the same way last night. I'll never again enjoy a cup of tea with her, or help her create bouquets from the flowers in her garden. I won't even be able to say good-bye. Heaviness sits on my chest, preventing me from inhaling properly.

Riot gets out and leaves the car idling in the driveway. It's clear he's not willing to stay here any longer than necessary. Although I suggested that I return, I'm secretly happy to be going back to Peaks Island. *I don't want to be alone. The thought of it terrifies me more than I'll ever admit to.*

We climb the steps of the porch in silence. As if sensing my unease, the knuckles of his warm hand brush against mine. It's comforting and annoying at the same time. The man has been hovering since the second my feet hit the gravel of the driveway.

Riot stiffens next to me as we approach the front door. Sliding the material of his peacoat to the side, he reaches into the inner pocket of his suit and retrieves a shiny black Glock. My heart skitters against my sternum at the sight of it.

What the fuck have I gotten myself into? It's not uncommon to see people carry around here, but to see him so brazenly whip it out of his jacket sets me on edge.

Who are you really, Riot Black?

"Stay behind me," he commands, using his free hand to cup my hip and slide me behind his towering frame.

An argument is on the tip of my tongue. I was about to tell him that I am fully capable of defending myself, but then I spotted the broken glass and blood in the foyer. Fear prickles the base of my spine and crawls up it like a centipede.

I came so close to death last night. So close, I can still feel James' death grip on my neck. My fingers ghost over where the worst of the bruising is as fear continues to consume me.

Would it really be so bad to let someone take care of me? Protect me?

Dark Angel.

His shoes crunch along the broken glass as he murmurs under his breath, "Cameron couldn't fucking clean this shit up?"

Seems he's still angry with his friend.

Well, that makes two of us.

Riot's hand lingers on my hip. His firm fingers rest on my ass like he's done it a thousand times before. I am practically bathing in his magical cologne with how close he has me pressed up against him. Or maybe that is just his scent. Whatever potent combination, its sorcery soothes my racing heart and eases my anxiety as we clear the main floor. He slows to a halt at the bottom of the staircase and swivels around, tucking the gun behind his back.

Intense emerald eyes capture my own. They really are beautiful, with lashes so dark and full, it's almost like he's wearing eyeliner. And if you knew me during my emo days... you'd know that's practically candy to me. I find myself lost in them and my heart rate kicks into overdrive for reasons besides fear.

Damnit, Sailor. Not good. Sooo not good.

"Stay here. I'll be right back." His jaw pulses as his gaze lowers, settling on my lips—*which may or may not be pouting after recognizing the extent of my attraction to him.*

My mouth has gone dry, my tongue too laden to speak, so I just nod. *God, why does this man make me feel things I have no business feeling for him? And why does his closeness pull the fight I have right out of me?*

The words that demand to go with him are nudging at my lips...But I can't get them to leave my mouth. Somewhere inside the ironclad fortress I built is a weakness. *I trust him.* Which leaves me doing exactly as he says.

An approving smirk forms on his kissable—*I mean, punchable*—lips as he heads up the stairs backward. Dark Angel studies me for another fleeting moment before turning around at the landing. He disappears into the bathroom on the left before returning and heading further down the hallway and out of sight.

The rigidity in my limbs comes back tenfold with him

gone. I shake it off and use the time alone to search for my phone. The snack table still holds my cup of tea and book, but my phone isn't there. Lowering myself to my knees, I bend over and search under the recliner. Coming up empty, I check under the couch next to it. Nothing but cat hair comes back as I scrape my hand forward along the hardwood.

Fuck. Where the hell did it go? Maybe I left it in the car at the club? My mind was so overwhelmed that night, I could have had it in my hand the whole time.

"Normally, I wouldn't object to seeing you on your knees, *Little Ember,*" Riot's deep voice penetrates my stream of thoughts, "but we need to leave in ten minutes. The house is clear. Grab what you need, change your clothes, and let's get the hell out of here."

My head snaps up so fast my neck lets out a nice little crack. He's standing above me with eyes burning into mine, blazing with heat. The apples of my cheeks flare at his brashness. A memory slams into me at that moment, the power of it knocking me forward onto my hands in front of him.

"I wouldn't normally object to seeing you on your knees for me, Little Ember. But right now? I need you to take my hand and walk through those flames with me." He points to the door behind him, which is now fully engulfed in them.

"Don't," Cameron warns, his voice barely a whisper.

The corner of the dark angel's mouth curves into an amused smile. "He doesn't trust me when it comes to you. But you trust me, don't you, sweetheart?" He stretches out his hand in offering.

I gasp as Dark Angel in the flesh and blood reaches his hand out to help me up. I'm too shaken up by the pieces of my dream flashback to accept it. Something deep inside me screams to grab his hand and never let go. Tears well in my lids as if I am about to lose him again.

What the hell? Get it together, Sai. It was just a dream, that's all.

I scramble to my feet and dip past him, but not before I see the amused look on his face. He knows his words just affected me—but for the wrong reasons. The infuriating man thinks a sexual comment rattled me. What he doesn't know is that I've been dreaming of him for the last few weeks.

That I've grieved him in them.

Coincidence that he's back in my life now? *I think not.*

I've read of fated mates in my fantasy books—and I hate to even admit it, but this is starting to feel a helluva lot like that. A trip to a psychic would help. *Though I'm sure a trip to a psych ward would be more appropriate.* But this crazy idea is already forming in my mind. And I know the perfect place to start.

What did that psychic Vanessa say to me? Or I think she said last night...

"Seek me out when you are ready to discover your truth... and his."

Unsteady legs carry me to the stairs. I'll be needing to collect a few of those outfits Liv sent me. If I am going to be working at *his* club, I'll need nicer clothes than the ones I wore at *The Rickety Fence.* Before heading up, I glance over my shoulder at the man who is watching me like he's about to pounce on me any second now.

Like a wolf dressed in a designer suit.

Wolf.

Oh God, what if all these fantasy books are based on

touches of reality? *No. You're losing it, Sai. Riot isn't a shifter...*
and he sure as hell isn't your fated mate.

Sifting and sorting through clothes and straw wrappers, my hands sweep around the floor of my car. *It's a fucking mess.* Boxes are still shoved into the backseat, and energy drink cans litter the passenger seat of my old Jeep.

"Ugh," I grumble. "It's not here." I slap my hands down onto my black leather leggings.

"I'm sure it'll turn up," Riot chuckles at my outburst.

He's leaning against my car and scrolling through his phone while impatiently waiting for me to finish my search.

"Got everything you need?" He looks through the window of my car skeptically.

"I'm not always a slob. It's been a rough few weeks, okay?" I say defensively as I slam the driver's side door shut with a little more force than necessary.

His hand collects mine, tugging me along. I slam into him, a little unstable in these black suede boots. My frustration instantly fizzles out as his presence and the heat radiating off his body soothe me. I release a deep exhale, a cloud of condensation filling the air around us. This weather is making me want to cling to him even more just to chase away the chill from my bones.

Riot picks up his pace, anxious to get to whatever the hell business he needs to attend to. He guides us towards the back door we left out of last night and shuffles me inside.

Almost immediately, that same familiar sense of peace wraps around me like a heated blanket. The scent of the air sets my heart rate back into a steady rhythm. Everything looks just as I had remembered. The exception being the velvet curtains that separate this hallway from the main room are now tied back.

A woman organizing bottles of liquor at the bar notices us and heads our way. Bright pink hair pulled up into a half ponytail sways over her shoulders. A gold nose ring shimmers in the dim light, enhancing her edgy look. *She's beautiful.* Her body language radiates *fuck off*, but there's something about her that tells me she would sit and talk with you for hours. Perfectly arched eyebrows raise as she takes note of Riot's hand in mine, and a low whistle escapes her lips. Which are the same shade as her hair.

"The Devil actually has a girlfriend," she jokes, a cryptic smile forming on her face.

Riot releases me and nudges me forward, his hand lingering on the space between my lower back and ass. The man sure loves to keep his hands there. *And if we are being totally honest here, I may get a thrill out of it, too.*

Even if he is an obnoxious cult leader who brainwashes people.

"This is our new employee, Sailor. She has bartending skills and will fit right in with the rest of my nosy staff." He lifts a menacing eyebrow in warning, but it lacks any real threat.

She snorts and rolls her eyes at him as she extends her hand to me. "I'm Rosemary. You can call me Rose." Her smile widens to reveal perfect teeth embellished with tiny gems on her top two canines and four bottom incisors.

I shake her hand and return the smile. *I like her.* She's got spunk. And if she isn't afraid of the Big Bad Wolf looming behind me, we'll get along just fine. Riot lowers his head over my shoulder so that his minty breath wisps over the shell of my ear.

"*Behave.*"

He taps my ass like he owns it and then disappears down the hallway we came in through. *The audacity of that man.* I let out a rattled breath. Once again, I've allowed the owner of this club to unravel me.

"Shall we?" Rosemary asks, her lips twitching as she holds back what she really wanted to say.

Thankful she doesn't ask what that just was between him and me, I nod. She leads us over to the Sun and Moon circular bar, opening a hatch and guiding us inside.

"Shifts usually start an hour before opening, which is at eight. The barbacks take care of most of the glasses, ice, liquor, and beer restock. If a keg is tapped, they take care of that, too. We offer small plates, mostly appetizers and late-night snacks. The kitchen is back that way." She points a black almond-shaped acrylic nail to the copper door behind the bar. "If the barbacks are running around and busy, it is our responsibility to restock or take the silverware and stemware out of the dishwasher." Her hand comes down on the stainless steel appliance below us. "Which is right here."

I collect the menu resting next to the POS system, getting familiar with the drinks and food. Many of the beers they have are local IPAs—which is a good thing. Wines I am familiar with—also good. The price tag on a few bottles makes my eyes pop. Nothing at all like *The Rickety Fence.* A few signature cocktails sound fancy...but will be easy enough to make.

I laugh at the one titled *Witch's Broom*.

How cliché for a club like this.

My index finger scans over the ingredients. Blood orange juice, a splash of pomegranate, ginger beer, and gin. All garnished with a few pomegranate seeds, a couple of cloves, a stick of cinnamon, and a star anise pod. The potpourri cocktail is served in a copper mug. Part of me is slightly interested in how good that can taste.

"That one is a club favorite." She lowers her voice to a whisper and cups her hand against her mouth conspiratorially, shielding the secret she is about to spill. "Even your man there orders it from time to time."

Her cheeks turn as pink as her hair as she discloses that little nugget of information to me. *Does she have a crush on him?* Something close to possessiveness stirs inside of me. I smack that thought down as fast as it came in.

WWE style.

With a chair.

"He's *not* my man. Did you two ever..." I point to the hallway as if he's still there and mentally smack myself for asking her that.

"Me and *Riot*? Ha!" Rose bends at the waist and actually grips the counter to laugh. "That beast of a man hasn't had a girlfriend for as long as I've known him. Which is...*a while*. That's why I thought you were his. He couldn't keep his hands off you! And that aura he was giving off while he was next to you? *Sheesh*, girl. Even if that vibrant ass aura of his didn't give him away... the lust and possessiveness rolling off him was more than enough to convince me."

"Aura?" I ask, confused. "Like colors?"

"Yeah, it's the electromagnetic energy field that surrounds all living things. It presents more strongly when your emotions are heightened. Seeing them takes practice, but working at a place like this, you get the hang of spotting them rather quickly. Here, I'll show you."

Rose grabs a white piece of paper from the printer under the POS system. She grabs my hand and places it in front of the paper she holds out. "Focus on your hand, then slowly shift your awareness to the colors *around* your hand. It will look like you took a highlighter and traced around it. What color or colors do you see?" she asks excitedly, happy to share this information.

"It's orange, I think. Like a reddish orange." I pull my hand away, feeling silly. Rose keeps her fingers cuffed around my wrist.

"You're right. Don't doubt yourself, Sailor.. It is orange and red. It's there but not as intense as Riot's. His was like a blazing fire when he had his hand on you."

"*You are the flames, Little Ember.*" The deep timbre of his voice pops into my head as the memory comes through.

"Okay..." I say nervously, gently tugging my hand back and tucking my blonde highlights behind my ears. "So what does that mean?"

"It means....that the elusive Riot Black has it bad for you. And you, my dear," she snatches a pink highlighter from a cup beneath the bar, "may be blind to it right now, but your soul has claimed his." She starts to giggle as she holds up the paper with a big heart and our initials drawn onto it.

I am anything *but* giggles. Cool air hits my face as I fan myself with the menu. *This is all too much. Dark Angel's* jade eyes watch me in my mind's eye, turning my body into a furnace. Heat spreads through my veins, flushing my neck and cheeks. It's to the point that I need to take off my cardigan that's covering my black lace button down. *Fuck, did I bring extra deodorant with me?* I haven't carried it in my purse since I was a kid, always being cold these days.

So, why the hell am I sweating again like I ran a goddamn marathon?

Bottles *clink* as Rose continues to organize and restock some bourbon while humming, "Chapel of Love" by The Dixie Cups. I can't even say I'm mad at the girl. In the twenty minutes I've known her, she's grown on me.

"I need to use the bathroom. Which way is it?" I ask, looking around the room.

"The guest bathrooms are behind that curtain back there," she points behind us to purple velvet curtains and a neon sign to match that says *Leaky Cauldrons.*

Hysterical. I roll my eyes.

Lifting the hatch of the bar, I let myself out, about to walk in that direction when she chirps, "You can use the employee bathroom. Head down the hallway–last door on your left, closest to the elevator."

"Thanks." I smile gratefully at her and head towards the dimly lit hallway.

CHAPTER 13

RIOT

C am greets me at the downstairs bar. He looks like shit. Almost as if he hasn't slept well. I love him like a brother, but he deserved the verbal beating he got from Sailor. He led her to believe his lies and twisted the knife even deeper after admitting what he did last night. Even I was shocked. I didn't know they slept together that night.

He slaps me on the back before handing me a drink in one hand and a box in the other.

"New phone. The guy at the store was a complete dick, but after a nice stack of cash was presented to him, he eagerly agreed to switch over her old number and contacts."

"Thank you. Did you happen to stop and get the other item I requested?" I ask, placing the box on the table we do meetings at, taking a sip of my drink.

"It's in there." He taps the cardboard box. "She just needs an account to get started."

"Perfect." I plop down in my seat at the head of the table, and he takes his to the right of me. "When is *The Bone Breaker* going to be here?"

"He and his wife will be arriving any minute. They can't

99

stay long. You know them, they try to get home before the kids go to bed."

"Right. Can't believe he has another one on the way. Bastard went from the underworld's most ruthless criminal to the World's Best Dad."

Cam lowers his head like my words triggered him.

"I want that. To be a good dad. I know how I acted back in college was awful, but I was scared, Ryder. I told you about what it did to Sailor, having her dad resent her and go off living a life without her. I didn't want that for me. I was young, and afraid to fuck up. Obviously now, everything I do is for my wife and kids. They are my whole goddamn world. If I could go back in time and change my behavior, I would. But since we can't change the past, I'll have to make peace with my sins. Starting with apologizing to Sailor."

I lean forward and link my hands on top of the table. "I gave her a job here. This way, we'll still be able to keep an eye on her, she can make her own money, and we can continue to run this club. Sailor isn't the only one who needs our help."

I purposely ignored his desire to apologize to her. She needs more time before he approaches her again.

He blows out a breath and leans back in his chair, cupping his hands behind his head. "She seems interested in you. And I can't tell why." He lets loose an amused chuckle that I don't reciprocate. "Come on, man, you two seemed rather cozy last night when I got there...and before I left."

"Trauma can do that." I write him off.

"I am only saying this because you are my brother and I know we respect each other enough to speak freely. You need to stay away from her, Ryder. She needs a man who will be there for her. Someone who doesn't have blood staining his fingernails. Sailor deserves to have a big old house and a husband who comes home and brings her flowers. Someone who will rub her feet after a tough day. Someone who will *stay*. Not a man whose life is constantly being put at risk. A regular, white picket fence life. Quiet. Safe."

"Not to be an eavesdropper," a familiar feminine voice interrupts from behind us, "but what if that kind of life is not what *she* wants?"

I swivel around in my seat, delighted to find Diego and his glowing wife, Madison, at the entrance of the room. Diego drapes his arm around her, dropping a quick kiss to her head as he smirks at us knowingly. She's always been bold, this one. And that's *exactly* why *The Bone Breaker* is in love with her.

Cam and I get up to greet them. Diego shakes my hand while Madison kisses Cam on the cheek before patting his face in a motherly way.

"Whoever this woman is to you *both*..." she looks back over at her husband and smiles, the two of them sharing an unspoken secret, "give her the chance to choose. You selecting that fate *for her* won't always work out the way you think it will."

I raise a brow at Cam, secretly thanking Madison for her words of wisdom. I was about to kindly tell my brother to fuck off with his bullshit—but she beat me to it, doing so in a much nicer way than I ever could have. I've never been one to coddle Cam. Not back in college and not now. Quite frankly, I've never been one to coddle *anyone*.

"Can I grab you guys a drink?" I ask as they take their

seats across from him. Diego places his hand on his wife's womb protectively; proudly.

"Coffee," they both say in unison, making me crack a smile.

Cam looks at me like he's seen a ghost. Smiles are a rare commodity for me. I guess being around a couple who truly loves each other will do that to you. It gives you hope. Makes you think about your own future. Finding love like that.

It most definitely has nothing whatsoever to do with the woman occupying my thoughts a floor above us.

Unsettled by my cheery mood, I snatch the corded phone and dial the number for the main bar. Rosie picks up all chipper. *Looks like I'm not the only one affected by Sailor's presence.* "You've reached the bar at *Mystical Mayhem*, this is Rose, how can I assist you?"

"*Rosemary,*" I clip.

"*Ryderrr.*" She mimics my tone, dragging my name out and making me shake my head.

"Have Sailor bring down a fresh pot of coffee and some pastries."

"Don't bother with the pastries," Madison shouts over to me. "I brought a bunch of goodies from our coffee shop." She reaches into her black leather bag and pulls out a box with white and red string wrapped around it, placing it on the table.

"No pastries. Just plates and silverware to go along with the coffee," I confirm, in case she didn't hear that.

"Sailor went to the restroom, and she's been in there for a bit. I bet Vanessa got a hold of her."

"*Fuck.* I'll be right up. Get that shit prepared for me. I have guests."

"Yes, *Sir*."

"Don't be a brat." I hang up on her.

"You will have to excuse me, I need to check on Sailor. Cameron can get you all caught up while I'm gone." Cam looks at me with a hint of concern but doesn't voice it.

I bolt to the elevator and repeatedly press the button like an impatient toddler. Like doing so will actually bring the fucking elevator here faster. It continues to take its sweet ass time. Time I don't fucking have. *She can't find out this way.* I need Vanessa to give me more time before she goes blabbing about the two of us.

Decision made, I grip the door handle of the staircase to the left of the elevator. The frosted glass nearly shatters as it slams against the brick wall. I jog up the two flights of stairs like a madman and bust open the door next to the elevator. My attention snaps to Vanessa's closed door. *Like I give a fuck about that...* I throw it wide open. Vanessa is sitting at her desk with a client.

Not Sailor.

"Mr. Black. Do you need help or can I get back to my reading with my client?" She raises a knowing gray eyebrow at me as I stand there like an idiot before shutting the door.

Anxiety simmers under my skin. If she's not here then she's still in the bathroom. There is no way James would have entered this building. I've got it armed to the gills with security. Still, the thought sends a stabbing pain into my gut.

I can't lose her.

I sprint across the hallway and shove open the bathroom door to the women's room. Sailor shrieks as we make eye contact in the mirror.

She has a wet paper towel pressed to the back of her

neck. Her long black hair is pulled over one shoulder and spills like ink over the swell of her full breasts. The lace of her shirt is nearly see-through, a black bandeau being the only scrap of material covering her curves underneath.

I grind down on my mint gum, which takes the brunt of the pressure threatening to shatter my molars. Any asshole entering this club can see her like that. Although we don't have a dress code per se, and what she is wearing is what most of our employees choose to wear, I can't help but feel a bit possessive. *Okay, really fucking possessive. Caveman status initiated. Mine. Mine. Mine.*

That irresistible body created specifically for my personal demise is for my eyes only.

In this lifetime and every other one.

The anxiety starts to ease out of me with the knowledge that she's safe. But her proximity and that damn intoxicating scent of hers keep the heat lingering inside of me. She still wears the same perfume as she did the day I met her. I take a step closer to her, unable to help myself. Completely drawn in by the gorgeous female before me. An invisible tether linking the two of us.

One *she* is completely unaware of.

And one *I* painfully am.

Both my hands grip the counter around her, caging her body between me and the sink. "What's wrong?" I rasp, my voice giving away the wave of lust coursing through me.

Her grip on the paper towel tightens and water drips down over her bruised neck, which she did well to cover with makeup. It glides slowly over her collarbone before disappearing into her cleavage. I watch its devious path, envious of a drop of water. Her eyes watch me in the mirror.

Our breathing accelerates. Our backs rise and fall at the same rate.

"I'm just really warm. Sorry, I'll get back out there." She tosses the paper towel into the trash next to us, dismissing my worry. But I don't move an inch. Not a goddamn centimeter.

Lightly wrapping her hair around my fist, I tug it back out of the way and begin to blow on her neck. On a gasp, she backs up, closing the gap that was between us. A delicious shiver runs down the length of her body. My own responds just as hers did. Goosebumps sprout up along my too-hot skin. Immense satisfaction in her reaction encourages me to do it a few more times before releasing her hair and stepping back.

"Better?" I ask her through our contact in the mirror.

"Much. Thank you," she whispers, dropping her eyes to the sink.

"I have my—I have Rosemary preparing a tray of coffee and plates for my guests downstairs. Let's grab them. I'd like for you to meet this couple. You'll like them—especially Madison. She reminds me of you. And she was a nurse. I want her to take a quick look at your wounds."

"Okay," she agrees as I place a hand on her lower back and guide her out into the hallway.

Vanessa is leaning against her door, her room now vacant, client gone. I shoot her a warning glare. *But does the stubborn lady ever listen to me? Never.* Her eyes grow wider as she notices my hand on Sailor. The one now lingering dangerously close to her ass—which looks incredible in these leather leggings. I nearly tossed her over my shoulder and was ready to take her on the nearest flat surface when she came down the stairs at Genevieve's.

"Ahh, Sailor. I heard you joined our crew. I offer a complimentary reading to all our new employees and would love to do a reading for you, dear."

I practically snort. That's a load of bull.

"Another time, Vanessa. Sailor and I have an important meeting downstairs." I increase the pressure on Sailor's back to keep her walking.

"The winds of fate are changing, Ryder," she says cheerily before stepping back into her office.

Sailor giggles and looks up at me. "So when can I claim my free reading?"

"Another time," I whisper in her ear as we reach Rosemary.

She greets us in the hallway with the tray I requested, handing it to me. A wild grin paints her face as she looks between the two of us.

"How was your visit with Vanessa?" she asks Sailor.

"I didn't get a chance to sit down with her. Riot found me first." She shrugs innocently.

"He did? Well, don't skip out on the opportunity. Vanessa is one of the best psychics I know. Ryder has her follow him around to all his clubs. At this point, she's become more of his own personal psychic than the clubs'."

"That's enough, *Rosemary. Mayhem* will be opening soon and we are understaffed tonight. Get back to work," I grit through my teeth.

"Aye, Aye, Captain." The sassy, pink-haired, pain in my ass salutes me before skipping away whistling, "Here Comes The Bride".

"I like her," Sailor giggles again.

The beautiful sound of it drowns out the taunting whistling coming from the bar. I pivot on my heel and head towards the elevator, feeling something akin to happiness. It's foreign and starting to take root in my system. Where I would usually gut that parasite right out of me, I can't help but let it engorge itself and take its fill.

This woman will be the death of me. I just know it.

CHAPTER 14
SAILOR

The second we enter back into the meeting room on the floor below, I am greeted by a stunning woman with dark hair and warm eyes. She stands, placing a gentle hand over her swollen womb. *Ahh. She's expecting.* Her eyes light up as they subtly take me in. Extending the manicured hand that was rubbing circles over her stomach, she introduces herself.

"Sailor, I'm Madison and this is my husband, Diego." She turns briefly to stare longingly at her husband, who offers me a slight smile in return.

He's handsome in the way a model would be. Sturdy nose, chiseled jaw speckled in stubble, beach wavy hair, and goddamn... Those eyes, so intensely blue, you feel as if you took a deep dive into the ocean. Swirls of topaz and cobalt snare my attention.

I've always been mesmerized by Cameron's baby blue eyes. These intimidating man's are something else entirely. Recognizing that I am being incredibly rude, I transfer my gaze back to her waiting hand and take it.

"It's nice to meet you both," I reply with a nervous smile. "Riot mentioned you were a nurse?"

"I was...Well, I *could* have been. After my graduation and passing my NCLEX, I never actually took up a position at a hospital. My...objectives in life had changed," Madison says hesitantly while sitting back down next to her husband.

Cameron pulls out the chair next to him for me. I take a seat, doing my best to ignore him, given the space we are in. Riot pinches his eyebrows together as his lips tilt downward. It's almost as if he's annoyed that Cameron beat him to it. A smirk grows on my face at the frustration rolling off his shoulders. It's amazing how carefully he crafts his expressions to not give a single fuck, only for that facade to slip in my presence.

Dark Angel gets right to the point, casually taking his seat at the head of the table with me adjacent to him. "Now that we have gone through introductions, I take it you were updated by Cameron on the recent events? You know I wouldn't reach out to you unless absolutely necessary, Diego. You're a busy man, and rumor has it you're trying to take a step back from assignments."

"I am. Family time is precious these days. I want to spend as much time as I can with my kids while they are little," Diego muses. "And of course my stunning wife, whom I can't seem to keep my hands off of." He shoots her a wink. Madison's face flushes even more than it was already.

Cameron sneaks a glance at me from over his coffee mug. Oh *yes, hearing about a father wanting to actually spend time with his family is admirable.* I can't exactly say the same for my own or the man I once knew. Who is now suddenly still as a statue next to me.

Riot, somehow always sensing my body language and inner thoughts, drapes an arm over my chair and scooches me closer to him. The chair screeches against the marble, directing my thoughts away from the spiral I was about to head down. Rather than just asking Cameron, he reaches over me to grab a pastry from the box in front of him.

A delicious looking cinnamon bun is placed on a plate before me. My eyes widen as I turn to look at him. The devil with green eyes sucks the leftover frosting off his thumb and leans in, his lips only a breath away from the shell of my ear.

"Madison owns a coffee shop in New York City and her pastries are fucking out of this world. The cinnamon roll happens to be my favorite. But considering there is only one... and you look like someone kicked your puppy, I'm willing to take the loss," he whispers, his tone playfully seductive.

Doing my best to ignore the heat between us or the intensity of his emerald eyes, I raise the pastry to my mouth and take a bite. A moan floats past my lips as my eyes practically roll to the back of my head. Holy crap, this *is* incredible. The perfect amount of sweetness. Riot's eyes blaze with desire, steadily fueling my own. I shift uncomfortably in my seat and look at Madison. Her eyes dance as she watches the two of us with interest.

"I'm going to need a box of these. They are perfection, Madison," I say between another bite.

She blushes, her cheeks even more pink than they were earlier. "Thank you. I found my calling to bake during a really difficult time in my life. Sometimes redirection leads us to exactly where we are meant to be." She smiles widely at me before sharing that light with her husband.

Without even really knowing this couple, you can just tell

how deep their love for each other runs. Where most times that kind of display of affection can be nauseating or fake as fuck—their interactions are unabashedly beautiful. Something I long for. I mean... I am a romance reader. Of course I want a love that will sweep you off your feet and make you feel alive.

One that consumes you.

But more than anything, I want someone who is willing to push me when I become stubborn and hard-headed. Someone who won't give up on me when I'm being a brat.

Someone who won't leave like everyone else.

Riot's index finger traces mindless circles on my shoulder as he begins to speak. "James is going to be a challenge. He's clearly out for vengeance. He feels wronged by his family and will stop at nothing to get to Sailor. You are the best in the game. Where would you start hunting? We've lost his trail after his stay on Long Island."

Diego crosses his arms over his chest, momentarily deep in thought. His eyes have darkened, like a massive storm is suddenly brewing behind them. The energy in the room crackles with static. That feeling just before lightning strikes. Madison reaches over and prepares coffee for her and her husband. He gratefully accepts the mug, takes a sip, then looks directly at Riot.

"How would you feel about drawing him in rather than chasing?" A mischievous grin paints his face. This is not the same soft-featured man we were just talking to. My heart beats in my chest with a little more force. *Holy shit.* He's like a shark. And this one seems to not just be out for blood—but for sport.

Riot's fingers shift from mindlessly tracing patterns on

my shoulder to a complete standstill. Not even a twitch, he's gone so still.

"What do you have in mind?" Riot's voice has dropped dangerously low, matching Diego's dark energy.

"Draw him here. Set the stage. Have her head back to Genevive's house on her own—obviously we will have eyes on her at all times. Then resume a normal routine. Sailor will come to the club for her shift. Make sure that night you host some sort of special—something that will further entice him to follow her here. Pack the place out so he feels more comfortable watching her in the crowd before attempting to lure her away from the bar... in which case you act."

"Sailor's birthday is coming up in a few weeks. We could host a birthday celebration here at *Mayhem*. The crystal ball marquee sign out front will announce the event. I'll have my staff post about it on our website and social media as well. That should give the asshole more than enough time to think he's no longer being followed and continue his pursuit."

I gasp loudly, turning a few heads and almost inhaling a piece of cinnamon roll. Riot's face softens briefly, the corner of his lips raising as he continues his invisible paintings on my shoulder.

"The fact that you remembered my birthday has me more concerned about you being the stalker than James," I say bluntly.

He barks out a laugh with Diego and Madison joining in. "Oh, come on, *Little Ember*. I owe you a birthday celebration. Remember the day you turned nineteen? You were angry with me and decided to barge into my bedroom at the frat house and help yourself to my private bathroom. All while breaking the original doorknob off my door, might I add. I tried to get you to stay, but you wanted to go home. Even took me up on my offer to drive you to the airport. You think I would forget a memory like that or a face like yours?"

Madison is now beaming, so completely enthralled she's biting her lip to hold back a simper. Her amused chestnut eyes volley back and forth between the two of us.

Shifting my entire body, I stare Riot down. "I certainly could *never* forget a face like yours. It haunts my dreams," I scoff abrasively.

Cameron sighs loudly, covering his face with his hands before sliding them up into his soft blonde curls. Diego chuckles deeply, shooting his wife a knowing smile while Riot continues painting invisible drawings on my skin.

Just when I think he has no comeback for me, he brushes his knuckles down my arm, eliciting full body goosebumps. I slide my tongue over my front teeth to hold back a moan. The skin he grazed beneath my sheer shirt is on fire. Again.

God, what the hell is happening to me?

"I guess we have that in common then," he ripostes before casually leaning back, arm once again draped over my chair as if he didn't just internally set me alight.

My mind spins. *Wait. Does he have the same dreams I do? The one where he dies saving me? Could that even be possible?*

"I think it's the perfect plan. It may not get him here though, if he doesn't see the sign or social media posts. Perhaps we'll need to have Sailor on the phone while entering Genevive's, explaining where she is going and that there will be an event," Diego says thoughtfully. "In the meantime, I'll do some digging and have my hacker Sebastian try and trace his phone. The guy's excellent at what he does. He may even be able to send over a digital flyer about her celebration via text message or email."

"This plan seems to be the best we can do for now. Let's hope we can draw him in," Riot nods, standing.

His hand drops from around my shoulder, breaking contact with the electric current running through the two of us. I almost inhale in relief. His touch, his energy, it's overwhelming and comforting all at once. I remain seated, trying to take in all this information discussed. Riot claps Diego on the back behind me.

"Thank you for coming out. I know this could have been discussed over the phone, but I'm not taking any chances with her." I can feel his heated gaze skim over me.

"I can certainly understand why, Riot," he laughs before turning towards me. "It was nice to meet you, Sailor. You've got an army protecting you now. Get some rest if you can. I can imagine the last few days have been exhausting."

And with those parting words, he moves over to say his goodbyes to Cameron–who has been nothing but quiet since I sat down.

"May I take a quick peek at your wounds before I leave?" Madison's sweet voice pulls me from my own mind, prompting me to stand up.

Jesus, Sailor. Could you have been any more rude sitting here as everyone says goodbye? They are all here to protect you, for fucks sake.

She gently guides me over to the side of the room away from the men. I smile gratefully and tug my shirt loose from my leather leggings. Madison's soft fingers palpate the area where the butterfly stitches are.

"Looks good, no signs of infection. You are very warm, though. Do you feel alright?" A perfectly arched eyebrow raises.

I let out a shaky exhale, tucking my shirt back in. "I'm *physically* okay. Riot is just getting on my damn nerves. Since the moment I met him eight years ago, he's embedded himself under my skin like a tattoo. I need to get rid of him once this is all over."

Madison lets out a silent chuckle. "Oh, girl. I've been in your shoes and I wish I could say that removing him will bring you peace. From past experience, that feeling only lingered and made me crave him more. Word of advice? Don't let those two choose what's best for you. Stand your ground–which I don't see you having an issue with."

She squeezes my arm twice before walking towards her husband's outstretched hand. "Take care, Sailor. Oh—and in case you didn't notice, Riot hasn't been able to take his eyes off of you since I've pulled you away with me." She shoots me a wink then leaves, the room growing awkwardly quiet as I turn around.

CHAPTER 15

SAILOR

Lights dance off the walls, and smoke permeates the air as patrons fill in around the bar. Some are already receiving various services behind closed doors down the dimly lit hallway.

I must admit, the place is pretty cool. And although it puts me in a foul mood knowing these places are the reason the mom and pop restaurants are closing their doors, it does bring a certain *charm* to our small community.

Rose and I have easily fallen into a routine as the night progresses. We are on the Moon side of the bar. Two other bartenders—Chris and Kevin are on the Sun side. We all briefly interacted before the doors opened. They are definitely not as entertaining as Rose and her energetic personality, but they are kind and gentle, willing to help with anything I need to get adjusted. Chris even wrote his number down on a napkin, offering to take me to work if I ever needed a ride.

He also lives on Peaks Island with Kevin. The two of them have been together for six years. It's actually quite adorable watching their dynamic and how easily they flow together while working. Where one tosses a glass in the air, the other catches it and fills it with beer. Supportive smiles and exchanges pass between them without words. They are a team at work and at home. I admire that.

Riot and Cameron had a drink at our bar after the meeting with Madison and her husband. Cameron still had a hard time making eye contact with me. Whereas Riot's eyes...never once did they wander far as I became familiar with the ways of the club. He did, in fact, order the *Witch's Broom* as Rose had suggested he would. He even insisted I try it so I would know what to expect while making it.

I must agree—it was delicious.

The flavors bursting on my tongue awakened a sort of ancient feeling inside me. If that makes sense. The first sip gave me a sense of sitting around a fire in the woods with old friends, sipping on the spiced citrus cocktail. The Moon is at its peak in the sky, and the buzz of cicadas singing their song. Across the fire sits a man, the shadows of the flames dancing on his chiseled face.

It brought up emotions of safety and comfort—and something else. Before I gave myself the chance to identify that feeling, I slid the copper cup back to Riot, whose fingers brushed against mine to receive it.

The organ in my chest began its incessant pounding, like it seems to do every time he touches me. At that point, I made sure to busy myself at the other end of the bar. Putting some much needed distance between the two of us.

Not that it helped much—the heat of his gaze on my back practically scorched a hole into the fabric of my shirt.

He may be helping me, and even laying on the protector vibes nice and thick, but he is still hiding something. That is exactly the reason I should steer clear of him as much as I can.

With him gone to do some more of whatever it is he does downstairs, you would think I'd have settled down.

Nope.

R ose and I interact with customers and make drinks. She laughs and shamelessly flirts with patrons. I smile at her, wishing I could siphon some of her energy. Ya know, let loose a bit and open myself up. *But, I can't.* I'm still fucking on edge.

All because of *him*.

The damn *Demon* a floor below us.

Rose lingered with the guys earlier, laughing and sending jabs at the two of them. That was the moment that I couldn't quite shake the feeling of jealousy that tried to creep its way through my veins. Especially after watching Riot interact back so playfully. *They have history.* And although she laughed that she and Riot hadn't been together, she never fully said it. The logical response is that I have no right to feel this way.

This ridiculous, primal need to claim him.

I don't want him. His presence is just hard to ignore.

But I'd be a damn liar if I said he didn't affect me at all. Not only is he involved in my waking life—now more so than ever—but he's also in my dream life, too.

One particular dream.

The one that has me gasping for air and begging and pleading for him to come back every time it ends. I try my best to focus on work, pushing those emotions to the back burner.

It's been a few hours since opening, and the entire club is packed. People are hovering by the bar, keeping me, Rose, Chris, and Kevin busy. The dance floor is buzzing with bodies swaying alone or passionately dancing together. While pouring a Captain and Coke, I fall into my own trance, mesmerized by the sight of them. That longing comes back full force, igniting my skin. Sweat drips down the back of my neck, my shirt and hair now clinging to my skin.

I hand the drink off to the young blonde and tap the computer screen to add it to her tab. Giving myself a second to breathe, I take a sip of my own *Witch's Broom* that is waiting for me next to the monitor. We are allowed two drinks per shift. Riot shot me a wink when he told me that my few sips earlier didn't count. This is my second. I shamelessly housed my first, to take the edge off. This one I've been nursing and is mostly watered down now that the ice has melted.

Rose comes up behind me and reaches over my head for a stein. If you order a local IPA, the refills are discounted when you purchase a wooden stein with the club's logo.

"You're doing great!" she praises as she lowers the tap handle to fill it.

I swipe the back of my hand along my forehead, collecting the moisture as I let out a laugh. "Thanks. It's a lot busier than my old job, that's for sure."

"It's already 1 AM. Two more hours and we will be out of

here. Can't wait to shower and jump back into my book. I finally got to the steamy bits, but had to leave earlier than expected after Riot demanded I get to the club. I planned on telling him to fuck off, but he managed to persuade me like he always does," she discloses, rolling her eyes dramatically. "What Riot wants, Riot gets."

My chest tightens again. *Persuade how?*

Stop it, Sailor. Not your problem. Stay out of it.

We get back to work, and before I know it, the lights rise, the smoke dissipates, and the DJ announces that it's time for the club to close. It's 2 AM. We spend the next half hour cleaning up and reorganizing the bar before cashing out our tips. And *holy fuck.* I made more than my entire weekly paycheck at *The Rickety Fence* in one night—in tips alone.

Rose hugs me goodbye as I take a sip of ice water. "I'll see you next weekend!" she trills in that sing-song voice of hers.

She passes Riot, who is walking toward me. Her arm swings out to playfully punch him in the bicep. He doesn't even acknowledge her, his emerald eyes glued to me as I down this water.

"Don't forget to send me the login. I'll make sure they are *extra spicy.* Just for you," she teases him.

Oh... I guess they are a thing. Maybe they aren't a couple... but maybe they fool around?

Cameron is lingering over by the door to the parking lot. He waves awkwardly and walks Rose out. *I guess he's still avoiding me.* Riot steps in front of me, but I barely notice him beyond the haze of my irrational thoughts.

"I can just get a ride to the ferry if you need to head back with Rose," I finally offer noncommittally.

He tilts his head, and his brows come together. "What are

you talking about, *Little Ember*?" The corner of his lips twitches as he mocks concern.

Now it's my turn for my brows to come together. "You two are hooking up?" I tried to voice it like a statement, but it came out as a question.

He bellows out a laugh and hooks his arm around my neck. *Ew, no.* I'm gross and slick with sweat. I swat his arm away from me—which he ignores—and continues to tug me along towards the back door.

His lips come ridiculously close to my ear as he leans down and whispers, "Jealous, are we?"

"No," I scoff. "Not in the slightest. I have zero interest in cult leaders."

I push him with more force until his arm slides off my neck. I'm sure it's now drenched in my sweat. Unfiltered embarrassment hits me. I need a fucking shower. A cold one. Because this conversation should *not* be happening.

It doesn't help that all night I've been restless. My skin has been on fire, my senses heightened. Something about that drink made me extra needy. *Maybe all the herbs?*

Perhaps the music didn't help. A thrumming started in my chest before spreading lower between my thighs. I noticed it slightly after the first sip, but couldn't put a name to it. After I finished the second one, my entire body buzzed. The desire to go dance with the others and feel a body against mine echoed within me. But it wasn't just *any* body on that dance floor that I wanted.

It was Riot's.

My reckless brain imagined us swaying our bodies to the tantric music, pressing my most sensitive parts flush against all his firm ones. The visions continued and intensified....*Riot taking me into the bathroom and spreading my thighs with his long fingers. Those green eyes of his glinting in the mirror with desire as his tongue sweeps across his lips, wetting them. His perfect white teeth clamping down on the fullness of his lower one as his fingers slip past the waistband of my leggings...*

Fuck. Now I am rethinking that damn vision.

HE IS OFF LIMITS, Sailor.

I chant it over and over in my head until we reach his car. He stares at me curiously before pulling open my door and gesturing for me to get in. That smile is back as he lingers there. The dimple in his cheek only tantalizes me further.

He leans over me, tucking my blonde strands behind my ears. The strong scent of palo santo overwhelms me, kicking my hormones into overdrive. That woody, mystical cologne mixed with the hint of mint from his gum is relaxing me and exciting me at the same time.

"For the record, Rosemary is my pain in the ass little sister. Also for the record... You're fucking irresistible when you're jealous." He rubs his thumb over the bruise on my cheek beneath my makeup before shutting my door.

I release a loud sigh as he rounds the front of the car. Relief floods me that he is out of my personal space. Because that feeling? Yeah, it's grown out of control now. My fists clench against the leather seat on either side of me. I'm so glad I didn't do something stupid like lean in that extra inch to kiss him. Provoke him. Anything that would get his hands to linger on me. But really, that sigh of relief was knowing Rose is his sister.

A small satisfied smile grows on my face.

Remember what happened the last time you opened up your heart and your body, silly girl.

That smile disappears as fast as it came. Riot is dangerous. Seeing these feelings through would only end in another mental spiral. I don't need that.

What I need is to focus on my new job and pray that James ends up behind bars. More importantly, I need to keep moving forward.

Let sleeping dogs lie.

CHAPTER 16

RIOT

My knee bounces up and down as I wait on the edge of Sailor's bed. She refused to sleep in my room—even though it has its own bathroom. So I offered her the spare. One bedroom down from mine. I insisted she use my en suite, though, since the other Demons share the bathroom in the main hall. The last thing I need is for them to drunkenly open the door while she's showering. They'd find themselves missing their eyes and half their teeth if that were to ever happen.

The door *clicks* open, and she saunters in. A white fluffy towel is wrapped around her perfect body, and another is wrapped around her head. Water droplets cling like diamonds on her porcelain skin. Clearly, she's not noticed me sitting here, masked in the shadows of her room. I should make my presence known...But I quite enjoy watching her when she thinks no one is looking.

She rummages through the cardboard boxes scattered around the room. My men brought them up for her while we were at the club. Delicate hands with healing cuts grip a t-shirt with a golden rose on it. There are about a dozen or so holes punctured through the fabric. *Why hasn't she thrown it out?*

Not the least bit concerned about her damp skin, she tosses it on over her towel before letting the terry cloth drop to her feet. The black cotton hangs low on her thighs, just shy of giving me a show. *Aaand* there goes my damn cock, jumping to attention at the forbidden sight of her.

She's stunning. More than stunning—she's a *goddess.* Makeup free, hair up in a towel, a tattered shirt loosely covering her soft curves. Her toes are painted a creamy shade of white. A few drops of water are still left clinging to her skin. Sailor shifts and digs around some more, leaning over another box. The shirt rides up and I look away.

Not because I don't long to get a closer look, but because she doesn't know I'm here. I'm not trying to be a Peeping Tom. In an attempt to announce my presence, I subtly clear my throat. Sailor gasps, clutching her white lace panties to her chest like a pearl necklace.

"What the fuck are you doing in my room, Riot? Get out!" she shrieks. "First, you watch me sleep, now you watch me undress? What the hell is wrong with you?"

Everything. But we don't need to discuss that now, love.

Embodying the monster she likes to think I am, I get more comfortable and lean back against the headboard, closing my eyes and propping my feet up on the comforter. I've already showered and changed, and have been sitting here for the last fifteen minutes waiting for her to come out. The woman took a half hour shower. What else was I supposed to do?

Honestly, I figured she'd have brought her clothes with her to my bathroom—assuming I could have been in my room at any point when she got out. Funny how she claims she's not into me, but her actions speak otherwise. She knew what she was doing when she walked out of the bathroom in just her towel. It was written all over her face when she saw me. Her shocked response didn't fool me. She's purposely trying to get under my skin.

And *fuck,* it's working.

I was delighted to get a glimpse of the lust in her eyes tonight. The green-eyed monster even came out to play when she thought my sister was my lover. *Ha. That made my fucking night.* I should give my sister a raise for whatever made Sailor think that.

But it wasn't just those moments alone that caught my attention. Watching my *little ember* work the bar... now *that* was mesmerizing. *I'll let you in on a little secret...* She wasn't the only green-eyed monster in the building tonight. I wanted to rip out every set of lustful eyes that landed on her and use them as a cocktail garnish.

Although I'm sure that would be bad for business.

Eh, what's a few bad reviews?

With violence no longer being an option, I left my place in the shadows of the main floor, made myself a drink, then parked my possessive ass right in front of the CCTV cameras a floor below. You better believe I had Sailor's beautiful face zoomed in on 4K.

Watching her fan herself while sipping on a drink full of aphrodisiacs had me wanting to jog up the stairs and offer her sweet relief. I nearly caved as her eyes softened and zoned out while admiring the tantric dancing a few feet in front of her.

Clearly distracted and riled up all night, I wondered

what it would feel like to pull her soft body against mine. To trace her curves with the rough pads of my fingertips. That desire only strengthened. My body demanded to know what she would sound like as she moaned my name. What her skin would feel like, taste like, as my lips pressed against the sensitive flesh.

In my fantasy, we were back in the employee bathroom. Back to the moment I had her pushed up against the sink. Except this time, my fingers didn't linger on her hips. Without an ounce of hesitation, they dipped under the waistband of those black leather leggings.

My lips trail down her neck as her head falls back onto my shoulder. My cock is pressed firmly against her ass. Begging for attention. But this isn't about me right now. I'm taking care of my goddess.

Perfect, full breasts rise and fall beneath the restraint of my forearm wrapped around them. Her breath fans my ear as her breathing becomes staccato.

Frantic, even.

Her pussy flutters around my two fingers, drenching them. The sound of just how wet she is joins in her echoes bouncing off the walls of the room. I quicken my tempo and grind my palm against her clit until she's tightening like a vice around them.

My thighs vibrate with the pure force of Sailor's legs trembling against them. They begin to buckle as she moans louder. Her back arches, and her breasts push against my forearm.

The firm grip I have around her is the only thing holding her up.

Satisfaction settles around me as I continue to draw out her pleasure, her beautiful body and mind like putty in my hands.

Sailor's muscles tighten around me one last time before relaxing. That's when my nickname rolls off her soft lips. "Riot..."

"Riot!" Sailor snaps her fingers in front of my face, interrupting my perfect fantasy. "Are you even listening to me?"

I can't help the chuckle that leaves me. She's cute when she's mad.

"Yeah," I rasp before clearing my throat. "I didn't know you'd be coming in here in just a towel. Relax, you were covered, and I looked away when you leaned over to get your..."

"Ugh! *Quiet.* Just...stop. It's late. What do you need? And close your eyes again!" she commands.

I do as she says, knowing she'll probably put her underwear on and add another layer of clothing just to spite me.

"I have something for you," I announce behind a smile, my eyes remaining closed.

She lets out a frustrated sigh. "You can open them now."

Sailor stands in front of me, arms crossed over her chest, hip popped out with sass. Surprisingly, she's still only in her t-shirt. I can't help the devious path of my eyes as they dip back down to the hem of it. Her cheeks flush red, but she remains standing there, not throwing any more accusations my way.

I hand her a Kindle, decorated with a sparkly case and a magnetic Popsocket. "I know that you like to read. And since I only need you to work at the club on the weekends when it's busy, I thought you might like to indulge yourself in some of the naughty books my sister downloaded for you. Seems you have a lot of pent-up aggression. It will probably help."

Her cheeks brighten to a beautiful shade of scarlet as she takes the device from me. I must have done something right.

All the tension she was holding onto visibly leaves her shoulders.

"I've always wanted one of these, but was never able to splurge the extra money on it. The library or Genevive's were my favorite places to go to borrow books."

A shimmer reflects in her lower lids as the screen lights up when she touches it. She looks at me, really looks at me. No mask. No armor. No fake bullshit. Just her stunning, makeup-free face, damp hair, and a sense of vulnerability she's not used to.

"Thank you," she whispers simply.

I clasp her hand in mine and tug her down next to me. "You're welcome. I added you to my account. Anything you want to download, just go for it. Apparently, my sister *highly* recommends the books already on there." I roll my eyes so hard I see the back of my goddamn skull. "Also, you need a new phone. So here." The iPhone box lands with a *plop* onto her lap. "It's already set up with your old contacts and apps. Same number, too."

Her plump, moisturized lips pop open. "You didn't have to do this, Riot. This is a lot for you to spend on me," she says reluctantly.

Sailor scrambles to her feet and darts over to the dresser, retrieving her purse. Money crinkles as she pulls out a few hundred bucks and hands it to me.

Absolutely not. I gently push her hand away with an insulted scoff. "These are gifts. I have a lot of money, *Little Ember*. It hardly broke my bank account to buy these for you. Honestly, seeing how you responded to receiving these has me wanting to buy you anything you want." I grin.

She scowls fiercely. *Alright, new approach.* "Listen, I get it.

I know what it is like to want what everyone else has. When I was younger, my family struggled pretty badly. The difference is, you had to grow up sooner than you were ready for. You didn't have the luxury of a special treat or gift from time to time. You had to choose between paying for your responsibilities or paying for leisure. It will never be like that for you again. I promise you that, Sailor. Not if I can help it."

She angrily swipes away a tear rolling down her cheek. Money is shoved in my face once again. An attempt to try and maintain her damn pride. "I'm not your responsibility, *Mr. President*. Please take this money and let me go to sleep." Her voice cracks as she says it. And it's like someone shoved a dull kitchen knife into my gut. *Pure fucking agony.*

"That's yours." I tuck her fingers around the wad of cash and shackle my own around her wrist, pulling her to me.

She surrenders immediately under my touch. The fucking shield she holds so tightly around her shatters. Her arms wrap around my waist as she lies her head on my chest. My own circle around her, swaddling her against me. A soul-crushing sob escapes her and rattles her back. I place my hand there and start drawing soothing circles over the tense muscles.

"Why are you doing this? You don't even know me," she weeps against my t-shirt.

"I do though, *Little Ember*. I know more about you than you may even know about yourself." My chest tightens at exactly how much I fucking know this beautiful creature in my arms.

This moment feels pivotal for us. A part of our journey that has spanned lifetimes. She doesn't know it yet, but her surrendering to this moment is huge. *Regardless of whether or not I think she'll give me the time of day.* Just bearing witness to her soul shining through the layers of fear she's shrouded herself in gives me a glimmer of hope.

Hope that we can make it work this time.

That we can get it right.

"Can you just stay here with me for a bit? I don't want to be alone tonight. I've not been sleeping great and...you... somehow make the ache in my chest go away. Even though you run a cult and are a complete ass most times." She quietly chuckles through the tears.

"Of course." I easily agree, laughing aloud and joining in her sense of humor. "You're safe here, Sailor. I won't let anyone hurt you." I smile against the top of her head and tighten my arms around her small frame.

Vanessa said this would be how it started. How the line in the sand would keep moving until one of us crossed it. For now, her surrendering to this moment of safety in my arms is enough.

She'll always be more than enough for me.

I just wonder if I'll ever be enough for her.

———

My eyelids groggily open to the sound of gentle snoring. I guess Sailor remained in my arms all night. Her head is resting gently on my chest, which rises and falls with each breath I take. Wild onyx hair cascades down my chest like a waterfall. I stroke it lightly, enjoying how peaceful she looks in her sleep.

We are still in the same spot as last night; the only difference is that we are a little more horizontal. Her smooth leg is draped over my hip, her foot hooked under my thigh. I take advantage of this time and admire her beauty, knowing this moment will probably dissolve as fast as a Listerine Strip.

Sailor's eyes and jaw are relaxed, no sign of a troubled night's sleep—which is reassuring after what she told me last night. I'm sure a lot still haunts her. Those blonde streaks of hair that halo her face are resting against her slightly parted lips. I gently tuck a strand behind her ear, sweeping my fingers along her jaw before brushing them across her soft lips. As I do, they raise, forming the faintest of smiles.

The sheets screech as she moves to nuzzle into me more, moving the hand that rests on my stomach to my waist before tugging herself closer.

Christ. This woman makes my heart race.

Long, dark lashes flutter as her lids slowly open. Honeyed eyes greet me and take my breath away. In the morning light, every shade of brown and tiny sparks of gold are visible in her irises. Never in my life have I seen eyes quite as unique as hers —aside from Vanessa's.

Sailor's smile grows wider as she shoots me a lazy smile, revealing straight white teeth. I'm tempted to grab my phone and snap a picture of her. A reminder that she is safe here in my arms. That she is actually looking at me the same way I am her.

"Morning," she rasps, her voice still groggy with sleep. It's sexy as hell and doing nothing to help this morning wood I've got going on—*that I'm sure she probably feels with how entangled we are.*

"How'd you sleep?" I lower my gaze to her arm, still wrapped snugly around my waist.

She doesn't remove it, making my heart beat a little more rowdily against my ribs.

"The best I have in a really fucking long time. Usually, I need chamomile tea and some melatonin to even be able to fall asleep—let alone *stay* asleep."

I lower my head, whispering my reply against her hair, "My chiropractor recommends body pillows to help facilitate sleep...or sex...I'd have to agree with him."

She chuckles beneath me as my hands move over her lower spine, needing to keep her close for as long as this will last. I pull her in until she is flush against me. A barely there sigh falls from her lips. Over the last few days, Sailor's body temperature has cooled my too-hot skin. But this morning, she's actually pretty warm, and I'm a few degrees cooler.

If that isn't the universe syncing our bodies, I don't know what is.

"As much as I'd love to enjoy a few more moments with you being pleasant towards me, I have to leave for a short business trip. Cameron will be coming by to keep an eye out. Help yourself to anything in the house. Whatever you want, it's yours. I've told my men to shadow you if you need to head into town. I don't feel comfortable with you walking alone with James' whereabouts still unknown."

She leans up and presses a palm down onto my chest, using it as leverage. Her face is only inches from mine. "And what if I don't want to be around Cameron?" A dark eyebrow quirks up, daring me to ignore her desire to steer clear of him.

"I do think you should talk, *Little Ember*," I preface. Her pink lips pop open, preparing to argue back. I silence those thoughts with my index finger pressed firmly against their plushness. Sailor's eyes flare with sparks of defiance and maybe even a hint of lust before I continue. "*But*...I also know you deserve time to process how you feel *away* from him. Would you prefer to come with me on my trip?"

She rakes her hands through her hair, flipping the loose waves behind her back. "So you're asking me to choose the lesser of two evils?"

"Oh come on," I tease, crossing my arms over my chest. "Being in my company is not *that* bad...You didn't seem to mind last night." I trace my middle finger down the curve of her spine to prove my point.

Her eyes narrow as she swings her legs over the edge of the bed. "Where are you going anyway?" she inquires. Her eyes remain glued to the floor, purposely avoiding my gaze.

"I have to attend a meeting tonight at one of my clubs in South Beach. I own a penthouse there. Wouldn't be the worst thing in the world to join me. You could spend the day in the sun, reading and relaxing, while I attend meetings. I should be free after noon tomorrow... Perhaps I'll join you if you decide to tag along."

She chews on her thumbnail, contemplating.

"I've never been to Florida. I haven't really been anywhere besides New York City and New Orleans that one time. That sounds...amazing, honestly. Although I'd rather use bleach as a coffee creamer than have to endure being bored to death on a plane with you." Her laugh captivates me as she looks at me with a grin on her face.

"Sorry, we're fresh out of bleach. I think we have ammonia if you'd like?" I cock my head to the side, waiting for her answer and loving every second of our banter.

"Alright, I'm in." Her eyes light up as she agrees. "When do we leave?"

Circling an arm around her waist, I lean over and lower my lips to her ear. "Oh, and by the way, *Little Ember*...the flight has the potential to be anything *but* boring...but I don't think we are quite there yet..."

I get up, not giving her the opportunity to respond, as I head towards the door. "Be ready in an hour. We'll have breakfast on the plane."

"I probably own like one bathing suit. I'll have to buy some down there. I don't think a place as nice as South Beach would approve of the ratty bikini I've had the last ten years."

"Don't pack a damn thing. It'll be taken care of." On top of a bikini, Sailor will have a whole new wardrobe by the time our tires hit the runway.

She rolls her eyes incredulously. "How will you know what I like or would even need to wear?"

Now I'm the one rolling my eyes at her before letting myself out of the room. "It'll be taken care of. Now get up, lazy bones. The beach is calling."

My mouth curves up into a goofy grin before shutting the door. *Smooth, Ryder. You look like a damn teenager with a crush.*

That foreign act of smiling has become a bit of a habit when I'm around my *little ember*. Waking up this morning was hell knowing I had to leave her for this trip. My hands were tied. I didn't have an option. In a matter of minutes, that dread has turned into excitement at the bone the universe just threw me.

CHAPTER 17

SAILOR

We get to the airport and instead of heading towards all the commercial terminals, the car takes us to a hanger in a private terminal. Riot gets out first. Like a gentleman, he opens my door and offers his hand to help me out of the SUV. You would never know these hands have ended a life...or touched me so intimately and softly...It's all hidden beneath the casual demeanor in which he carries himself.

I meekly smile up at him as his hands rests on my waist while assisting me out of the SUV. Why am I suddenly so shy around him? *God, he looks good.* So much more relaxed than he was while attending the club. His eyes penetrate mine, holding them captive...

Fuck me. Why does he have to be sweet and hot? *He's still a cult leader, Sailor. Don't forget that.* I lower my sunglasses that rest on my head, grateful for the reprieve.

Dark Angel is sporting a pair of tan golf shorts that do well to show off his impressive ass, along with a black linen shirt. The short sleeves are highlighting his sculpted biceps...which are doing their best to escape the confines of said shirt. A hint of his dragon tattoo peeks out behind the open button at his collarbone.

My teeth clamp down on my lip, holding back a groan as I continue to drink him in. He catches me staring, a playful smirk playing at his lips. Warm fingers lace through mine as he tugs me along towards the stairs of the private jet awaiting us. *How much fucking money does this guy make? A private jet? What is life right now?*

"Come along, *Little Ember*. There will be plenty of time to ogle me on the flight there," he teases.

"I was not *ogling* you. I was admiring the plane. I thought we were flying commercial?"

He shifts me in front of him, nudging me up the airstairs. I glance over my shoulder at him, still waiting for a response. "I have a private jet for the luxury of privacy. What my team and I do demands it."

"*Right.* I'm still trying to process exactly what that is..." I snide, still annoyed that he holds all these secrets he now has me involved in.

A flight attendant greets me with a genial smile as I step into the main cabin. My jaw practically hits the floor at the *luxury* he just spoke of dripping all around us. From soft white leather with black embellishments to warm under-lighting. The jet *screams* more than just a tax cut.

Where I currently stand is a small bar and kitchenette. On both sides of us are two sets of chairs facing one another. A rich walnut table rests between them. Towards the back, the light plush carpet leads to a comfortable looking sofa and another table. At the very back is a black door. *I wonder...*

Riot leans over to rest his chin on my shoulder, following my gaze. "That one leads to the private bedroom and bath."

His voice drops to a gruff baritone, making goosebumps spring up along my arms. Heat rushes down my body and pools at my core while a blush creeps up my neck and darts straight to my cheeks. I take a step forward, giving space to the desires he is stirring in me.

Riot silently chuckles behind me before taking a seat in the chair to our left and resting his elbows on the table. I move to take the seat opposite him, curious how far I'll let this flirting go. His eyebrow raises, probably wondering the same thing. I mimic his stance, going a step further to steeple my hands. *If the man wants to play chess, by all means, let's play chess.*

A noise from the back snags my attention. Riot looks past me at the same time I swivel my head. The door to the bedroom opens revealing a woman with bright pink hair. She leans against the doorframe to casually inspect her nails.

"Oh, for fuck's sake," Riot groans, placing his hands over his face.

"Ryder, you won't mind if we join, do you?" Rose chirps with a big ass smile on her face.

"*We?*" he mumbles beneath his hands.

"You did offer for Vanessa and I to get a little reprieve from the club..." she goads her brother in the same moment Vanessa fills the threshold of the door next to her.

Riot's hands fly off his face at the mention of Vanessa. The woman who appears to hold a world of ancient knowledge within her unique violet-blue irises raises a gray eyebrow at him. A satisfied smirk grows on her face at his unease.

"That was *before...*" he practically growls his irritation at seeing the two of them.

"Before...?" Vanessa presses.

"Before your aura went from muddy gray to blazing orange and red?" Rose adds. "Or before Sailor agreed to come with you?"

"Ya know what? Just sit the hell down and *behave.*" He gestures to the matching set of chairs and table across the aisle from us.

"What's the big deal?" I question the cranky asshole in front of me. I mean, Rose is awesome. We already get along great. And from what I learned last night, Vanessa travels with him all the time.

"This was supposed to be a time for you to *relax. And me...*" he says the last part under his breath. "That likely won't happen now that those two have joined." He glares at them behind his sunglasses while leaning back to sulk in his chair.

"Don't be such a grouch, Ryder. I'm sure the three of us will have a lovely time together while you're stuck in stuffy business meetings all day," Rose chimes in from her seat.

"Your definition of lovely and mine are wildly different, Rosie," he raises his aviators to his forehead, revealing intense emerald eyes. Ones currently shooting daggers at his sister.

Why is he so upset? We were just together less than twenty-four hours ago. If he was that adamant about us not being around each other, he wouldn't have had her train me.

"I asked you for your measurements this morning, not for your goddamn attitude to join Sailor and I," he adds irritably.

"You're the only one here who seems to care. You don't mind, Sailor, right?" Rose giggles, knowing she's tickling the talons of the beast across from me. It's actually quite amusing.

I stare up at him with the hint of a smile, enjoying how much his sister can rile him up. If Riot were to take the form of the dragon etched into his skin, he would currently have smoke pouring out of his nose. Even his muscles are bunched as he sits on the edge of his chair looking prepared to abandon us here in lieu of taking another flight.

"I don't mind, Riot." I reach over and place my hand on his formidable forearm. The once tense muscles relax at my touch, quickly followed by his anger and anxiety that were tightly coiled into his facial features. "It will be nice to have someone to talk to while you're in your meetings."

"Fine," he grits out through his teeth.

"Wonderful," Vanessa agrees happily as the flight attendant starts setting up place mats in front of us. "I even brought my tarot cards. We'll have plenty of time to do your reading, Sailor."

"Yay! That's awesome!" I turn towards Vanessa with a pleased grin.

"No." Riot hisses furiously at the same time.

"*Yes*. It's about time she understands her journey and *who* she shares it with," Vanessa says calmly, completely unaffected by Riot's temper.

"Can I get you something to drink, Ms. Monroe?" The beautiful blonde flight attendant smiles down at me, temporarily putting Riot's argument to rest.

I take my sunglasses off and place them in my purse

before looking up at her. "I'll have an iced coffee if you have —light and sweet, please," I reply.

"I'll do the same, Alyssa. Please and thank you," Rose adds while reclining her chair all the way back and taking out her Kindle.

"Of course, Ms. Corbin." *Corbin?* I thought she and Ryder were siblings. That would make her Vanessa's...

"Rosie and I are adopted. Vanessa has raised us since we were young kids." Riot explains, noticing my confusion. "When my mom was murdered when I was thirteen, my father wanted nothing to do with the two of us. He gave up his rights. Having no living relatives, we were placed in the system. Both my father and mother were only children. The only stipulation that piece of shit requested was that we be adopted together."

The floor rumbles as the jet's engines start up, preparing for our flight. Riot leans back in his chair, getting comfortable.

"Vanessa came along when I turned fifteen and Rosie thirteen. She was never able to have children of her own. Over the years she gave up on that dream, shifting her goals. Eventually, she and her husband opened up a crystal shop in New Orleans. They had a beautiful life. Half the time they offered classes and sold crystals and trinkets, the other, they explored the wonders of the world. The year she lost him to pancreatic cancer, my sister and I apparently came to her in a psychic vision. That's when she knew it was the right time to fill her home with love and laughter again." Riot chuckles wryly, trying to lighten the mood, but his eyes are still glazed in sorrow.

I use the knuckles of my index fingers to swipe at the

tears inching down over my cheeks. Now I feel like a complete asshole, disgusted with how wrongly I have judged Riot since the day I met him. All while his past was filled with as much grief as mine.

He didn't come from money like I thought. Which I was only just made privy to last night. Discovering he and his amazing sister were abandoned by their father after losing someone precious to them—and murdered nonetheless...it's almost too much for me to digest. My heart pounds an unsteady rhythm against my ribcage with the similarities we all share.

The grief. The trauma we all endured.

Riot reaches across the table and squeezes my hand. "Don't cry for me, *Little Ember*. Vanessa was an incredible parent to us. She gave us a loving home. *Strict*—" he gazes over at his adopted mother with nothing but kindness now, "But incredibly loving. Rosemary took Vanessa's last name in the adoption. I chose to keep my birth surname, hoping one day my father would discover the kind of man I became. That my worth never left with him leaving us."

"Why do they call you Riot?" I press, still needing to understand the nickname.

"When Vanessa first met me, she told me that she knew one day I would start a riot for love. That she had *seen* it. I was destined to meet another who would do the same for me." His green eyes soften as they lift to mine. Suddenly, I can't look away, clinging to them like drops of dew on freshly cut grass.

"Since that day, I introduced myself to everyone outside of my family as Riot. It was a new life for me. I could be anybody I wanted to be. And that was something *I* got to choose. Upon entering college, it became my entire personality. The name Riot just felt...right. Like perhaps this was the man I was supposed to be. Because it was true. I would start a damn riot for all those who didn't have the power to do so themselves. That's when the plan to form *The Demons* came into play. I started to recruit like-minded individuals who could help me carry out that vow. Around that time, a song named "Start *A Riot*" came out by Banners. The lyrics..." he pauses, a radiant smile forming on his face as he reflects on the memory.

That smile does me in. Or maybe it's the way he's looking at me... Goosebumps sprout up along my flesh and an overwhelming sense of pride fills me as he continues to tell this story.

"I remember one of my friends showing me it in the car, and something major clicked into place for me. It wasn't just a name anymore. It was my life's mission to help others. To give them the justice or peace they deserved. *The Demons'* responsibilities were all I could focus on besides my studies in business. Every once in a while though, a little flicker would arise in my caged off heart. A pulse not my own. *A palpitation.* I wondered if what Vanessa had seen would perhaps come true. That one day soon I would find the woman who would start a riot in my own soul."

"And did you find her?" I ask boldly.

He squeezes my hand twice before releasing it, along with a heavy sigh. *Soo... is that a yes?* The uncertainty and even a bit of unwarranted jealousy prompt me to do the same.

Leaning back in the chair, he retrieves his phone and starts answering texts or emails. Maybe he's playing Candy

Crush for all I know. His face isn't giving anything away. That vulnerability he showed me earlier is nearly tucked away again.

The engines prime and the plane picks up speed, soaring down the runway. I clamp my eyes shut as we lift off the ground, climbing higher and higher. My ears start to pop, making me uneasy. I never enjoyed flying. Not that I did it much. Each time always resulted in me having a mini panic attack.

Riot's soothing scent filters through my nose as I inhale deeply. A useless attempt at settling my racing heart. The jet hits a bit of turbulence, jostling me in my seat. Ice spreads through my veins thinking of all the possible scenarios that could unfold at the moment. *"Please God, Please God, Please... Please... Please,"* I mentally pray, my eyes still screwed shut.

A firm hand lands on my knee beneath the table, pulling my attention back to reality. My eyelids pop open. Riot sits across from me unbothered, still absorbed in his phone, but his hand remains on my knee, his fingers tracing circles on my thigh.

Alyssa comes back with our drinks and a tray of muffins, scones, and bagels galore when we finally reach a safe altitude. Jam, cream cheese, and fresh fruit are spread out amongst them. I snag a croissant and load it with Nutella before taking a sip of my iced coffee.

Holy shit, this coffee is heaven. I take another satisfying sip before devouring my croissant like a ravenous squirrel. When there is nothing but crumbs remaining on my plate, I move on to the freshly cut strawberries. Also drenching them in the nutty, chocolatey goodness.

Riot looks up at me over his phone and smirks. Those

panty-dropping eyes of his have me glancing back down at my plate. A sudden wave of desire rushes over me. *Damn him and his beautiful eyes... and lips...and that little piece of hair that sits out of place on his forehead... Ugh!* This path we are heading down is going to be a disaster for my heart...

Although the more I learn about Riot, the less I actually believe that.

I power on my Kindle and dive into a book about an arranged marriage between a vampire and his blood source. Typical enemies-to-lovers, forced proximity, touch her and die, and lots of delicious banter. Based on my reading history, it's right up my alley. A perfect distraction from 'ogling' Riot. Because we all know that is exactly what I was doing earlier...

Every time we hit some turbulence, I glance up at the flight path on the monitor above Riot's head. His penetrating, yet understanding eyes always lift from his phone to offer a semblance of unspoken comfort. The more severe bouts of them, he would place his hand back on my knee.

Where that should have helped...I'm more on edge now than ever. This book has gotten around to the spicy scenes, and I'm about to lose it. I'm sure it's become plain to see. Riot's lingering gazes and occasional fingers on my bare flesh have not only heated my face, but my core as well.

It's been too damn long since I've been intimate with someone.

The last hookup I had was with a local patron at the *Rickety Fence*, who, after repeatedly and annoyingly asking me out, I finally caved and gave my number to. We went on a few dates. And when I say 'dates', I mean takeout at my apartment after my shift and some *Netflix and chill*. It was nothing special. Or memorable for that matter.

And he snored like a warthog.

My eyes drift away from my book and back up to the more poised, tuskless predator in front of me. He's deep in thought, brow furrowed, scowling at something on his phone. The straw to his iced coffee is hanging loosely between his lips after he drank deeply from the plastic cup. I can't help but be enamored with him.

He *is* ridiculously handsome. The type of exquisiteness that is kind of hard to ignore.

It doesn't help my libido with his muscles on full display. As if hearing my praise for his brawniness, he clenches his phone in one hand and the cup in the other. Even his hands are nice... Liv has this theory about thumbs. If a man's thumbs are long, it suggests their ... *FOCUS, Sailor.*

On an overly frustrated sigh, I keep reading. Instantly, I regret it. The second sex scene just started up.

The turbulence decides to settle—*Thank God.* I take the opportunity to stand and stretch. Riot's eyes flash with fervor as my tank top rides up, exposing more of my heated skin to him and the healing wound on my side. Unable to stay a moment longer wrapped in this alluring space, I head for the bathroom at the back of the cabin.

The coffee I downed ran right through me.

Along the way, I pass Rosemary, who is passed out in her seat, hoodie up, Kindle resting on her chest. Vanessa shoots me a wink as she takes out her tarot cards and spreads them across the table.

"Come see me when you're finished," she says. For the second time now, I realize her lips aren't moving. My eyes widen a fraction, and Vanessa sends me a knowing look. One of pure amusement. *She knows then? But... how...?*

I have so many questions.

When I press the bedroom door closed behind me, I'm met with resistance. Of course, it's none other than Riot Black who greets me. The man setting my skin aflame. He weasels his broad body through the gap with a determined look on his handsome face. His energy and domineering proximity hit me like a damn meteorite, overwhelming my already heightened senses and apparently sizzling the rational part of my brain that's good at setting boundaries.

Is my body buzzing? Because it feels like the closer Riot gets, the more my body vibrates. Similar to that of a magnet getting closer to another. It's almost as if I can feel his excitement as much as I can feel my own. The anticipation that's building.

"Can I help you?" I narrow my eyes at him while crossing my arms over my chest, covering my now agonizingly hard nipples.

"You can, actually. Stay still. This has been driving me fucking mad all morning." He lowers his head and licks the corner of my mouth. Slowly.

Excruciatingly slow.

On instinct, my palm slaps his firm chest, shoving him back. The vibrating only gets more intense. My ears start to ring with a frequency that makes me dizzy. *UGH*. These frustratingly lonely hormones, along with my scrambled brain, start to scream at me to pull him back in. Because what he just did has my pulse hammering against my neck.

And I want more of it.

More of him.

All of him.

"You had Nutella there the entire morning. And I have a sweet tooth. Especially for chocolate."

Eyes as green and round as Granny Smith apples project all sorts of mischief. A dare sits within them. He inches back just enough to seek out my response before his lips slam against mine. The door crashes shut as he kicks it with the tip of his boat shoe before slamming *me* back against the bathroom door. His teeth graze along my bottom lip as he sucks it into his mouth. I moan loudly as his tongue slides over the flesh, easing the sting his teeth left behind.

"You had some there, as well," he whispers against my lips.

Butterflies swarm my stomach as he presses me flush against the wooden door. The hard planes of his muscles and something even more firm press against me. I open my mouth, inviting his tongue in. He takes full advantage, caressing mine in a dance only we seem to know. It's as if we've done this a thousand times before. His fingers wind into my hair, angling my face to kiss me deeper as mine cling to his sculpted back.

"I've wanted to do that since the moment you knocked into me on the staircase at my frat house," he growls between kisses.

"*You* knocked into *me*," I argue playfully, and can't help but laugh in disbelief.

I felt the same pull the night we met, but was so hung up on Cameron, I brushed it aside. Then, to add insult to injury, I turned Riot into the villain in order to keep the feelings I had towards him at bay....or use him as the punching bag for the anger I truly had towards Cameron.

Only when he entered my dreams as the *Dark Angel* did I recognize the extent of just how much this man affected me.

"There are things Vanessa is going to tell you that will probably change how you feel about this," he gestures his index finger between us. "I selfishly wanted to make sure you knew how I felt about you before she did," he says cryptically, even nervously, as he steps back. Long fingers rake through his onyx hair as he releases a forceful breath.

"Okaaay? Does it have anything to do with how I can hear her talking to me in my mind? Or how you have shown up in my dreams over and over again?"

His eyes widen to saucers and his face pales. "You're dreaming about me?" he asks, tilting his head slightly.

"That's all you got out of that? I just said I can hear Vanessa in my mind, and you focus on me dreaming of you?" I laugh.

He reaches out and cups my face in his hand, running the pad of his thumb over my cheek. "I dream of you, too, *Little Ember*. And you'll soon discover why."

A gentle kiss is pressed to my forehead before he slips back out of the bedroom door, leaving me to my racing thoughts.

Okay, what the fuck just happened?

With my mind running a marathon, I use the bathroom

quickly and wash my hands before splashing some cold water on my face. My skin is on fire. Specifically, the places he *touched*. I pull my hair back into a low bun and let the blonde pieces hang loose around my face. Taking a steadying breath, I exit both rooms and head straight for Vanessa.

It's time to meet my destiny, I suppose. Who better to gather the information Riot's been so afraid of being exposed, from none other than the best psychic around—and also his adoptive mother.

CHAPTER 18

RIOT

Fuck. Fuck. Fuuuuuck. That kiss was everything it should have been and more. Yet it's everything I fear is about to be torn away from me. Possibilities of our life flashed before my eyes when she moaned as my lips devoured her. Sailor clung to me like I was the only one who had ever elicited that feeling out of the depths of her soul. And quite frankly, I *am the only one* who has ever done that.

In every fucking life before this one.

Sailor has been mine longer than I can remember. Vanessa is about to disclose that to her during her reading. Which is why I am freaking the fuck out. Why I've *been* freaking the fuck out. It took me years to process what this journey is and the stages involved. Beyond that, it requires dedication and practice to even begin to comprehend the flashes of memories that come back. As far as I understand, she's a novice. Completely unaware of the inner workings and practices of divination.

"Ryder, why don't you come and take a seat. I'm sure Sailor needs a few minutes after your intimate aura merging," she chuckles deeply, her voice giving way to her age.

I plop down next to Rosie. She startles awake, her Kindle tumbling onto the floor. "What'd I miss?" she mumbles, looking around bewilderedly.

"Your brother and Sailor had a 3D moment of passion."

"Vanessa..." I groan, lowering my face into my palms.

"He did?!" Rosemary shrieks.

She sits up excitedly and claps her hands like a fangirl shipping her favorite characters before reaching down to retrieve her Kindle. Inclining the seat back to normal, she carelessly tosses the device into her purse—the one covered in little locks that hang on a thick chain attached to the handle.

"Shh, settle down, child. We don't want to frighten her. She most likely is processing a lot right now. So many memories and feelings are going to surface soon, which can be overwhelming for someone who hasn't fully awakened yet."

"You're right, Nessa. Sorry," Rose whispers sheepishly before resting back in her chair and patting my arm.

Just when I think she'll behave, she shifts her body towards me and pretends to wrap her arms around an invisible figure. She mimics making out—including tongue. I really do wonder if she'll ever grow up. My sister can take down a grown ass man. Rosie truly is a badass. Yet somehow she manages to still act like an adolescent.

Amused by her antics, I shake my head, doing my best to hide my smile. Rosemary may operate to the beat of her own drum, but she certainly is my biggest cheerleader. And as much as I complain, I wouldn't have it any other way.

The bedroom door clicks open. We all subtly exchange looks with each other in anticipation. A few seconds later,

Sailor's footsteps grow closer, and she appears at the table. A red flush still kisses the apples of her cheeks. She does look calmer, though. Caramel curls frame her face; the rest is gathered into a bun at the back of her neck.

I wonder if she's hot? I know I fucking am. I'm going to need to change this damn shirt before my meeting. The amount I've been sweating the last few minutes...

"I think I am ready to join you, Vanessa," Sailor says first.

"Of course, my dear. Come have a seat next to me." Vanessa pats the seat beside her, which is directly across from me. "I take it you are starting to understand there are larger things at play here than just a simple kiss?"

"I wouldn't call what I did *simple*—" I retort defensively. Vanessa holds a palm up and a stern look on her face to shush me.

"Ryder William Black. Please do not start. If I am to read with you being here, I would like silence unless she or I requests information from you."

"Yes, ma'am," I reply, feeling like a goddamn child again. Vanessa always ran a tight ship. She kept me out of trouble for the most part–but not *always*. My rebellious side begged to come out and play every now and again.

Still does when I'm on the hunt.

"To answer your question... *Yes.* I can't keep trying to convince myself that running into Riot again was just coincidence. Or even the result of a bad decision I made listening to my friend Liv's advice on where to go if I was ever in trouble. After having him in my dreams, and it being recurring at that, I know there has to be something more to it. More to... *us,*" she practically squeaks, her eyes rising to meet mine briefly before turning back to glance at Vanessa.

Vanessa covers her hand over Sailor's trembling one. She tilts her head and focuses, peering at Sailor as if she's speaking to her telepathically. Goddamnit, she *is*. She plans on keeping this information from me.

Sailor giggles nervously. "How can I respond... using this?" She taps an index finger to the center of her forehead.

"Just follow the thread of energy I just sent out to you in reverse," Vanessa responds for us all to hear. "Imagine you are at the bank drive-thru and I am the teller. You are going to place your signed documents I sent you back in the tube or drawer and send them back to me. Use that same theory to send over information."

"Got it—I *think*," she says ambivalently before smirking. A sense of hope brightens up her features.

"Good. Now show me the dream you keep having," Vanessa encourages gently.

She closes her eyes even though she doesn't need to. I'm sure it's to ease the pressure off Sailor. Or perhaps to make her feel more relaxed and open spiritually. Sailor follows suit, closing her own eyes. Inch by inch, her shoulders drop and her jaw unclenches.

A few heartbeats later, and at the same time, their eyes snap open and widen. A gasp slides over Sailor's swollen lips. The honey of her eyes has deepened into a dark caramel and her pupils have dilated. *She's doing it.* She's communicating and sharing her visions with Vanessa telepathically. *Damn, I'm so proud of her right now.* That skill can take years to master.

And she's done it in a matter of minutes.

Rosemary and I aren't even able to do it yet—and we've been trying since we were little kids.

Vanessa claims that Sailor is a powerful psychic medium like herself due to her near-death experience when coming into this world. Rosemary and I never had such a close encounter with death, so we aren't as easily able to use the gift as they are. That's not to say that we *can't*. All of those awakened can grow and develop their psychic abilities. Some are just naturally better at it than others.

"My dear, what you showed me is the *exact* same dream your counterpart has," she affirms, nodding my way. You are what we call *mirrored souls*. Or the more modern term would be *twin flames*."

"Like... fated mates?" Sailor asks innocently before worrying her lower lip.

Rosemary burst out laughing. "*Exactly* like that, girl. Except your mate is this big guy right here." She juts her thumb out at me and scrunches her face. "And unfortunately for you, he doesn't have an impressive wingspan. Or maybe he does," she wiggles her eyebrows suggestively. "Who can really say without those leathery appendages making his endowment status known?"

Fucking Christ, Rosemary.

My *Little Ember* snorts a laugh, cupping a hand to her mouth. Another one follows as she howls with laughter, my sister joining her in the cacophony. Even Vanessa joins in, her wrinkles becoming more prominent as the first sign of a smile shows.

"What the fuck are you even talking about, Rosemary? This is the kind of shit you read? That sounds *disturbing*. I think I may need to delete all those books off Sailor's Kindle. You're corrupting her innocence."

Rosie completely ignores me.

Sailor rolls her eyes dramatically.

"He's basically followed you around like a Golden Retriever mixed with a Doberman in every life you've lived together. Such a loyal little beasty you are," my sister coos while patting my head.

"Fuck *off*, Rosemary." I snap my teeth at her like a real dog. She's pissing me the fuck off today. Sailor is going to run for the fucking hills. Who the hell would want to get involved in my world, let alone deal with my over-the-top, frankly, *batshit* crazy family?

"*Language*," Vanessa glares at me.

The gorgeous woman in front of me contains another giggle by biting down on her lip and driving me insane with need. I just had my teeth, my tongue, and my lips all over hers. I'd like to do it again, soon. If only my family, *correction* —my *sister*—would shut the hell up.

Sailor eventually finds the strength to calm down, forcing her face back into a casual demeanor. Vanessa smiles at her again. I can't say I've seen my mother smile in such a long time. Not *truly*, anyway.

Not since we were kids.

"Have I ever really gotten a say in who my heart would belong to?" Sailor questions.

Ahh. And here comes the doubt. The questions. The fucking mindfuck of a spiral.

"Of course. Nothing overrides free will. Not even the Universe's workings. Believe it or not, you and Ryder spent most of your past lives dating karmics," Vanessa explains.

"What are karmics? People who teach you lessons?" Sailor asks, loosely understanding the concept.

"Yes, Sailor. To sum it up, they are romantic partners or

people in your life who teach you important *soul* lessons. These lessons are usually learned the hard way in order to be able to encourage growth. They are a catalyst. Sometimes these connections trigger a massive healing that leads you closer to your counterpart. And sometimes they don't. Understand that these individuals were *never* meant to linger in your orbit. Not for long. They aren't able to complement your life the way a true counterpart would. Most of the time, these connections are toxic and abrasive. Karmics were never the ones to ignite the flame inside you or continue to stoke its fire. Those would be a twin flame or soulmate. And their role is very rare and very beautiful. Your mirrored mission is to awaken the best parts of your soul until you are in harmony and union within yourselves, and therefore, with each other. Ultimately, your union will help uplift humanity as a whole."

"Is that why I feel such grief at the end of my dream, when I... when I lose Ryder?"

Hearing her say my real name has blood rushing south. *Do you know how many times I fantasized about Sailor saying my name? About her finally switching up the syllable at the end?*

"Yes. Many of your past lives you two spent leaving each other. Right as you were on the cusp of finally recognizing what you meant to one another on a soul level. There hasn't been many lifetimes where you are physically able to stay together. Only a few that I can pick up on from Ryder's past life regression sessions. I'd be interested to see what your sessions would bring up."

"I'd be interested in learning more. What do those cards have to do with our situation?" Sailor asks curiously.

"These cards," Vanessa waves a hand above them, "are a

tool used to see the path ahead for you and also your twin flame. It is always subject to change; however, what is shown now is the current trajectory based on your mindset and energies. We are going to be using the traditional Rider-Waite deck."

"Understood. Can we see what's ahead?" Sailor asks with a twinge of excitement in her voice. Which does well to ease the anxiety still coursing through me.

At least one of us is calm right now.

"Of course. I think we are all a bit interested in your path ahead. We've been anxiously awaiting the day you reunited with Ryder. And as much as we wish it were under different circumstances, the timing has been quite divine," my mother muses.

A beautiful pink blush flushes Sailor's face. She looks up, sharing a hesitant smile with me. *Perhaps this will work out? I expected her to have freaked out already. Cue the runner stage.*

"I am going to have you select ten cards. We are going to do a Celtic Cross spread. It will give me a good indication of where you're at and where you're headed," Vanessa explains.

Sailor reaches out, slowly hovering a hand over the cards and selecting carefully. She's clearly putting thought into which ones she chooses. It doesn't seem random at all.

"May I ask how you are selecting the cards?" Vanessa asks as Sailor hands her the ones she's already claimed.

"Some make my hand tingle more than others," she replies skeptically.

"That's a great way to understand how energy and our intuition guide us. *Clarsentience*. Perfect job, Sailor," Vanessa praises, pride lighting up her face. My mother is in her teaching element right now, and I know she's loving every second of it.

Sailor collects the remaining five cards and hands them off to Vanessa, who adds them to her pile. My little ember leans over to observe the spread before us. A vertical card with one horizontally crossed over it is located in the center. Those two are surrounded by four other cards in vertical positions. To the right of that cross—or circle—depending on how you look at it, are four other vertical cards lined up in a row top to bottom.

Vanessa collects the card on top and places it off to the side, pointing her bony finger at the one beneath it.

"The first card here," she taps the vertical card in the center, "will tell us about where you currently stand. And you have the Six of Swords. That card is a great representation of transitions. Which seems to be where you are in life. Moving locations, switching jobs, meeting new people, leaving behind chaos and that of the past to seek safety in the calm." Vanessa's finger glides over the artwork to circle around a child. "See that other person in the boat? That can represent someone here helping you during this transition and healing journey. Perhaps it is your spirit team...or it could even represent Ryder."

"Wow," Sailor nods.

Rose hands Vanessa the card she had placed to the side and smiles savagely. She's just as excited for this as I am. "The *Lovers*." She taps her black almond-shaped acrylic nail on the card.

"Beautiful!" Vanessa sighs in awe. "This card is a true twin flame indicator. It represents Gemini energy of the twins. Mirrored souls. You and Ryder. See how the pair reaches for each other, completely naked and exposed? That is part of the soul's journey. It's reaching a point where you are entirely open and vulnerable with your counterpart. No need to hide anything or allow the ego to drive you. The sun here and the angel above show happiness, union, and how this connection is divinely guided and protected by angels such as Archangel Metatron and Archangel Michael."

Sailor observes the card, lips twitching at the nudity.

If you wanna see me naked, baby, I'm ready when you are.

As if she heard me, she lifts her head and rolls her eyes at me. *Wait. Hold the fuck on. Did she just hear me?*

Her gaze drops to the next card Vanessa picks up. The one directly below the two that are crossing. Vanessa's thumb skims over the card thoughtfully.

"This card represents where your focus *should* be at this time. You have the Four of Swords. It represents a need for relaxation—" She playfully nudges Sailor in the ribs. "Which you'll be doing a lot of this trip. As well, it indicates a need for healing and to find your center. What's important now is to make peace with your past. Try to be open and vulnerable enough to allow others, including Ryder, to help you heal those wounds and trauma."

Sailor nods her understanding solemnly. She reaches forward and collects the next card, the furthest to the left.

"What's the Three of Swords? It looks and feels like betrayal or really bad heartbreak. I hope that's not what my future looks like." She laughs it off, but her body language says otherwise. A deep V forms between her eyes as her arms fold across her chest.

"That card is in the *past* position. Thank fuck for that," I reassure her. I damn sure won't be breaking her heart. And I'll do everything I can to prove that to her.

"Ryder. If you don't mind your mouth in front of Sailor, I'll make you go to the back of the jet," Vanessa scolds me again.

I raise my hands in surrender and mumble under my breath, "You should hear Sailor's mouth."

"It's alright, *really*. I'm actually just as bad," Sailor sheepishly agrees with my statement. "So... The Three of Swords is my past? I'm assuming it's full of heartbreak and painful moments?"

I mouth a *thanks* and shoot her a wink. In return, I receive the most devastatingly beautiful smile. It's the first real one I've seen on her since we met. And it steals the air right out of my lungs.

CHAPTER 19

SAILOR

"That's right. And from what I've seen in my visions and what Ryder has told us after you came to him, it seems you have been through quite a bit. What further encourages that you and Ryder are in fact twin flames is that you each share a similar upbringing. Your mission in this life together is to heal the parts that have left you feeling unworthy or undesired. This will allow you both to come into full union much faster."

Union? Like marriage? We need to slow the hell down. I may be open to exploring this thing between Rio—Ryder and I but... marriage? I'm not sure I want that.

I release a nervous laugh and clench my fingers together in my lap. "I'm not sure I'm ready for all that yet."

"I knew you'd scare her off. It was only a matter of time," Ryder complains, a look of disappointment clear on his gorgeous face.

"Do you see her running, Ryder?" Rose prompts with a raised eyebrow, the mannerism so similar to her brother's.

"It's not like she can escape this tin can," he snides.

"Play nicely, you two. I'm not running, Riot. I'm just letting you know that my view on marriage has changed over the years. So if you're looking for a wife, maybe you're better off finding a new twin flame."

"You can't just *find* another twin flame, Sailor. The soul we share is split in two. Like a unique, one-of-a-kind locket or a friendship bracelet. My vessel holds half, your vessel holds half. Don't you understand that? That's why we yearn and mourn for each other in our dreams and waking life. We are searching for ourselves in one another, for the other half of our soul. Once whole, no one can ever replace that connection. So if you think some other random *charm* will fit into yours—I can assure you, it won't," Riot spews. He stands abruptly and storms off into the back room, slamming the door behind him.

"Oh, sweetheart," Vanessa wraps an arm around my shoulders. "I know this is a lot to take in. Marriage isn't the endgame of this journey. It's peace and harmony with another. And most importantly, within yourself. It's showing the world what love and oneness can look like. Marriage won't change the depths of how you feel about him. Ryder *is* right, but that doesn't mean you must be together romantically. If you don't feel the connection or it doesn't lead you to union, there are soul mates who can also pop up in your life. Forgive my son, he is just frustrated. He's known about you for longer than you could imagine. You just finding out now is somewhat of a tease to him. So close, yet so far," she chuckles to herself. "He so badly wants this to work out. His biggest fear now that he has you back in his life is losing you again."

I swipe angrily at the tears pooling in my lower lids and huff out a sigh. An overwhelming feeling to go to him and comfort him slams into me, making my hands shake. Vanessa collects the card above the two in the middle.

"Your strengths at this time," she states, flashing the card at me with a gentle smile. *"Incredible,"* she says in awe. "You have the best card you can have here– *Strength.*"

Rose reaches across the table to collect my hand in hers, gently squeezing it. "You and Ryder have the strength to push through every obstacle laid out before you on this journey. And you, my love, have the strength to tame the beast in him. You both will find the courage to move beyond your fears and doubts. It's not an easy journey, Sai. It's not for the weak of heart. But I can promise you my brother will give his all to this. From the way I've already seen you push through your fears with dignity and grace—I know you will give this your all, too."

A tear drips down onto our conjoined hands as I take in an unsteady breath through my nose. "The way I feel when I lose him in my dreams is not anything I ever want to feel again. How can I be sure that I won't in this... lifetime?" I ask Rose.

"You can never be one hundred percent sure. But so far, the reading has been pretty clear that *you* have the power, and will soon have the knowledge and intuition to pursue this journey. He'll fight with everything he has in him to not leave you in this life. It's broken him too many times. Ask Vanessa how his past life regression sessions went. She'll tell you just how shaken up he is coming out of them. These sessions have forged the confidence he needs in making it work this time."

"It's true," Vanessa adds. "You've both come a long way. I wholeheartedly believe this is the life you get to be together in union. Would you like to see what's still to come in the near future?"

"Yes," I nod encouragingly.

She collects the next card to the right of the cross. "Ace of Wands. A card that suggests things could heat up between the two of you. It's a card about new beginnings based on a spark. That nickname my son gave you has been carried along for lifetimes. All it will take is for you to open up to him. Give him your trust and time to explore this journey with you. Doing that will ignite the flame you still hold smoldering in your veins."

"I think we may have had that moment before this reading," I admit abashedly.

"Keep that flame alive, Sailor. This vacation will give you the time you need to explore it further. I think we should take a break. I'll take a picture of the spread on my phone. We can go through the remaining five cards while my son is in meetings."

"I think that's a good idea. Do you think I should go talk to him?" I glance at the closed door.

"If he is going to hear anyone out, it would be you. Go ahead, child. We should be landing soon," she glances behind her at the flight path.

The lovely women in Riot's life release me and fall into quiet conversation on their own, allowing me to head back to the bedroom. I knock first, waiting for a response. When I get none, I knock again. The door swings open, and his piercing green eyes hold mine captive. We stay that way for longer than should be comfortable—yet, it feels safe. Like coming inside after being stuck out in a raging storm.

He leans against the threshold of the door and tugs me

closer by the waist. My heart thrashes against my sternum. He has changed shirts, now wearing a similar one as before, but light blue. The color complements his warm skin tone perfectly.

"I owe you an apology. Come in, we can talk briefly before we need to get back to our seats. We should be landing in ten minutes."

He tugs firmly at my waist, pulling me into the room and leaving no room for negotiation. The door closes behind us as his hand clasps mine. He leads us to the edge of the bed before he sits down and pulls me between his open thighs. Big warm hands cup my waist, right at the waistband of my jean shorts.

I wrap my arms around his neck almost out of habit. For the first time in a long time, I feel at peace. This feels so natural. Not forced, not awkward. Just... *right*. The corner of his mouth tugs up with my change in mood.

"I've grown up with Vanessa teaching me everything she knows in the spiritual community. For someone like me, I had access to every energy healer and light worker around. Because of that, I learned more about my past lives than most have. The night we met, I had just woken up from a dream about you. I thought nothing of it because I never felt worthy enough to have a relationship. Every woman who entered my life, I gave a three-day rule. Three days of dates or fucking and they were out of my life. Cut off. I never wanted more. Until your irresistible body slammed into mine. The second I saw your face and those mesmerizing eyes of yours met mine, I knew something bigger was at play."

"Is that why you were reading a book on past lives the

morning after?" I ask, the pieces of the puzzle falling into place more and more.

"Yes," he laughs, tugging me closer so that he rests his forehead against mine. "I know this feels accelerated, our attraction to each other, but I've waited so long for you. Vanessa always said fate would bring us back together after our first meeting. But I lost hope of that when you distanced yourself from Cameron after I dropped you at the airport. I was willing to wait an eternity for you. *Never* did I expect you to stumble into my club. And of all things, seeing you bleeding and scared. It nearly broke me. I felt what you felt and more. As a divine masculine, I am a protector. I struggled with the decision of either staying with the woman I've been thinking and dreaming about for years, or go hunt down the fucker who hurt you and make him wish for death over what I had planned for him. Does that scare you?" His jade eyes search mine, desperate for an honest answer.

"No," I reply with candor. *Because it doesn't.* My fingers glide over his stubbled jaw before my thumb traces over his lower lip. He inhales a sharp breath before I close the gap and replace my thumb with my lips, kissing him tenderly.

It's not like before.

Not rushed.

Not curious or confused.

It's everything that this moment demanded of us. An overwhelming desire to thank him, to show him I feel this, too. I'm no longer running away from him or making excuses as to why I can't feel what I feel for him. He's done nothing but prove to me how much he cares for me, how much he wants to protect me. And I've done nothing but throw snide remarks, name call, and pin the blame on him.

"I can't lose you again, *Little Ember*," he whispers against my lips.

"Just promise me you'll be patient. I am not an easy person to deal with, and this is a lot," I smile hesitantly against his lips.

"No, really?" he laughs before kissing me deeply.

I pull back when the door pops open. Rose sticks her head in, smirking at the two of us. "Oh, good, you've made up. We are landing in five. Captain wants us to take our seats. Sai, celebratory drinks are in order once we get to the penthouse and my brother stops occupying your lips."

This is the start of a beautiful friendship between Rosemary and me. We are going to be great friends. After years of being on my own, it finally feels like things are looking up for me. I can't believe I didn't see how similar she and her brother are. That I thought they were together. I shake my head at the thought and step out of Riot's arms. He follows closely behind me, placing a hand at the small of my back.

For the first time since I was a kid in Cameron's arms, I feel safe. Truly safe...and this time, genuinely desired.

I just pray the rest of my reading is as encouraging as the first half.

CHAPTER 20

SAILOR

Entering Riot's penthouse has me regretting my decision to see this thing through. The man must have more money than God. You thought his private jet was lavish? If only you could see the interior design of this place, the money put into each and every detail, every slab of marble.

I'm way out of my league here. And it's becoming abundantly clear we are both in very different social classes. I said I misjudged him from assuming he knew nothing about growing up the way I did, but damn, his current lifestyle is so far from what mine is, it's almost comical.

Our bags are delivered right behind us. Once the staff are done unloading them into the entrance, Riot tips them generously. He closes the door and takes my bag by the handle, rolling it down the hallway past the kitchen—which is incredible, by the way. The massive center island looks out through floor-to-ceiling windows towards a reflective turquoise ocean.

The area of the beach below must be private; only a few ant-like specs of people are visible from my vantage point. Turquoise and white umbrellas are lined up immaculately in sections right past the small beach bar that sits directly off the infinity pool below. A couple lounges in the corner of it, looking more than cozy, wrapped in each other's embrace.

Wheels thudding against the marble floor catch my attention. I quicken my strides to follow Riot and his family towards what I assume are the bedrooms. Rose and Vanessa respectively head off to the rooms to the right and left of us, knowing already which is theirs. I'm sure they have done this quite a few times before. Riot continues to the doors further down the hall, adjacent to each other. He guides my suitcase inside a room to the left, then lifts it, placing it on the bamboo luggage rack at the foot of the bed.

"Feel free to take some time to unpack and get settled. I'm sure you could use a reprieve from my family. He reaches into his pocket and pulls a black shiny card from his wallet, handing it to me. "The refrigerator is stocked, but if you want anything specific, use this."

My stubborn streak kicks in. "We have already been over this this morning. I have money. Might not be a lot, but I can take care of my needs on my own." I gently push his card back towards him.

Riot arches a dark brow at me and then nods to the walk-in closet. "Right. So now would be a bad time to tell you that the closet is also stocked with all the clothes you might need while down here?"

A smile creeps its way onto my face. "You work quickly, I'll give you that."

"I did say it would be taken care of," he smirks proudly before reaching for my waist and pulling me closer to him.

I place a firm but gentle hand against his chest, feeling the steady thump of his heart beneath my palm. Craning my neck, I look into his eyes—which are more emerald than jade at the moment.

"I know I said we can try this, Riot, but I still need time to adjust to all of it. Not just in the spiritual, romantic sense, but the change in lifestyle, too. I appreciate you wanting to make me comfortable and feel cared for. I really do. I just need a minute to grasp how easy it is for you to hand over that card, when the amount of money it would take for me to even rent out this place would be a lifetime's worth of savings. If we are going to see how this goes, we need to go slow. Like, really fucking slow."

He tucks the blonde pieces of my hair behind my ears and cups my face with both hands. "I have meetings the rest of the day, but should be able to get in a little fun before dinner. If we are lucky, I may get out around two. Wear the clothes, Sailor. Or don't," he shrugs, "I just want you to be happy. You are making it sound like you are a charity case. And that was never my intention, so I am sorry for that. But I am going to say this as nicely as possible without sounding like a total dick. Get used to being treated like a goddess, *Little Ember*. Because you are one. The sooner you realize that, the better. It doesn't matter what your upbringing was, what your financial status is, or your views on a lavish life. You deserve to be adored, worshipped, and praised." He brushes his lips over my slightly ajar ones and leaves.

The intensity of his smoky scent is left in his wake, cloaking me like a protective blanket. My eyes track each of his confident steps as he enters the hallway and vanishes through the door to my left.

"Okay then," I murmur before releasing a shaky breath.

The lid of my suitcase lands with a smack against the

footboard as I open it. I need some space to think straight. So much has happened in the last few days that my mind is spinning, tripping, tumbling blind in the dark.

Do I feel something beyond reason for Riot? Yes. Did I agree to this? Also, yes. But am I freaking the fuck out over what it would be like to truly trust someone and give them my heart and soul?

Hard yes.

My scrappy bikini mocks me from the top of my suitcase. Once again reminding me how Riot has been nothing but caring towards me. *I may have been a bit harsh earlier.* I'm just so used to taking care of myself, relying on me and only me for my needs, that it's strange and uncomfortable allowing another to do so.

I chew on my thumbnail and glance over at the walk-in closet to the right of the massive king-sized bed. Curiosity gets the best of me, and I find myself walking over to it with a hint of excitement. I've never really been gifted any clothes or purchased any for myself that weren't secondhand.

The lights automatically turn on upon entering the space. Beautiful, tropical prints and colors surround me. Everything from sundresses to satin pajamas, to cover-ups hangs delicately from gold metal hangers. My fingers glide across the rows of clothes, causing the hangers to clink together as I approach the set of four white oak drawers.

Tugging the first drawer open, I discover more panties and bras than I could ever have dreamed of. Matching sets, scandalous lingerie, padded, non-padded, bralettes, cotton, lace, mesh. Any style—all in my size—at the touch of my fingertips.

Gently closing the top drawer, I move on to the next. Workout gear. Leggings, shorts, sports bras, tank tops. Anticipation sparks within me as I close that drawer and open the next. Filled to the brim with casual comfort. Sweatshirts of all colors and thicknesses, zippered, pullovers, yoga pants, cotton shorts, cotton leggings. The final drawer is full of more than a dozen bathing suits. Mostly bikinis—which I'm sure Riot had a lot to do with.

Scattered throughout the separates are a few beautiful one pieces that snag my attention. A black one with a low scooped back and a decent-sized V in the front sings to me. There is a gold seashell clasped between the cups, adding just the right amount of 'extra' for me. When it comes down to it, I like to stick to my color palette of mostly black, occasionally brown or nude. It makes me feel safe, confident, and I am able to blend in.

I scoop up a black oversized hat, pull a sheer black coverup off a hanger, and make my way to the en suite. The bathroom is just as glorious as the whole space. White marble floors glimmering with a pearlescent sheen surround a spa-like glass shower with black lava rock tiles and teak walls. There is a rain showerhead and about four or five different matte black jets jutting out from the wall.

This has to be the most intricate shower I have ever seen.

My shower time has always been cut short due to the hot water running out, but I've always cherished the calmness I felt while it lasted. While the hot water cascaded down on me, washing away the day's chaos and imbuing a sense of calm. I can hardly wait for the hour-long one I'll take later tonight.

After freshening up and getting dressed, I toss my clothes into the black metal laundry basket provided. There is a wicker beach bag hanging from the back of the bathroom door. I laugh to myself when I discover that it is already filled with the essentials—sunscreen, tissues, gum, lip balm with SPF, and a wad of cash.

Doing a once-over in the mirror, and frankly impressed with how gorgeous this whole outfit is, I make my way back to the bedroom.

The ocean view draws me closer. I gaze at the sliding door, the soothing space of the balcony beckoning me to come take a peek. Gripping the door, I pull firmly and slide it open. *Damn, these doors are hard to open.* The white linen curtains blow into the room on a breeze as salt and warmth brush across my face. I lean over the balcony railing, feeling overwhelmed with gratitude.

This is paradise.

I can't believe I'll be waking up to this view over the next few days. A sense of calm washes over me as my eyes close and I inhale deeply. This could easily become my new favorite sanctuary.

Riot was right, this *is* what I needed.

The hairs on the back of my neck stand up with a knowing feeling. *He's near.* My eyelids flutter open, and I turn to the right, finding two emerald eyes observing me. He's mirroring me, leaning over the railing of his balcony, closer to the shared glass separating our rooms. The corner of his mouth tilts up, revealing a lickable dimple indenting the apple of his cheek.

I turn my attention back to the ocean, lowering my sunglasses back down to shield my eyes. The sound of my racing heart overrides the sound of the crashing waves. His presence is always intense. Now more so than ever, I understand why. If this theory of twin flames is true, he's literally my perfect match. Cut from the same cloth as I.

"I thought you had a meeting?" I ask, eyes still trained on the shoreline.

His eyes still hold their focus on me as he responds, "I do. I just felt called to this view before being held hostage in an air-conditioned office all day with some truly boring companions."

"You could try my bleach trick?" I offer on a laugh.

"Eh. I'd prefer my organs to remain solid." And with that, he leaves my peripheral, the sound of his glass sliding door closing being the only indication that he's gone.

CHAPTER 21

SAILOR

The cabana we have on the beach is amazing. Fully equipped with snacks and fans. It even has its own staff, who have been nothing but extremely accommodating. I barely take the last sip of my mango mojito when a new one appears. The refreshing cocktail has me feeling buzzed and alive—or maybe it's the riveting book I'm reading on my Kindle that nearly has me melting into the mattress.

Rose and I rest side by side on a daybed, the wind gently stirring the curtains and creating the most relaxing environment. Vanessa lounges on a similar bed next to us, shading herself more than we are. She sips on a blended cocktail and reads a book titled "Mastering Union." They are all so invested, it's kind of adorable.

I am just getting to the part of my book where the MMC is about to confess his feelings for her after the entire first half of the book was banter and filthy, delicious sex, when a deep rumbling laugh grabs my attention.

Peering over my heavily tinted shades, I find Riot talking with a beautiful brunette outside our cabana. She's in a barely there red bikini that has gold jewelry draped between her breasts and dripping down her midsection. She reaches up with red manicured nails and clasps his bicep, her eyes crinkling as she beams at him. He lowers his head and whispers something in her ear, which creates an even bigger smile on her face.

Fuck, she's beautiful.

And I'm... well, *me.* Soul contract or not, maybe Dark Angel is just appeasing his mother. Maybe all his talk about wanting me, even if it seems rushed, is just a load of bull.

I toss my Kindle into my bag—no longer interested in reading about a steamy romance while watching him flirt with another. This is *exactly* why I don't get my goddamn hopes up. I'm let down time and time again.

With frustration coursing through me, I clasp my drink and drain the rest of its contents in two sips. The condensation on the glass dampens my hands, which I swipe along the back of my neck.

This man makes me so hot. *Burning* hot.

And irrational.

Gah!

I swing my legs over the bed, my feet angrily hitting the sand. Rose shoots an anticipatory glance and a brief smirk at her mother. If they think I am going to go "get my man", they are about to be sorely mistaken. There is no way in hell I'm going to vie for his attention.

As I approach them, the gorgeous brunette runs that lingering hand over the swell of his bicep and squeezes his shoulder. "I'll see you later, Ri," she sings before jogging down the beach towards a Jet Ski.

Now my mind is as red as her nails. *Christ, why is this bothering me so much?* I'm not the jealous type. *You want to make me look like a fool? I'll make you look like an even bigger one.*

It's then that I remind myself he's not mine. It's not like we are exclusive. This thing between us just clicked into place a few hours ago. I agreed to *see* where this went, he never said we were dating or anything of the sort.

Free will and all that jazz.

His smile widens as he sees me, those green eyes sharp as blades as they slice down my body, exposing me right down to my core.

Okay, fine. I am fucking jealous. Now leave me alone and let me wallow in peace.

I allow myself to do the same. To drink him in, all the tattoos, abs, and sharp cut of the V where his swim trunks sit for all of two heated seconds before I bypass him. My route is direct. I jog down to the water's edge and wade knee deep before deeming it far enough. As clear as this water is, I'm sure there are all sorts of poisonous or deadly sea creatures in it.

The mid-evening sun beats down on my back, and I instantly regret not being courageous enough to wade out deeper. My name is Sailor for fuck's sake. Yet, here I stand, knee deep in the water. Too afraid to face the depths of the unknown. It's not like my Dad was around to really adjust me to his life on the sea. *He certainly loved it more than me.* If it wasn't for Cameron, I wouldn't even know how to swim. Not that I'm the best at it.

A prickling sensation erupts across my back as a shadow looms over me. My pulse picks up, and the tips of my ears scorch with heat. I swivel my neck over my shoulder to glance at him. I'm sure it looks more like a glare than a glance.

"Here I was, wishfully thinking you might have missed me while I was gone, but I can't even get a proper hello," he muses.

"You were pretty occupied," I snide as he takes his place next to me.

He cups his hands in the clear water and wets his black hair. *Fuuuck.* I really need to simmer down my attraction to him. It's becoming unhealthy. Borderline out of control. Although I understand the validity of this connection and what Vanessa was explaining earlier, my heart is still very much guarded. That being said, I'm still a hormonal woman who hasn't been laid in God knows how long.

Plus, all the steamy romances aren't doing me any favors.

I try. Truly, I do. Even going as far as to slowly count to ten. But I can't resist his pull any longer. Like the moon's gravitational pull on the tides, I keep up this dance, the ebb and flow of coming closer and then retreating.

A crack forms in the thin shield of resistance I have up before it shatters. I peek out over my sunglasses to admire the way his muscles ripple and flex while he drags his fingers through his scalp. Butterflies scatter around my stomach and flutter up through my rib cage, stealing the breath from my lungs.

"You angry with me, *Little Ember*?" He tilts his head to the side as he inches closer to me.

"Nope." I pop the p, feigning nonchalance as I circle my hands in the crisp water at my sides. "I'm as calm as a clam."

Oh, kill me now. The sand should just swallow me up and be done with me. Why did I even open my mouth to respond, let alone use a beach pun? Thank God for heavily tinted sunglasses. I can practically see the back of my skull with how hard I'm rolling my eyes at myself.

"Is it because of what I said earlier?" He takes another step closer to me.

His scent mixed with salt and sweat assaults my senses, almost making me turn my head to acknowledge him. *Or ogle him.* Instead, I shrug.

Calm as a clam, Sailor. Remember?

Jesus, why am I like this? I mentally smack myself.

Without warning, I'm falling backward, my distracted mind not quick enough to notice an ambush. Riot's muscular arms sweep my feet out from under me before pulling me tight to his body and flinging my sunglasses onto the dry sand behind us. I jostle against him as he hops wave after wave, guiding us past where they break to deeper waters. My heart pounds in my chest as I let out a yelp and cling to him like a cat thrown in a bathtub.

Satisfied by our location and impressively treading water, he loosens his grip on me, causing me to smother him even more. My arms wrap tighter around his neck as my fingers white knuckle my elbows. I squirm until he releases my legs before wrapping and locking them firmly around his hips.

White hot fear rushes over me as I tuck my head into his neck and squeeze my eyes shut. The muscles of his firm arms flex as he tightens his hold on me, his breaths coming on more quickly for an entirely different reason than why mine are.

"Scared of a little water, Sailor?" he rasps, his chest rumbling against my breasts with silent laughter as his toned thighs continue to tread water beneath us.

"I…I can't see the bottom!" I stutter, my teeth chattering with anxiety.

"We aren't far from the shore. Open your eyes, sweetheart," he says it calmly, sensing my increasing anxiety as my chest heaves with each staccato breath.

"I don't care how close we are to the shore! Sharks can attack in ankle-deep water, and we are clearly unable to touch the bottom." My voice wobbles and squeaks as I practically crawl up his body. If it wasn't so sexual and it didn't drown him, I'd crawl up even further and lock my thighs around his shoulders.

"There is a much larger and more intimidating predator in this water than sharks," he chuckles darkly. I'm so glad he's getting a kick out of this. *Divine masculine, my ass. He's supposed to protect me!*

"Oh yeah? Wh…what?" I ask, horrified, letting my mind conjure up beasts straight out of a nightmare. All sorts of grizzly-looking sea creatures with sharp fangs and bulbous black eyes.

"*Me,*" he growls, lowering his head and playfully clamping his teeth over my neck before soothing it with the warmth of his tongue.

The delicious move startles me right out of my panic. Heat grows between my thighs— which is pressed up against the now 'solid organ' he mentioned needing use of earlier. *Shit, he's huge.* Like bigger than I've ever been with— including Cameron.

A groan passes my lips as I instinctively press them to the skin of his neck, beaded in salt water. As my anxiety eases out of me and on whispered breath, I question, "And who will protect me from you?"

He drops his arms from around my waist and tugs my arms loose from around his neck, resting them on his shoulders. He's now standing, slightly closer to shore. The pads of his fingers trail their way up from my wrist, his forearms brushing against my breasts, before his fingers slide under my jaw to cup my face. The reflection off the water is making his eyes shimmer like precious polished stones. Humor and an intensity I can't place swirl behind them.

"You'll never have to worry about that, *Little Ember*. I'm here now, and I'm not going anywhere. I'm not your father, or Cameron, or that psychopath, James. I'll protect *you* with my life. I know these last few days have been scary. And I know what I do for a living can seem even scarier." His thumb scores over where my bruise is healing. "But you don't have to worry about needing protection from me. I'd *never* hurt you. Your heart already knows this. It's your brain that needs catching up and perhaps even time to rationalize. This is something that seems unworldly or written in one of your fantasy novels, but guess what, baby? I'm the fucking dragon in those books you read. And I will take down any threat that comes your way. You were mine to protect and adore way before either of us even realized."

His thumb brushes over my lower lip again, sending a ripple of need coursing through me. Dark Angel's eyes have grown heavy, the black of his pupils expand, darkening his irises. Those beautiful eyes dart back and forth between mine, seeking silent permission to lean in and close the gap. To kiss me senseless as I open myself up and trust him.

Fully letting him in.

What he sees there must be enough, because his lips clash with mine. Roughly. Savagely. Our breaths are mingled, our moans in sync. We pull each other in again, the heat of his touch a delicious addition to my own as he drags me impossibly closer. I'm burning up. Even the backs of my eyes are on fire as a zip of pleasure snakes its way up my spine. His tongue swirls with mine as I moan euphorically into his mouth.

Scary sea creatures be damned, they are now a distant memory. All I can think about, all I can *feel* in this moment is Riot.

"Still mad at me?" He smiles against my lips, his chest heaving like mine is.

"Nope." I pop the P again just to annoy him.

"Brat." He tweaks my nose, and I smirk before giving myself a second to catch my breath. My body is still buzzing from our fervent moment.

"Riot, who was that girl earlier? I know we aren't exclusive or anything... but I just thought... I don't know. Maybe you wouldn't entertain anyone else on this trip." I look down at the water, ashamed of even voicing my jealousy and insecurity.

This is so new, so foreign, so *raw*. It's hard to be this vulnerable with him. With anyone, for that matter. I nearly resort to raising my shield again— or at least try to.

"Ahh," he sighs as he stands, his hands sliding down my back and over the swell of my ass before gripping it. We've made it back to waist-deep water now. "You were jealous of Shelby." His nose nudges mine so that I look at him again.

"She an ex or something?" The assumption slips so easily off my tongue. My heart races wildly waiting on the confirmation.

"I already told you my three-day rule. Even if she was

one of the three dayers, it's a far cry from categorizing her as an ex. To ease your mind, no, she's not. She's the watersports facilitator for my building and someone I helped survive an awful situation a few years ago. I offered her a new life here. She was just helping coordinate something for us later, but now I'm not so sure you'll enjoy it." He laughs deeply as his eyes lower to where we're still pressed together beneath the water.

"Eh, I'm sort of enjoying it now," I flirt, rolling my hips against his.

His grip tightens around my ass, and his solid length twitches against me. I release another needy moan.

"Don't look now, but my sister and Vanessa are watching us." Riot nods his head behind me.

I angle my body to look as he drops us below the surface. We sink under the water, and my ass hits the sand before he stands back up. I splutter and wipe off the hair clinging to my face.

Asshole.

"Sorry, sweetheart. I know you wanted to take things slow. We... *I* got a little carried away there and needed to cool things off a bit." He smiles smugly while lowering his hands to collect my own and guides us out.

Rose and Vanessa are both grinning from ear to ear as we enter the cabana. Riot's hand remains firmly wrapped around mine. He grabs two towels and tosses me one before shaking his hair out like a wet dog over his sister.

"*Ugh.* Riot! You're such a fucking child!" she shrieks, using her own towel to dry off the screen of her Kindle.

"Not as much as you. I could have had a nice romantic

trip with Sailor, yet, here you both are, acting like camp counselors and watching our every move."

He runs the towel down the center of his chest before scrubbing it over his hair, making it stick up in all different directions. His fingers rake through its dampness, slightly taming it. The desire to run my own fingers through it nearly has me stepping closer to do so.

But he's right.

I did ask for this to go slow. I should behave...*for now*.

It's becoming abundantly clear that I've gripped this live wire that's buzzing between us with both hands. Now the only way to let go is if the power supply gets shut off.

CHAPTER 22

RIOT

Okay. So she doesn't like the water. Correction—*ocean*. Interesting, because her goddamn name is Sailor. Her father is a real piece of work—I already knew that, though. Fucking asshole gives her a name that represents passion for the sea, and the sense of freedom and adventure it brings, and then leaves her feeling exposed and fearful of what lurks beneath its surface.

She may not fully trust me yet, but today we made the kind of progress I wasn't expecting. To be completely honest, I was worried my family would scare her away. Rose is a lot on her own. Vanessa and Rose combined? Absolutely lethal when it comes to their pursuits.

My little ember is as tough as nails, though. I had a feeling she would be receptive to them. I just feared it may have been overkill when they got into every fucking detail.

Part of me wished she were able to come to this realization herself, but she's never even dipped her toes into any type of spirituality as far as I know.

So fine. I guess I'm fucking glad my family came. Their little plan worked. Now it's up to me to do the rest and prove to my girl just how good we can be together.

Starting with getting her to trust me more.

———————

I shut off the water and step out of the shower, wrapping a towel around my hips. My fingers connect with the mirror, swiping against the moisture gathered on it. The reflection staring back at me is different than normal. This man is... Dare I say happier than he's been in a long while?

For the first time in a long time, I feel *hope*.

Finally, I have connected with the woman of my dreams. Without jinxing it, it seems I've got an actual shot here at making this work. I grab the shaving cream, spray it into my palms, and lather it over my face before grabbing a fresh razor. Tonight, Sailor will see the put-together version of me. Not the wild and untamed beast that so readily lurks beneath my skin.

————

The kitchen is lit up in a warm, romantic glow. Candles flicker against the walls, casting their shadows in a dance all their own. The lights under the counters and the two hanging above the island are dimmed to an ancient amber hue. Music hums through the speakers surrounding the space. There is an open bottle of wine chilling in an ice bucket by the sink, along with two glasses. And the island is nearly prepared with all the ingredients we'll need to make dinner.

"It's GO time," I mentally prep myself while rubbing my palms together.

I grab myself a rock glass from the bar and drop in an ice sphere from the freezer before pouring myself three fingers of my favorite bourbon. After only the first sip, the amber liquid starts weaving its magic on my nerves.

This. This is what I needed to take the edge off.

Movement directs my attention to who is currently occupying the space beyond the sliding doors. Vanessa is out there relaxing on the balcony. A nice chilled glass of white wine is in her hands. Her head is tilted back as she rests on a cushioned wicker chair, enjoying the twilight.

Oranges and pinks swirl with purple, creating an ethereal sky that adds charm to tonight's energy. The pastel pink reminds me of my sister. Will she barge in at any moment with her typical theatrics?

Curious as to why she's not already complaining about dinner, I pad over to her open bedroom door and pop my head inside.

"Rosie?" I call out, confirming what I already know.

She's not here.

I step over her damp, used towel on my way to her en suite. The bathroom counter looks like a bomb went off. Makeup products are scattered all over it. Her hair brush and straightener sit in the sink—still plugged in. I reach over and unplug it while shaking my head in disbelief. She can be so damn careless at times.

Hair spray, fake eyelashes, and other random products sit atop the closed toilet lid. Various styles of clothing litter her bedroom floor. I'm sure all of them at some point had the potential to be her outfit for the night.

A clothing and makeup graveyard is typical Rosie. It's something I've grown up around and can manage. But a goddamn bucket of glitter?! *Literally!* That shit is in an actual sand bucket next to her dresser. Shovel and all. Don't even get me started on the fact that it's fucking sprinkled like fairy dust all over the carpet.

Jesus Christ, this woman gives me a headache.

I press at my temples and take a deep breath. I'm sure Rosemary is off doing what Rosemary does best—searching for men or partying at some unknown pop-up rave.

Fantastic. That's one down.

Pulling my phone out, I shoot a text to Kael, one of my men traveling with us, and let him know my demands. He's more than used to it by now. Rosemary can have all the fun she wants. She can be a goddamn fairy or unicorn for all I care, but I want eyes on her. That's my baby sister. He responds right away, already in the car and heading towards the club she's at.

Great.

Vanessa, on the other hand, will probably order some food and disappear to her room, subtly giving Sailor and me some privacy. She may have been stirring the pot earlier, but now that she has set the stage, she'll let me take the spotlight.

I head back into the kitchen and take another swig of my drink, which brings heat to my chest but cools down my body.

Sailor wanders in at the same time. Her aura and our connection alert me before her feet even hit the threshold. That addicting perfume of hers hits me next, softening the sharp edges of nerves that were plotting to ruin my night. I gaze at her over the rim of my glass as she approaches the opposite end of the island from me.

She is absolutely stunning in her flowy coral sundress. The hem rests just above her knees, showing off the length of her toned legs. Capped sleeves rest loosely around her biceps, exposing slightly tanned shoulders. *It's a step up from her usual ivory complexion.*

Her freshly washed hair is pulled back in a low bun, which rests at the nape of her neck. The blonde streaks are curled and left loose to frame her face. Only a dusting of makeup accentuates her natural beauty, illuminating it in a dewy, sun-kissed glow.

Fuck. I rake my fingers through my hair as I continue my perusal. Her entire body is glowing. Whatever she used on her face, she continued with on the rest of her exposed skin.

"I wasn't sure what the plan was for dinner, so I figured... you couldn't go wrong with a sundress. As far as the shoes go..." She looks down at her bare feet and shrugs nervously, plopping her beaded sandals onto the floor next to the stools.

If I hadn't already witnessed her stand proudly in her own skin, I'd say it was kind of cute how she was acting. But you know what's even sexier than a woman being shy? A woman who knows that when she enters a room, everyone will bow, regardless of what the hell she is wearing.

Gentle honeyed eyes framed in thick black lashes scan over the counter full of ingredients as she takes a seat on a stool.

"You are perfectly dressed, sweetheart. After seeing how much you thoroughly enjoyed today's *surf* adventures, I decided perhaps we would partake in the *turf* portion of the evening," I quip.

Her laugh and the light behind her eyes pull loose the last remaining threads of anxiety clinging to me. I step forward and cup her face, tracing her highlighted pink cheek with my thumb. The bruise is way less noticeable than yesterday.

"You look beautiful, by the way. What can I get you to drink? I have white wine chilling if you'd like?"

She nods, biting her lower lip before smiling up at me. "Sure, thanks."

How badly I want to close the gap and pry her teeth off that lower lip with my own. The only thing stopping me is that I'm *trying* to stick with the yellow light act. Where, for some, including myself, it means step on the gas, right now it means to ease off.

She wants slow? I can show her slow.

Ever try squeezing the last bit of honey out of a plastic container? That's exactly how this will go down. Dripping so fucking slow, excruciatingly so, until finally you end up banging the goddamn cap on the counter to get it to move along faster.

Part of the twin flame journey is a lot of push and pull. If I pull back, she will feel comfortable moving forward. When she is ready or when the temptation to close the gap becomes too much to bear, I'll be here. Ready and *more* than willing.

The energy in this room is already pulsing with desire— and we haven't even been around one another for more than a few minutes.

When I step away, her eyes trail me the entire time. *See... just like row crew. Push, pull. Push, pull.* No matter how much you push away and pull back, you're still making strides.

Ice jostles against the metal bucket as I snag the bottle from it. I pull out the cork with my teeth and pour her a glass. Then, using the island as a sort of barrier between us, I slide it over the granite towards her. Her brows furrow as she tracks her drink.

Is she sad I didn't hand it to her? Or that I put some space between us?

She brings the glass to her lips and takes a small sip, then looks over at the ingredients. "So...what are we making for dinner?" she asks with genuine enthusiasm.

"Homemade spinach ravioli and a horseradish and herb-crusted skirt steak."

I take another healthy sip of my bourbon, trying to calm my returning nerves. I'm not used to being so open and vulnerable, either. It's not in my nature, just as I'm sure lowering her shield around me is incredibly difficult. Being an asshole, savage, *'cult leader'* as she likes to call me...Not a fucking problem. *That comes easily.* Trying to be more relaxed and romantic? *Not simple.*

Although it feels as natural as breathing, being emotionally and physically romantic with her, actually trying to add a bit of zest and impress her is hard as fuck. I'm completely out of my element here. I never really did the dating thing. Unless, of course, you count a movie in bed with maybe some takeout then fucking like rabbits a date? *Didn't think so.* That wasn't goddess treatment. *Not that those women minded.* They knew what they were signing up for with me. And they definitely left pleased.

Sailor deserves so much more than that.

So this... *all of it..*it's foreign as—

"*Shit.* The bottle of white was already chilling for Vanessa, but if we are eating steak, would you prefer I open a bottle of red?" I ask nervously, already stepping towards my wine rack to evaluate which one she might like best with this meal. The woman's a bartender for fuck's sake. I probably just made a rookie mistake.

She slides off the stool and comes around to grip my forearm. The soft pads of her fingertips skate up to mine, which are clenching my rock glass. Sailor loosens my grip and takes the glass into her own hand, sipping a healthy portion while her eyes smirk at me from over the rim.

"I actually would prefer what you're drinking. I lied earlier. I don't mind white wine, but I definitely prefer this. I should have spoken up. If we are going to get to know each other better, I should start with being honest." She hands the glass back to me and walks over to the food processor on the counter.

I'm smiling like a Cheshire Cat at her openness. It's time to calm the fuck down and attempt to do the same. "Angel's Envy okay?"

"Perfect drink for a dark angel such as yourself," she quips.

"And you?" My voice is downright husky and filled with lust.

My back is to her as I prepare her drink. If I dare look at her now, I'll lose all sense of control, and we'll both be skipping dinner. I'll satiate my other hunger first and indulge in her for hours before either of us gets a solid meal in. The *clink* of an ice ball against the glass increases the static between us as I wait to hear what she has to say.

"It's perfect for me, too, because I want what I shouldn't really have."

My brow arches as I step towards her with her drink. "And what is that, *Little Ember*? My voice has deepened to a low rumble as my fingers brush hers. I press the glass into her hand, keeping my own wrapped around hers as I gaze down into her penetrating eyes.

"Hope," she whispers, smiling up at me.

CHAPTER 23

SAILOR

"They say hope is a dangerous thing," he counters, a delicious smirk growing on his handsome face. He cages me in against the island, resting his hands against the cool granite at my back.

"Maybe I'm starting to like a little danger," I tease, bringing my fingertips up to brush against his clean-shaven jaw. I kind of miss the bite of stubble. It suits him better... ya know, dark angel vibes and all.

"So the shark diving excursion is back on, then?" He ups the ante, lowering his face so the bridge of his nose rests on mine.

"Whoa, whoa, *whoa*. I didn't say that. Perhaps the kind of *dangerous* I am interested in is a 6'4, dark angel who haunts my dreams and now my reality. Who also happens to be the leader of a secret cult in the basement of some esoteric club."

"Hmm..." he purses his lips as if thinking. "Oddly specific. Let me know if you find him." He winks at me before pushing off the counter and sauntering over to the cutting board at the other end of the island.

If my heart doesn't slow the hell down, I'll surely have a

heart attack. Or pass out. *Calm down, Sai.* I take a sip of my drink and attempt to casually walk over to him. He tosses a dish towel over his shoulder and starts chopping the stems off the parsley. *Mmm, that's just straight up hot.* Watching his muscles bunch as he works and seeing that towel draped over his traps like he's done this a time or two is making me want to skip dinner and head straight for dessert.

"What can I do to help?" I ask awkwardly, feeling so out of my element in the kitchen.

"Can you crack two eggs and one yolk into that food processor there? I'll get these ready and then toss them in."

"Sure," I chirp, more than happy to focus my attention on anything but the man in the room. Or my heartbeat drumming in my ears.

I flip open the carton and collect three eggs, placing them on the counter. They nearly roll off onto the floor. So I place them back before they embarrass the shit out of me. *Stay.* From the corner of my eye, I spot Riot holding back a laugh. My cheeks heat instantly.

Real smooth, Sai.

One by one, I crack the eggs into the bowl, using extra caution not to drop any shells. The third, I separate between the shells before adding the additional yolk. I'm pretty sure I got some whites in there, but it'll be okay... or at least, I sure hope so. *What if it completely fucks the recipe?*

Riot leans over me and tosses in a cup of spinach and the parsley, then sprinkles a bit of salt over the top. He smacks the lid on, locking it in place, and pulses it twice before handing me the bottle of olive oil. From the look on his face, he's encouraging me to add it to the small spout at the top.

"How much?" I ask warily.

"About a tablespoon." He shrugs, clearly eyeballing the recipe. *Good, maybe my little egg white incident won't do much harm.*

I may not cook often or would consider myself even a decent cook, but I am a bartender and do know a tablespoon by eye. Dark Angel presses up against me with a finger hovering over the pulse button as I add in the oil. When seemingly satisfied with the texture, he opens the lid and unlocks the base, leaving it on the counter beside a bowl of flour.

"Have you ever made ravioli before? Fuck, do you even like pasta? Kinda late now for me to be asking. I just figured this would be a fun meal to make together."

He's just as nervous as me. It's cute.

"No," I laugh, practically snorting. The liquor is definitely starting to loosen me up around him. "I can barely cook. I love pasta, but I usually buy frozen ravioli or order it from the pizza place. And sauce? *Yeah... It's* jars for me. This meal sounds delicious, Riot. Thank you for planning it."

His smile widens to reveal his dimple, and I just can't stop my eyes from lingering. "Focus, *Little Ember*," he tsks before dumping the flour onto the counter.

I rise up on my tiptoes and lean over him, eager to learn. "How much flour is that?"

"About two cups of oo." He points to the bag on the counter. "Now, watch." He forms the flour into a round pile, then makes a little well in the middle. "You're going to want to make a well like this to place the wet ingredients. Then we will gradually introduce the flour until it's all blended."

I'm mesmerized as his deft hands slowly work the flour

in. It's amazing how hands that have more than likely ended someone's life treat making raviolis with such delicacy.

"You going to continue ogling me again, or do you want to give this a try?" he laughs heartily.

I slip under his arm and stand in front of him, not confirming nor denying if I was or wasn't ogling him. It doesn't help that the heat he is radiating brings my own body temperature to nearly scorching. Yet...it's not burning me up like it normally does. It's almost comforting, like being wrapped up in a blanket doused in his scent.

Safe, is what it is.

That feeling, along with the hint of bourbon on his breath as it fans my neck, has me wanting to lean back against him. To sink even further into his potent energy.

So, I do.

Riot's large frame towers over me to observe as I work in all the remaining flour. To my surprise, he moves his fingers on top of mine to help knead the dough even further. His neck rests on my bare shoulder as his firm body curves around mine.

"That's perfect, Sailor," he rasps.

Clearing his throat, he steps away, then pulls a sheet of plastic wrap out and hands it to me. "Can you wrap this up and place it in the refrigerator as I prep for the next step?"

I take it and silently let out a breath as he starts chopping rosemary on the wooden cutting board. Once I place the ball of dough in the refrigerator, I take up my position beside him again. Honestly? This is a lot of fun, and I'm genuinely enjoying learning how to cook with someone of a higher skill set.

The sound of expert chopping and the smell of fresh

herbs are awakening all of my senses. Memories of cooking with him once before start to spark in my mind in little, shortened clips. Just as I try to focus on one memory, another rolls in... and then another... and then they stop altogether. Just the sound of his chopping comes back to the forefront.

What was that?

I shake it off and focus back on him. Riot's movement with the knife is oddly sexy. *Did he master that skill in the kitchen or... Stop, Sai. You don't even know that he kills people.*

He pauses his work to finish off his drink, and I do the same. The burn is a good distraction from my tug-of-war emotions. On one end of the rope, you have the fact that he is an extremely dangerous man. Someone who runs a secret society of vigilantes. Someone who more than likely has killed people. Someone who still probably has a lot of secrets. On the other end, you have how incredibly sexy, protective, and also extremely generous he is.

In his defense, the reason for the dangerous lifestyle he leads is to protect others like me. *UGH!*

And right smack in the middle, where the red flag is, is the fact that he is my twin flame.

Either way you pull, I'm his.

Wait? Am I?

A glass mixing bowl slides against the counter and snags my attention back. Riot tosses in the roughly chopped rosemary and a tablespoon of horseradish from a jar. Two small bowls of salt and pepper are thrust into my hands.

His arm wraps around me as he tugs me closer to him by the hip. Long fingers rest on the top of my ass, finding his favorite placement on me so naturally. I shiver as his heat once again swirls over me. With intention, I step closer to him, soaking it all in.

"Add in some salt and pepper. Enough to use as a rub for the steak," he prompts.

He gathers the bottle of olive oil and drizzles it over the top until satisfied. Then he grabs a wooden spoon and mixes the blend, all while keeping his other hand right where he left it. Leaving the spoon in the bowl, Riot grabs the tray the steak is resting on and slides it in front of us.

"Can you do the honors of rubbing this into the steak? My hands are going to be a bit preoccupied in a moment." His innuendo sparks heat between my legs.

Are we going there? Can we pleaaase go there!?

He lowers his lips to my ear, sending a shiver down my spine and making me delirious with need. I clench my thighs together to relieve this ache while hoping he'll touch me even more.

His other hand joins my other hip as he steps behind me, pulling me back against him. His arousal presses firmly against my ass, making me push back. A low growl emanates from him, turning me on even more.

It's extremely difficult to focus on the task as I pour the mixture onto the steak and begin massaging it in. Mentally, I encourage his hands to explore more, but they stay firmly planted where they are. Vanessa said twin flames can telepathically communicate. I wonder if what I was able to do with her earlier, I can do with him? Might as well try. At least if it doesn't work, I'll only look like an idiot in my own head.

Kiss my neck, Riot. God, I need to feel your lips on my neck right now.

His left hand slides from my hips. Keeping contact with

my body, he uses his index and middle fingers to graze up my spine, causing me to arch into him more. My head rests on his shoulder as his lips find my neck. They are gentle at first. As if he just placed them there to test the waters. Feather-light kisses start to trail a path from the curve of my neck to right below my ear. I tremble in his arms as my eyes close, basking in the bliss of this moment.

Mark me.

What? Where did that come from?

The softness of his lips wraps around my throat first, followed by the pressure of his teeth as they start to make contact. A moan escapes my lips as his hand inches up my stomach and grazes the bottom of my breast. It's cut off abruptly by the sound of the sliding door opening.

I spring out of Riot's arms and head over to the sink to wash my hands. *What the fuck?!* I didn't know anyone was home! Rose told me she was going out. Nearly tried to drag me to some secret rave with her.

"Sorry to interrupt you. I'm going to head down to the Japanese restaurant in the lobby and pick up something to eat. I should be back in a few hours. I'd say behave, but it is a beautiful thing to be able to share our sacred bodies with another. Especially with how close you two are spiritually. I remember when my kundalini was activated for the first time..."

"Jesus, Mom. Can you please just...GO?" He's embarrassed. I almost want to laugh, but it wouldn't be right.

"We are making dinner. I'm sure it'll be ready in a few minutes. Would you like to join us, Vanessa?" I offer kindly.

"No, don't be silly, my dear. Take advantage of the privacy." She winks a knowing violet eye at me before leaving out the front door.

I dry my hands off with a paper towel and toss it in the trash can drawer I saw Rose use earlier to get rid of her gum.

Leaning a hip against the counter, I cross my arms over my hardened nipples and stare Riot down. "You could have told me she was out there the whole time," I say bitterly.

"Would you have treated me the same way if you knew she was?" he asks, moving the tray of steak and placing it next to the massive stainless steel stove. There's an entire grill down the center of it.

"Probably not," I scoff.

"I think you would have. Chemistry like ours can't be denied for long. Keep telling me pretty little lies."

Woah. I heard the first part of what he said in my head. Like I caught on to how he was feeling. Maybe even his direct thoughts... but I only heard him vocalize the 'Keep telling me pretty little lies'.

"Did you hear me before?" I ask excitedly. This is too similar to the books I read. No fucking way. *How cool?*

"You were extremely specific earlier. Now not so much. Use your words, *Little Ember.* It's not like I can read your mind." His lips twitch, giving him away. He *did* hear me, that motherfucker. *Why is he making this into a game?*

"Did. You. Hear. Me?" I emphasize each point by tapping his temple with my index finger.

He grabs me by the wrist and tugs me closer until we are a breath away. His head bends down to rest against mine. "Yes, I heard you, you irresistible, violent little thing. Not specifics...*not yet*, anyway. I just knew what you needed, what you were asking for. It was a first for me."

I raise a brow and look up into his shimmering eyes. Excitement and mischief swirl behind them. "And what about now?"

Suddenly, I'm lifted off the floor and placed on the counter. Flour plumes up all around us, but it doesn't stop him. His lips are on mine greedily, biting the sensitive flesh and pulling it between his teeth before soothing it with his tongue. His fingers dig into the back of my neck as his thumbs press against my cheeks. I moan loudly into his mouth as I open my legs, inviting him to step closer.

His one hand drops down to caress my breast over the dress as my hands rake up his back, pulling him closer to me. *I need him so much closer.* And with far less clothing on.

My fingers slip under his dress shirt, slinking up the hot skin of his back until they reach his carved shoulder blades, imagining black wings there. I tug him to me more firmly, as his mouth devours mine, his fingers rolling my nipple through the fabric still dividing us.

Touch me where I ache, Riot.

He breaks away, leaving both of us panting and me feeling disappointed as hell at the loss of him.

"I can't, baby. You asked for this to go slow, and we should. Plus, I need to feed you, and I wasn't done with my lesson on how to make the best goddamn raviolis you ever had."

"I did... but... this thing between us. It's... yeah, it's fast... but I can't help the thread pulling me closer to you. Can you?" I ask, chest heaving, adrenaline and lust zipping through my body.

"Let's make one thing perfectly clear, *Little Ember.* I have chased you through a thousand lifetimes. This one is no different. The only difference this time is that I *will* catch you. And I sure as shit am not letting you go. The last few days have been overwhelming. I want you to be able to process them so that when I do get between your pretty little thighs, all you see, all you think, all you feel *is me.*"

A woosh of air leaves my lungs at his proclamation. I focus in on his aura. It's a deep shade of red. I can imagine mine is the same. Red must mean passion and lust, and uncontrollable *need*.

He extends a hand and helps me jump down from the countertop. Placing a brief kiss to the top of my head, he suggests, "Why don't you go get cleaned up? I'll fix this mess. By the time you get back, the dough will be ready to be rolled out and filled."

"Okay." I hate the way my voice wobbles, betraying my need for him. It's as if a bucket of ice water has been poured all over my libido.

When I get to my room, I stop in front of the stand up mirror and just laugh. Flour is all over my hair, face, and neck. An imprint of Riot's hand is on my breast and hips. I even have some on my swollen lips. I strip the dress off and toss it into the laundry bin in the bathroom. Padding over to my closet, I snag a lavender hoodie and matching sweatpants out of the drawer.

With haste, I tidy up in the bathroom, then pull the sweatshirt and sweatpants on. They are made of the softest, butteriest material. Just like Riot's sweatshirt I once had... and the new one he let me keep back at home.

Home. That's what he feels like. The thought makes me smile. I have never truly had a home. Yeah, I've had a city I've lived in. An empty house. Single apartment. But never have I felt like I was *home*. Suddenly, being around Riot, I know that it wasn't a place I was missing or longing for...but a person.

Already feeling flushed, I drop the pants and fold them, placing them on the bathroom vanity. I mean... I have underwear on, and the sweatshirt drops down to above my knee. He saw me last night in less than. Shoulders rising, I say, *fuck it,* and head back towards the music floating in from the kitchen.

CHAPTER 24

RIOT

I 'm preparing the mixture of ricotta and Parmesan cheese for the filling when she walks back in. I smile up at her and go back to mixing before doing a double take. Her sassy little smirk says it all. The sexy as sin thighs I mentioned wanting to get between earlier are on full display, barely covered by a lavender sweatshirt.

Fuck it. She wants to play that game with me? Just watch...

I toss her the ball of refrigerated dough. *Think fast, Little Ember.* She catches it with deft precision. *Impressive.* Even more impressive than that catch? Her sweatshirt slinks up her body from the elevated throw, exposing her black panties to me. I catch a brief glimpse of the radiant skin above the satin and want nothing more than to run the pads of my fingers over its softness. Or my tongue.

Fuuuck. She isn't playing fair.

"I just made the filling. Let's get this pasta rolled out, shall we?" I practically growl my frustration. If I wasn't trying to give her some time to process this all, I'd already have her sprawled out right here on this fucking counter. And the only thing being rolled would be her nipples under my fingers and her clit under my tongue.

"Problem, Ryder?" she asks sweetly. *Tauntingly.*

Fuck, baby. Say my name again.

I inhale and exhale slowly through my nose...

Once.

Twice.

On the third, she hops up onto the counter and takes my drink, draining the rest of it. Crème brûlée eyes never stray from mine. Not even a blink. They hold steady with a twinkle of mischief. Her cute sun-kissed button nose even twitches as she continues to toy with me as she continues holding my gaze. She collects the wooden pasta cutter beside her and twirls it around her hand.

"What are you waiting for, *Ryder*?" she teases seductively. *And there goes my fucking self-control.* My name on her lips has me gravitating closer to her. The little vixen is giving me the choice here. Continue where we left off and fuck her til the sun comes up, or finish making our dinner.

I sigh dramatically, knowing more than likely I won't be the one *finishing* here. Reaching out, I tuck her blonde hair behind her ear as my thumb traces over her swollen lips. A trace of bourbon coats them from the drink she downed, and suddenly I've become an alcoholic, desperate for every last drop. I lower my head and claim her lips.

She tastes like vanilla, caramel, and *all fucking mine.*

Sailor leans into the kiss, sighing into my mouth. That noise alone has me ready to come undone. Knowing I won't claim her body for the first time while she's drinking, I take a step back. Fucking Cameron already did that ten years ago. Look where it got him. If she wants this. *Us.* She's going to have to be sober for it.

Doesn't mean I can't give her a little taste until then...

I step back between her legs, and her arms circle around me. "We." I kiss her neck. "Are." Her collarbone. "Making." The tip of her nose. "This." The corner of her lip. "Damn." Her lush lips. "Pasta," I demand before my tongue delves into her mouth.

Hers greets mine with the same sense of delirium. A heady, drawn-out moan leaves her lips as she tugs me closer by my dress shirt. Her fingers tremble and fumble with the buttons. She gets frustrated and tugs hard, scattering them across the floor. *God fucking damn.* Warm lips collide with my chest as she slides the fabric off my shoulders.

"Sailor," I whisper my temperance as my shirt hits the floor. Determined fingers skim over my tattoos, then sternum, dipping lower over my abs and getting dangerously close to my dick. I jerk nearer to her as her lips place featherlight kisses along my collarbone.

Prying the ravioli cutter from her grip, I toss it with a *clank* on the counter. She startles before looking over at it with curiosity. "What is that thing, anyway?"

"A pastry wheel...but it has other uses as well..." I pick it back up and tug her hand from around my waist, spreading it palm side up in front of us. Gently, I roll the wooden teeth over her hand. "This is your Heart Line. All to do with emotions and relationships," I murmur as it skims along the highest horizontal line running from her pinky to her middle finger.

Lifting the tool, I move slightly lower, "Your head line. Decision making, intelligence, problem solving."

I drop the wheel lower to the one that spans from her wrist to the space between her index finger and thumb. She squirms, her thighs clenching tighter around me as small appreciative gasps leave her lips. "Life Line. It's all about vitality and major life events. Are you giving your all to this thing called life, or are you letting it pass you by?" I rasp.

"Then finally, right here," I apply more pressure to the fainter line running vertically up from the bottom of her palm through her head line, "Fate Line. Are you destined for the stars, baby?"

Her intake of breath lets me know she likes the sensory pleasure she's receiving from this, as well as the bit of knowledge I'm providing.

"Well, what does my palm tell you?" she questions, her eyes on where the wheel is still applying pressure to where her fate line intersects her head line.

There are two X's there—mystic crosses, indicating transformative connections and psychic abilities. A smile forms on my face, knowing it's further proof that she's destined for this journey.

"A lot." I chuckle my amusement. I barely read the rest of her palm. I tried the other day, as well, but I could hardly focus on analyzing anything while under her captivating spell.

Her fingers wrap around mine, leading my hand to her inner thighs. She applies pressure, inching the tool upwards. I watch greedily as it disappears under the limited cover of her sweatshirt.

"And what does it tell you, now?" she asks lasciviously.

Breathtaking eyes greet mine, her intentions sketched out clearly in which direction she wishes for this to go. Indecision must have been written in Sharpie all across mine. She notices and lowers her head, avoiding my eyes.

Instantly, her aura shifts from blazing red to pulsing

violet. *Embarrassment*. Even regret. Her hands release their hold on me, moving to grip the edge of the counter instead.

"*Fuck*," I sigh, my forehead clapping with hers. I tug my hand away from between her thighs and back to neutral territory, plopping the pastry wheel on the counter. I clasp my hands on either side of her head and tilt it up so she looks at me. "I want you more than the air I breathe, but we need to—" Her hands push against my chest, attempting to shove me back. She pouts when I don't move much.

"*Go slow*. Yeah, I know. It's fine. Let's just finish making dinner. I'm starving," she clips, sliding off the counter and sidestepping me.

"Sai, it's not that I don't want this. Trust me, I've been fucking hard since the second you walked into this kitchen. I'm *trying* to do the right thing by you. You've lost someone you cared about just the other day, you were nearly killed by James, and you've had a falling out with your oldest friend. I don't want to be your escape from that. I want you to choose this because it feels like coming home, not because you're running away from what or *who* you once knew as that."

Her tear-lined eyes seek mine out, and she nods. Even her damn lip wobbles. I hate seeing her cry. I hate that she has gone through so much trauma. And more importantly, I hate that what she felt was rejection from me made her guard slam back into place.

Closing the gap, I tug her closer to me and just hold her, resting my cheek on her head. "I'm not going anywhere, Sailor. I know you've grown up with rejection stinging you left and right, and experiencing the ones you love push you away. But I am NOT them. I'm here and I'm not fucking going anywhere. So take your time. Process all of it. Let me help you through it. And when you have, I promise you, you'll never feel at home anywhere else but here in my arms."

Her back vibrates with small sobs as she nods her head against my bare chest. Tears drip onto it, rolling their way down towards my stomach.

"Thank you," she whispers against my shoulder tattoo. "I'm sorry that I'm such a mess."

"Stop. You have nothing to apologize for," I say. But what I really want to say is *"I love you"*. Those three words sit at the tip of my tongue. But I know if I say them now, she'll run for the hills. I've known for years just how deep that feeling goes for my girl. Sailor, however, has only just begun the journey. She hasn't seen our love grow and blossom in every lifetime, in every cup of tea I bring her in the morning, in the moments leading up to an argument—and then *after*—or how safe she feels falling asleep in my arms every night.

But she will. Because I'm not fucking this up.

Slowly, I loosen my grip on her before sliding the pasta machine towards us. I guide the dough through the machine a few times until it thins out to the appropriate amount. Sailor watches with clear eyes. She's silently observing each number I turn the dial on the machine to, how I angle my hands to feed the dough through. It's adorable how interested she is in learning to cook.

"Flour the surface for me?" I ask, nodding to the bowl of flour.

She sprinkles it out across the granite, like a real professional. *Looks like someone is starting to get the hang of this.* Or perhaps our little moment just subconsciously reminded her of all the times we did this in our previous lives. Minus some of these modern kitchen appliances. I smile at her reassuringly, then place the dough out on the counter.

"This is *the* best pasta I've ever had in my entire life. Holy shit, Riot. You are an amazing cook," she praises over a forkful of ravioli.

"*We* are amazing cooks. You did most of it, *Little Ember*."

A radiant smile forms on her face as she finishes chewing. "Did I ever cook with you in our past lives? I had these... *visions* earlier. They were short little snippets of us in different kitchens or settings, but we were always cooking together like we did tonight."

I slice into my steak and answer her. "We did. Whenever we got the chance to, we would make meals together. It was my favorite time of the day. Most of the time, it ended in skipped meals. The two of us just couldn't keep our hands off each other. Although the times we did finish our task, we always made incredible meals with more than enough leftovers to feed the whole town. You made sure of that. Always so generous and loving to everyone around you. When I wasn't home, you would make batches and batches of freshly baked bread and homemade butter and deliver it to the locals who struggled financially. So many people looked at you like you were an angel. I know I did. I still do."

A beautiful blush tints her cheeks before she speaks. "It definitely felt natural and familiar cooking with you tonight." She smiled up at me again before digging back into her pasta. "I'd be interested in doing those past life regression sessions Vanessa told me about."

I swallow down the bite of steak and nod my head. "When we get back to *Mayhem,* I'll introduce you to Sonya. She is incredibly gentle when navigating you through the hypnosis process to obtain the memories."

"Will you stay with me for the first one?" she asks hesitantly—as if I'd say no.

"Of course. I'll be wherever you want me to be," I vow, meaning every word of it.

One of these days, I'll have earned her trust enough to give her the peace of mind that I'm not like all the others. *I'm not going anywhere, damnit. I won't abandon her.*

We wrap up dinner after a bit of small talk. Sailor offers to do the dishes as I box up the leftovers and wipe down the stove and counters. The two of us orbit one another so perfectly, like a choreographed dance. Her eyes track my movements every few minutes, a peaceful smile gracing her face when my gaze connects with hers.

Fuck, this feeling is incredible.

The last dish is placed in the dishwasher. The kitchen is officially cleaned up for the night. I lead her to her room and linger against the door frame with my arms crossed over my chest.

"I have a few meetings tomorrow. I should be back here around dinner time. You going to be okay on your own for a bit? Of course, you always have Rose and Vanessa to keep you company if you want it."

Her warm hand gently wraps around my forearm. "I've lived alone my whole life, Riot. I'll be just fine."

She steps into her room and slowly closes the door, hesitating before it closes fully. "Thanks for taking me with you. And... for everything else you've done for me. I may not have shown it so well, but I am grateful for you. I've learned over the years not to rely on anyone but myself. This time I needed help. Without hesitation, you gave it to me. So... yeah... thanks."

The front door opens, and the sound of a plastic bag being sorted into the refrigerator alerts me to Vanessa's return. Sailor swivels her head, looking down the hall nervously, like we are two teenagers sneaking around. She starts to close her door, avoiding another run-in with my mother.

I press my palm to the wood before it clicks shut. "You don't have to face everything alone. Not with me here. Not anymore. If you need me, my door will be unlocked. Just hop right on in my bed, *Little Ember*. I'll keep the nightmares away."

"I thought you said no sex tonight?" she whisper-shouts with a sassy brow raised.

I cluck my tongue and roll my eyes at her. "Who said we would be having sex?"

"*Psh*. The notoriously reclusive Riot Black wants to cuddle?" she asks incredulously before repressing a giggle. Her eyes go to the hallway again, checking that Vanessa isn't making her way over here.

I shrug my shoulders. "The only person I enjoy cuddling is you. Everyone else would have been tossed out of my bed if they even tried."

"We didn't cuddle last night. Or the night before. That was more like comforting," she refutes.

"We *so* cuddled. You were coiled around me like a goddamn vine. I don't wanna hear it."

She can't even argue that fact. Instead, she bites her lower lip and closes the door in my face.

Stubborn woman. *My* stubborn woman.

Meet you in our dreams, baby.

And if I'm really a lucky son of a bitch—in my bed, later.

CHAPTER 25

RIOT

A warm body is wrapped around me. A heavy head rests on my chest. Snoring. My eyes crack open as I shift in bed to cuddle Sailor closer as a wrapper crinkles between us. *I knew my little ember would seek me out.*

With a smile growing on my face, I glance down to where the soft snores are coming from. Pink messy hair and Taco Bell wrappers litter the space between us, along with shreds of cheese and lettuce. *The fuck?*

"*Rosemary,*" I grunt, shaking her gently before pushing her hands off me. She's still dressed in her going out outfit. Her face sparkles in the dimly lit room. Blue eyeliner is smudged under her eyes.

She stirs awake and stretches like a cat, the crumbs from her late-night snack tumble off her and onto the white sheets between us. It pisses me the fuck off. This is my goddamn bed. Why isn't she in hers?

"I want a new bodyguard," she grumbles.

I sweep the cheese, lettuce, and tomatoes away from me and sit up against the headboard, glancing at the clock. It's nearly 6 AM.

"What's wrong with Kael?" I swipe the sleep from my

face, running my hands over my face and then through my hair.

"He's a brute and I can't stand him."

"That's his job, Rosie. He's not one of your little rave buddies."

"Fucking asshole made me leave early. When I refused, he tossed me over his shoulder and brought me out of the club. Trust that I made a scene. And did he care one bit? No. I was in the middle of dancing with this incredibly hot guy from Portugal when Kael decided I had to go home. He's a fucking cockblock, Ry. I need a new bodyguard."

"Sounds like I need to give him a raise. Dealing with you is already a nightmare. I can't imagine having to stand by at a rave while everyone is high on Molly and doused in glitter. I'm sure he had good reason to take your ass home. Looks like he even got you Taco Bell," I say irritably, glancing down at the mess she left.

"That was *after* I ki–called him every name under the sun. Fucking asshole. I want a new one. I'm a grown ass adult." She crosses her arms over her chest and pouts before collecting the half-eaten taco from the wrapper and taking a bite.

I roll my eyes dramatically. "Really?"

She sighs and closes her eyes as the taco soaks up the rest of the alcohol still in her system. "Yeah, jerk," she mumbles over a mouthful.

"He's the only one who will put up with you, Rosie. And he does a damn good job of it. Especially when you try to make your guards' lives a living hell, or dodge them every chance you get. You know how many men begged me to find a replacement? How many were afraid to tell me they lost track of you? How many I've had to punish for losing you? Kael stays. Deal with it."

"Whatever. He can suck a huge—"

"Rosemary! Get out of my fucking bed. And take your crumbs with you." I pinch the bridge of my nose, losing what little patience I have left. When will she just grow up?

Being the brat she is, she tosses the rest of the taco into her mouth and brushes the crumbs and glitter off her shirt onto my bed before skipping out of my room.

Crumbs, glitter, and wrappers are what remain on my bed as I decide to start the day.

The coffee machine hisses as I collect the carafe and pour two mugs of steaming French roast into it. I add a splash of cream to mine and then cream and sugar into Sailors. I noticed how she takes her coffee the other morning before we left for Genevive's and then again on the flight here. She's got a sweet tooth, that one.

Padding down the hall in just my sweats, I spot Vanessa in her room. She's awake, sipping on tea at her desk. Tarot cards are spread across it over a burgundy velvet altar cloth. She leans forward, running a finger over The Tower card with her brows bunched. She's so immersed in the moment she barely registers that I'm in the hall.

I brush off the uneasy feeling that just gave me and continue my route to Sailor's room. With both hands full, I use my elbow to knock on her door.

Silence.

I knock again. More silence.

It *is* early. I guess she's slept in. On a shrug, I head back to my room, kicking the door shut with my foot. My feet carry me to the sliding glass door, where I try to shove it open with my hip. These doors are meant to withstand hurricane-force winds. The thing isn't budging.

I shift the drink by the handle into my right hand and pull the door open with my other. Coffee sloshes over the rim of my cup and splashes onto my gray sweats. *Mother-fucker.* First crumbs in my bed and now this shit. If it's any indication of how my day is going to go, I might as well just go back to bed and call it.

Deciding not to, I place both drinks down on the table and take a seat in a wicker chair. It's a beautiful morning. The beach is empty, the waves wash against the shore as a squadron of pelicans fly by. I spread my legs and allow the warm breeze and morning sun to dry out my pants.

Pulling the coffee mug to my lips, I take a sip and savor the peace of this moment. The irritation that had my heart beating fast slows, and once again, all is okay.

I make a mental list of the meetings I have today and the things I need to get done. Collecting my phone from my pocket, I shoot out a few emails. One of them is a grand opening notification for our Tennessee location. After that, I sent another text to Carlos to confirm if there were any leads on that scum, James.

My phone chimes with a notification.

My heart picks up rhythm in my chest, and I know exactly why. I glance over my shoulder to find my little ember all sleepy-eyed and adorable as fuck. She is in a baby pink satin cami and shorts set, leaning against the railing of her balcony. Dark, wavy strands blow in the wind as she turns to face me. When she notices me, her eyes light up before a smirk grows on her face.

"Aren't we a little old to be peeing the bed still?" She giggles, biting her lip, her eyes remaining glued to my crotch before traveling up over my abs and then settling on my eyes.

"I..." I stumble over my fucking words, tongue-tied. Comebacks are easy for me. I practically live and breathe sarcasm. But for some reason, this beauty has me stuttering.

"It's coffee," I finally say. "I knocked on your door a few

minutes ago to bring you some. When you didn't answer, I came out here to get a few emails sent. I spilled it while opening the door."

"*Mhm*. Okay." She giggles again, and it has a smile forming on my face.

"Well, if you want your coffee, you'll have to join me over here."

"Alright," she complies before disappearing behind the billowing curtains. The sliding door clicks shut, and goddamn butterflies swarm my stomach.

Tell anyone I said that, and I'll kill you.

A few moments later, my sliding door opens, and she comes out with furrowed brows.

"What the hell happened in there last night after we went to bed?" She jabs a finger towards the bed.

"*Rosemary* is what happened," I growl. "I woke up thinking you changed your mind and came to cuddle me. I was irritatingly disappointed to discover my little sister and a bed full of her fast food."

Sailor chuckles as she takes a seat next to me before collecting her mug and taking a sip.

"That's why I woke up to a Chalupa at my door. She must have left it for me."

I sip my coffee and shake my head.

Comfortable silence sits between us as we enjoy our morning coffee and view. It spurs on memories of us from other lives. Sailor and I would share these quiet moments together as much as we could. Sometimes we would make it down to a beach and watch the sunrise with coffee or tea. Sailor would always bring scones or something she had baked the night prior. Other times we would stay in bed or by the hearth. Each of us basking in the silence and enjoying the presence of one another. Reveling in the little slice of peace that comes before the rest of the world wakes up.

"Do you know what they did with Genevive's remains?" she asks in a whisper, still trying to maintain that bubble of tranquility.

"Landon, one of my men, investigated what happened. They have her ashes in an urn she had selected in her will. The lawyer, Donovan Creed, is currently in possession of it. From my understanding and what Landon has gathered from one of his assistants, he will be contacting you soon to discuss the will and her possessions.

"Okay." She takes another sip of her coffee and stares out at the horizon and the glow of the sky with its first streaks of daylight.

I angle my body towards her, resting my hand on her smooth, bare thigh. She's warm, far warmer than she has been the last few days. "Are you alright?"

She shrugs. Another sip.

"We can do something special for Genevive when we get her ashes. A memorial garden, if you want."

The corner of her mouth raises. "She would really like that."

"Then we absolutely will." I release a frustrated sigh. "I have a few meetings today. I'll be back again by dinner. We can go out to eat, if you'd like?"

"Do what you have to do, Riot. I'll probably read on the beach the rest of the day."

She's not okay. But the last thing I want to do is push her. So I just remain quiet again.

"Ryder," Vanessa's voice carries through the open door.

"The rest of Sailor's reading is...OH! Sailor, you're here." My mother places a hand to her chest.

Her eyes flick over to mine for a second. *Just a second,* but they held enough of a message to let me know that reading wasn't good. And I'm now more than positive that the reading she was doing this morning was Sailor's.

The Tower card is about collapse.

Chaos.

Destruction.

Fuck.

CHAPTER 26

SAILOR

It's been two weeks. Two weeks since Vanessa finished the remainder of my reading. Two weeks since I started my trip to Florida, finally understanding the connection between Riot and I. And two weeks since I knew we would *never* head towards anything but hurt and heartbreak.

And *betrayal*.

Vanessa tried explaining that not everything the cards show is written in stone. That we should look at the reading objectively. Putting aside the fact that she's Riot's mother, she tried convincing me not to make any rash decisions about the romantic connection.

Well...*Too late*. I'm not doing this.

My heart has been broken too many times. I'm not setting myself up for another failure. We haven't even slept together, so it will be a cleaner break than most.

Today, I plan on telling Rose that I'll be putting in my two weeks. She probably won't be happy with me. The two of us have really created a beautiful friendship while working together these last few weeks. After the reading, I mostly spent my time with her, avoiding Riot at all costs. The beach called our name, and Rose and I only continued to grow closer.

When we got back from Florida, we got together after work or before our shifts to talk about books or binge-watch our mutually favorite series on Netflix. It was so easy for us to fall into a routine. *Perhaps I knew her in a past life as well.*

One night while we painted our nails in Riot's living room, Rose told me all about her broodingly hot bodyguard, Kael. And how he annoys the absolute shit out of her. How he is always so overbearing and too attached. I had to laugh at how familiar that sounds.

Stupid, Riot. Why does he have to be a pain in my ass and also charming? Why did that reading have to show me that, once again, there is no hope for me?

Beyond him and what he could mean to me, I finally found a friendship outside of Liv. Even *that* connection is long-distance. I mean, for fucks sake, our get togethers are limitedly spaced and planned throughout the year.

Losing Rose is going to sting as badly as it will losing Riot. *There, I said it.* But that can't be the reason I stop pushing forward. *I have to.* I will not make it through another breakdown.

I physically and mentally can't.

Which means I can't look behind me when I go.

Rose was there when we did my reading. The three of us sat around the desk in Vanessa's room and went over the cards she had set up from the original reading. Riot was already neck deep in meetings when his mom finally agreed to sit down with us.

For a wise woman so poised and calm, she was visibly shaken up by it all. Rose knew immediately it was going to be bad news; her eyes, full of trepidation, always darted from the cards to her mother. Vanessa had mostly spoken about what the cards suggested, never once about what she had *seen or heard.*

I almost wish she did.

The violet-eyed woman is a very talented clairvoyant psychic medium, from what I've been told. She can channel spirit, *feel* and *see* the energy, receive messages from those who have passed on, or those a part of our spirit teams. From what I understand, every person has a group in the spiritual realm guiding and comforting them through challenging times, important lessons, and overall, throughout their life.

This *'team'* was put together before you even entered the world. Their main goal is to help you achieve your highest potential and fulfill the mission you were sent here for. A spirit team could consist of ascended masters, ancestors, angels, and gods and goddesses who offer their insight and protection.

I sure hope mine are around for this next dooming chapter of my life.

"There is a darkness I cannot see past. This Tower card, next to Death, is a strong indicator that something big is about to happen. It feels like chaos and a major turning point for your journey. I'm not trying to scare you, Sailor. This reading is just extremely dark. This card," Vanessa points to The Tower. *"Although this is a positive sign of transformation and letting go of what no longer serves you, I keep getting this vision of a storm, like you see here in the artwork. There is a fire like the one you dream of. Ryder is there with you...and then he isn't. Perhaps this is just a representation of the Phoenix,"* she trails off, speaking

more so to herself. Firm lines of worry etch her features, steadily increasing my anxiety.

Those daunting words have been on repeat since we left Florida. They have infiltrated my dreams and kept me tossing and turning each night. Riot seems to be the only one to keep the bad dreams away, but I refuse to let him sleep with me.

In fact, we have barely spoken since returning to Peaks Island. I avoided him every chance I got. He knows something is up. The man's not stupid. He tried to ask me about the reading, knowing my mood had changed dramatically since then, but neither I nor Vanessa would tell him what it was about.

I asked her not to.

Keeping my distance from him is what's best. Riot is traveling to the Tennessee *Mystical Mayhem* grand opening tonight, and I am heading to Genevive's after work to start the process of luring James in.

Which, honestly, couldn't be better timing.

Sebastian, the hacker helping us, has confirmed James received the text promotion for my birthday celebration tomorrow. They want me to call Liv and tell her of my plans while walking into the house. If luck is on our side, James will have confirmation that I am heading to *Mayhem* tomorrow.

That is, if he's actively watching me.

The thought of that sours my stomach.

Riot promised that I will have eyes on me at all times. And though he won't be able to be with me tonight, he'll be notified of my every move. That *should* comfort me, knowing he's doing all he can to bring James to justice and keep me safe.

But all it does is frustrate me.

He is *everything* the reading is not.

Kind. Caring. Protective.

Yet, the cards clearly show destruction and chaos. Heartbreak and betrayal. So, let's face it. People change. Their true colors always come to the surface. I'm just not willing or strong enough to stick around and find out.

Once James is detained, I'll leave this job and stay at Genevive's. Not that *that* would stop Riot from trying to convince me to come back. He's too stubborn and prideful to allow me to just walk away.

Which is why I've contemplated moving.

Starting over.

My heart skips a beat and I inhale sharply the same moment my phone chimes with a text notification.

> RIOT
>
> Still ignoring me? I was hoping for a goodbye kiss. You look good enough to eat in that leather skirt.

I scoff and lean against the bar, my eyes scanning the room, wondering where he's lurking. He hasn't been here all day. How does he know what I am wearing? When I don't find him, I look directly at the red light of the camera in the corner and flip him off.

The phone chimes again.

I have to bite back my smile. He can't affect me like this.

Cut it off by the head, Sailor.

RIOT

So… is that no? I must say, your version of foreplay has a flair for dramatics. I like it. 😉

SAILOR

NO. It was fun while it lasted, Riot. I made a lapse in judgment. My emotions were all over the place the last few weeks. I'm not interested in a relationship of any kind. It just felt nice to have comfort from someone familiar when I needed it most.

RIOT

You're a fucking liar. You know damn well what you felt in New Orleans and what you FEEL now is real. And raw. And it scares the hell out of you. Whatever the fuck Vanessa told you in the rest of your reading spooked you. Can we talk about it? Please? I have a few minutes before I need to leave for the airport.

When I don't respond, the bubbles pop up on the screen and then disappear before a new text comes in.

RIOT

I'm in the black van outside in the parking lot. I have chocolate… 😬

SAILOR

You do realize you offered me candy out of a sketchy black van, right? I'm gonna pass.

RIOT

I did offer myself up first…but now writing it out does sound pretty sketchy. Fuck. Just come say goodbye, Sailor. I'll toss the candy out the window… and I won't even try to kiss you.

I bite my thumbnail. *He deserves some closure, Sailor.* Even if just to tell him you appreciate his help. After tomorrow, you can officially close the door.

Instead, my fingers fly over the screen.

SAILOR

> There's nothing to talk about. Have a safe flight.

"You're scared, Little Ember. I won't let you push me away."

I hear his response in my head, and it freaks me out how that works. How, sometimes, especially lately, I can pick up on his thoughts. Vanessa even uses the channel to send me messages when she is checking up on me from her office down the hall. She also promised to work on strengthening my psychic abilities when I'm ready.

Little does she know, I won't be around long enough for that to happen.

The rest of my shift is miserable. I have a splitting headache, and Tylenol and Redbull aren't doing a damn thing to help. That chocolate could have worked wonders...

No, Sailor. Don't go there again.

Rose has been preoccupied, texting every chance she gets and leaving me alone with my anxious thoughts. A smile graces her beautiful face every so often. She's quite literally glowing. I wonder if that has anything to do with her...what did she call him? Oh, yes... *"King of the Assholes"* bodyguard.

We finally cash out our tips, and everyone says their goodbyes. Rose stops me before I reach the door, curling a gentle hand around my arm.

"You sure you don't want to have some company at Genevieve's? We could find a new show to watch and do some face masks. I'll bring that matcha tea you love and the melting flower oatmilk bombs." The crystals on her teeth sparkle as her face contorts with a convincing smile.

That sounds so fucking perfect. Especially after the last few restless days I've had, but doing anything more to lock in our friendship will only hurt her in the end. And me. A heaviness sits on my chest like a damn elephant.

I don't want to say goodbye.

"It's going to be an empty house tonight; most of the guards will be stationed with me. I'm sure Kael will be with you, which means the two of you could..." I shoot her a knowing look.

She rolls her eyes before winking at me. "That *is* true. Why didn't I think of that earlier?" She places a kiss on my cheek and starts rapidly texting as she makes her way to the back parking lot. "Call me if you need us," she shouts over her shoulder.

I smile, despite my current mood, and head for the main entrance. Carlos is waiting to drive me to Genevive's.

A text comes in with the promo and details for my party tomorrow. Butterflies take flight in my stomach just thinking about all the eyes that will be on me. I don't care for the attention, let alone James' beady ones feasting on me all night.

Ugh. A shudder runs up my spine as I hop in the front seat. I shoot a quick text to Liv letting her know I'll call her when I get home to talk details of the party. She wants to try and come, but Ethan may have family in from out of state.

Sucks. I really miss her.

"You're *so* worried about getting in a sketchy van with me, yet, you don't even pay attention to your surroundings while I'm gone," a familiar deep voice reprimands, then tsks. "Anyone could have been in this car, *Little Ember.*"

I startle at the sound of his voice, and my phone goes flying onto the floor below us. "Jesus, Riot." I press a hand to my chest, my heart thrashing against it from beneath.

"Why aren't you in Tennessee?" I ask as I lean down to collect my phone.

He bends forward at the same time as me, and we smack heads. "Ow!" My hand flies up to touch the tender spot above my brow.

Riot smiles all goofily and hands me the phone. "Sorry. Are you alright?" His fingertips brush against my hair before he pushes my hand away to inspect the area.

I snatch his hand away and place it on his lap. "I'm fine. Answer my question, Riot. Why aren't you in Tennessee? Aren't you the *big man* who is supposed to be in all the photos?"

"I sent Cameron instead. I have zero patience for that shit today and have a splitting headache. With James more than likely lingering close by, I didn't want to be away from you. At least not that far. And we need to talk."

He grabs the brown bag on the floor between us and

drops it into my lap. Loads of different chocolates and snacks fill the bag nearly to the brim. A few pieces fall out and he chuckles to himself before snatching one from between my clenched thighs.

"I call dibs on the Kit Kats. The rest are for you."

This man. Tell me how I can break his heart—and mine, for that matter—when the next two days are through? He has burrowed himself so deeply under my skin already, I think he's hit muscle. A little further and he'll have completely infiltrated the tissue, shimmied his way through bone and sinew, and I'll find him dancing on my heart strings.

I'm fucked.

So. So. Fucked.

I steal the unwrapped Kit Kat out of his hands and bite both pieces at the same time. *Mm. They are my favorite, too.*

He looks at me like I'm a wild animal. Which, to be fair, is probably accurate. I *feel* like a caged animal right now. All day I've been pacing. And pacing. And sweating. *Which has been really fucking annoying.* I miss being cold. Even my normally tame hair is wild and frizzy from my shift. And I'm starving.

For pizza.

For this candy bar.

And for him.

"You little savage. You don't break apart the pieces before eating them?" Eyes the deepest shade of green are splayed wide as he stares at me in shock and disbelief.

They glaze over as he watches me suck the melted chocolate off my finger. *Oops. I didn't mean to do that. See what*

I'm talking about? This man has me so rattled, I don't even realize I'm flirting with danger.

"Nope." I pop the p to add that flare of dramatics he was speaking of earlier.

He shakes his head with an expression of mock horror and pulls us out of the lot.

CHAPTER 27

SAILOR

Past

Riot turns right, pulling out of the student parking garage in his black Jeep Grand Cherokee. This one may be a year or two younger than the one I've had my eye on back at home. The one that belonged to Mr. Sanders. A sweet old man who used to frequent the bar I work at.

He passed last weekend. Complications after his heart surgery. His wife, Anne, can't drive anymore and is selling it for a really great price. *A steal, if you ask me.* I've got a tiny bit of money tucked away for it. Even left a deposit before I left.

His right hand rests on the wooden gear shifter, his elbow pressed against mine on the center console. The other, loosely holds the wheel as he navigates us towards the highway, heading towards the airport.

Thank God I was able to get a last-minute flight out. I'm seated in the very front by the bathrooms—but, fuck if I care. Anything is better than spending another second here. I have absolutely *zero* desire to face Cameron or all the emotions spreading like wildfire throughout my body. I just need to get on that flight, and leave it all behind me.

Riot collects the black thermos sitting in the cup holder and hands it to me. "It's black tea with honey," he offers.

I stare at his extended hand and the thick veins that are bulging from his grip on the mug. I almost want to laugh at the way he's holding it, like it's a deadly poison, or a bomb that could explode any second.

"Thanks," I say hesitantly, accepting the oddly kind gesture.

Mr. President isn't all that bad, I suppose.

Still a cult leader.

Still the reason Cameron has chosen to cross over to the dark side.

He clears his throat as he watches me blow on the steaming lid before taking a sip. I hide a smirk and the comment I have on the tip of my tongue–which is now burned, all because I am an impatient fool. An amused smile is hidden beneath lips pressed together as his fingers fumble around with his phone. A few seconds later, Sam Smith's *Latch* filters throughout the car.

Nice choice.

Ugh. Why do we like the same things? I'm supposed to hate him.

"So, what now?" he asks, interrupting my mental sing-along.

"What do you mean?" I turn towards him, taking another sip of the tea.

"With... Cameron," he clarifies softly.

I bite down on my lower lip, biding my time in answering. Because, truthfully? I don't know. I just know that this was my last fucking straw with him.

"I don't know." I shake my head before looking out the window. Stupid hot tears fill my lower lids.

The car in front of us slams on its brakes, and Riot's hand jolts out to press me back against the seat. My damn heart nearly bursts out of my chest as he swerves and narrowly avoids an accident.

Jesus Christ.

I blow out a harsh breath as he does the same. His hand stays glued to my chest, right over my breasts. The warmth of it spreads through my Spice Girl's t-shirt, easing the pounding below my sternum.

"Fuck," he croaks.

Riot pulls his hand back and runs it through his hair before laying on the horn and flipping off the asshole next to us that nearly got us killed. His piercing green eyes flare as they dart back to me before descending, taking inventory of every inch of my body.

"Are you okay?" he asks. Stress coats his throat, making it raspy... and hot...*Fuck.*

Bad Sailor. NO.

"Yeah. Your floor, not so much." I nod to the spilled tea all over the floor mat below me.

"Don't worry about that. Did it burn you?" Riot rests his hand on my thigh, which has a few wet spots on it.

"No," is all I'm capable of saying, while trying my best to reassure him.

My leg could currently have third-degree burns on it, but I wouldn't have even noticed. I'm more concerned about where my brain is at right now. Must have gotten rattled around.

This man is supposed to be the Devil. Not some angel. Some sweet savior. Perhaps I can find some middle ground, something in between... to keep things grey and not so black and white.

Ah...Dark Angel...

That certainly suits him.

His hand trembles on my thigh. All that adrenaline finally kicked in. Without consciously directing it, my hand covers his, and our fingers intertwine. He glances back over at me, and I can't stop staring at those eyes. They really are beautiful... *for a serpent, that is.*

Snakes are beautiful too, Sailor. Doesn't mean you should pet them like you are doing now.

I laugh at myself, breaking the weird spell we were under. I pat his hand twice. "Thank you for keeping me alive. And thanks again for taking me to the airport."

He tugs his hand back and replaces both on the wheel in a 10 & 2 position. The tension in his shoulders slowly eases as he relaxes back into his seat.

We remained quiet the rest of the drive. Occasionally, a song would come on that I approved of, prompting me to quietly hum along. Riot would smile and sing along. *Pretty well, I might add.* Luckily, my pants dried as we approached the drop-off area. Nothing like walking into the airport looking like you pissed yourself.

Riot hops out, opens the latch of the trunk, and collects my suitcase. He rolls it towards me and awkwardly keeps his hand wrapped around the handle.

"I'm sorry Cameron is an asshole. It doesn't justify it, but he's been going through a lot lately."

I hold up a hand to stop him. I don't want to hear it.

Any of it.

"Thanks again," I say, tugging my bag from his hold.

I turn around and start walking towards the terminal doors. Back home to literally no one. Me, myself, and I. Party of one.

My name on his lips stops me from entering those doors.

"Sailor, wait."

Turning around, I see him dodge a taxi and a bicyclist, narrowly avoiding death or bodily harm, once again.

Soft but firm hands come up to tuck the blonde streaks of hair behind my ears. Eyes as green and clear as emeralds gaze into mine. It's like I am suddenly caught in a spell. A dream. I can't look away. It feels like a fucking fishing hook is lodged into me. And I know, without a shadow of a doubt, if I were to walk away, he would reel me right back in.

Honestly? I don't even think I would care.

Except this is *not* one of those stupid fairytale airport moments like in the books I read.

Not some Hallmark movie.

This is catch and RELEASE.

I need to swim far, far away from this place.

From *him.*

We stay like that for what feels like an eternity. *How long was it really?* I'm not even sure. His thumb brushes against my cheek first before it's replaced with his soft, warm lips.

No. No. Why do I like that? Why does that have goosebumps springing up along my arms?

"No one deserves to feel unwanted or forgotten. Especially on their birthday," his minty breath tickles my cheek as his whispered words reach my ear.

Sliding his hand into his back jeans pocket, he pulls out a business card and hands it to me. His fingers curl around mine, tucking the stationery into mine for safekeeping. I stare down at our conjoined hands and then back up to his eyes. The black of his pupils has expanded as our breathing turns shallow, our chests rising and falling perfectly in sync. The chaos and noises around us have dulled, becoming muffled. My peripheral darkens like I have blinders on.

All I see is *him*. All I feel is *his* hand in mine.

Taking one step back, he smiles widely. "Happy Birthday, Sailor. I hope you have a safe flight. If you ever feel lonely, or bored...or just need someone to talk to..." He barely looks over his shoulder as he starts to walk backward. A taxi blares its horn at him as he chuckles and holds up his thumb and pinky finger to his ear in the gesture of a phone. "*Call me*," he mouths.

I can't help but laugh at how ridiculous this moment is. I am running away from my problems, not trying to start new ones. My hand rises and I do a little wave before I turn back around and enter through the sliding doors.

When safely behind those doors and standing in line to check in, I lower my head to look at the card in my palm. His name and fraternity information are on there, along with his phone number.

Feeling flustered, and a little breathless, I pull my phone out of my purse, ready to enter his information. But then the rational part of my brain kicks in, and I'm reminded he is a cult leader.

He cannot be trusted.

Clearly, my heart disagrees. It skips a beat. Like a built-in lie detector telling me that just isn't true. *Well, fuck what my heart thinks.* It's done nothing but lead me in the wrong direction. I tear up the stupid card and toss it in the trash bin next to me.

Inhaling deeply, I remind myself that I can't rely on anyone.

Not even dark angels with green eyes. The dangerous kind that will haunt me for the rest of my days.

CHAPTER 28

SAILOR

J ust as requested by Riot and Diego, I made sure to walk into Genevive's while talking on the phone with Liv about the details of my birthday tomorrow. She so badly wants to come, but doesn't think she'll make it.

Sucks, really. I miss my best friend.

Like the silk of a spider web, the type that can't be seen but felt, an eerie feeling crawled over my skin as my feet crunched along the gravel. Movement next door, where my childhood abandoned house remains, sent ice shooting up my spine. It took everything in me not to rush to the front door. The second I was through it, I latched the lock and released a bone-chilling sob.

How did I get here? Being hunted by a psychopath?

Riot circled the block a few times before parking in front of my old house and walking back to Genevieve's. He made sure neither he nor the other men stationed somewhere out there were noticed. *At least that's what his text message assured me of.*

This was the plan. The more vulnerable I appear, the more comfortable James will be in approaching me again.

242

Another wave of adrenaline judders my body as I welcome Riot in through the back sliding door. I slam it closed behind him, toss the lock, and swiftly pull the curtains shut. My goosebump-riddled arms come up to wrap around myself. An unsuccessful attempt to keep the nerves at bay.

James could be out there right now for all I know. Watching me. Waiting. Jerking off. *Ugh.* Another violent shudder runs through me at the thought.

The *clink* of Riot's keys and the bag of goodies hitting the granite have me jerking back and yelping. *He's* here now, my dark angel.

It's okay.

It's *okay.*

Deep breaths, Sailor.

Riot steps towards me slowly, approaching cautiously, like one would a skittish animal. "I'm not going to let anything happen to you, Sailor," he vows. He gently pulls me in by the back of my head and cradles my face to his chest.

Numb and gripped with fear, I can barely move my still crossed arms. I inhale deeply. The heat radiating off him and his calming smoky scent wrap around me and ease some of the tension in my rigid limbs.

After a few moments of being held in his embrace, the adrenaline starts to dissipate out of my system, and I relax into him. A weighted breath is released from my still trembling lips. My arms, more viable now, find their way around him as the tips of my fingers dig into the carved muscles of his shoulder blades. The way I cling to him is the same as it was in the ocean a few weeks ago.

Like he is a life vest, and I have been stranded and swimming for a very, *very* long time. All alone out in the vast ocean without a coastline in sight. He keeps my head above water when I get tired.

Too tired to keep up this fight alone.

Riot inhales deeply, tightening his hold on me and lowering his cheek to rest on the top of my head. "I've got you, *Little Ember.*"

My dumb ass brain chooses this moment to pick a nice fight with my heart. Damn, how good it feels to be wrapped up in the safety and sanctuary of his arms. To know I could stay here forever. That, in fact, I have apparently done exactly that in so many lifetimes before.

The craving for everlasting serenity is a dangerous thing. Because being right here in his arms brings back that hope all over again.

That thought is quickly overshadowed by the fear of getting hurt again. *I don't even really know him, do I? Hardly. Yet, this connection...it's undeniable...*

Nope. I can't do it.

I just...

A warm knuckle slides under my chin and guides my face up. My eyes greet his. They are intense today—an endless forest of lush green fields and moss. Pain and hope reside there, warring with each other. They are a mirror to my own thoughts. He must know, must *sense* that I'm retreating. Throwing up a white flag.

I don't want to run.

But I have to. I have to preserve what's even left of my abused heart.

Soft lips crush mine in a blinding kiss. Making me forget all the reasons why. White is all I see behind my closed lids.

Surrender. This is what surrender should feel like.

All previous thoughts go out the window. Immediate feelings of belonging and undeniable *need* filter through my veins. It sets me alight internally, racing up my spine and burning away all my worries and fears. In this moment, all I can think of is that I don't want him to stop kissing me.

Please, please don't stop kissing me.

A sigh floats off my lips as a smile grows on his face. Our lips are still firmly pressed together when a wave of boldness takes over me. I clasp the back of his neck and align our bodies until they are flush, until I can feel every hard ridge of his muscles. I'm burning up, desperate with desire. And it only gets worse. The internal temperature of my body soars exponentially as his heat, his scent engulfs me.

Riot's lips savagely claim mine, bruisingly so. Teeth nip at my lower lip as his tongue swipes away the sting. His strong hands cup my ass, lifting me off the ground. My legs inch up to encircle his waist as he leads us out of the kitchen and up the stairs. They creak as we make our ascent. I break our kiss to press feather-light kisses along his jaw and down the column of his neck. He growls low, his Adam's apple bobbing and vibrating under my tongue as I swipe it along the pebbled skin there.

We enter a room I haven't been in yet. I stayed a few doors down in the guest room. This must be another. Riot removes a gripping hand to blindly search the wall for the light switch as his lips easily find mine in the dark. There is a shared urgency vibrating between us. One that was missing the last few weeks.

Riot wanted slow... because I wanted slow...and ultimately that left room for me to freak the fuck out. Put distance between us. Which I should still do...

It doesn't mean I won't—but let that be tomorrow's problem.

Right now, I need his lips on every inch of my skin. I want his tongue to trace every crease, every curve. And then when he's had his fill, I'll get mine, memorizing every inch of him, so I never forget.

Reading my cues—or maybe hearing them–he releases a low chuckle as his lips break free from mine. He gave up on finding the light switch, our eyes slightly more adjusted to the darkness with the bit of light pooling in from the cracked door. The back of my thighs hit the mattress, and he careens over me until we fall onto the soft down feather comforter. It smells of lavender and vanilla.

Soft lips and a wicked tongue trace a path down from my racing pulse to the dip by my collarbone as his fingers work the buttons of my black satin dress shirt.

"Tell me what else you want, Sailor," he murmurs, his breath hot against my flesh, right below my navel.

I lean up onto my elbows and watch as his tongue lavishly traces the waistband of my skirt. Goosebumps erupt across my skin, pulling a satisfied hum from deep within me. Approvingly, he guides his fingers into the waistband and tugs gently, leaving a few more seconds for me to back out.

"Words, Sailor. I need words. I promised you slow, but I can't fucking do it anymore. You've driven me fucking crazy these last two weeks. I told myself I would give you the distance you craved, but I have exhausted any restraint I had left. I need to taste you. Touch you. Need to feel your racing heart pressed against mine as I bring us both to ruin."

Hot, noisy kisses are peppered along my exposed hip bone—and I lose it.

"*You.* I need all of you, Riot," I whisper, wanton need lacing my voice and making it breathy.

He doesn't respond with any words other than another agonizingly heated kiss pressed to my other hip bone. His fingers clench around the leather material, dragging both my stockings and skirt down my legs until they are tossed behind him. He follows through, adding my panties to the pile.

I lean forward, capturing his lips with mine. We only break contact when he reaches behind him to tug his sweater off. My greedy fingers skim his waistband and stop at the gun tucked in his waistband. With a grunt, he removes it and places it on the end table. At least *we have protection should someone breach the men outside while we are...distracted.*

Redirecting my thoughts away from the fear, I reach for the button of his jeans. Of course–it gives me a hard time, only delaying the desire rolling through me. With a smirk, he kisses me quickly before releasing his fly and swiftly removing his pants, boxers, socks, and shoes. As he carelessly tosses them behind him, I drag the satin shirt off me and chuck it aside.

We are a mix of breaths, moans, and giggles as his body presses against mine. We fall back, and he gently pins me to the mattress. *And—ohhh.* Liv may have been right about her 'thumb theory' because... *holy crap.* The thick, hot length of him rests heavily between us, twitching against my sensitive flesh as I shift beneath him. A knowing smile grows on Riot's face as he makes quick work of my bra, his deft fingers snapping open the clasp with one flick.

"Fuck this contraption," he laughs, throwing the scrap of lace over his head. That irresistible dimple on his cheek appears as he admires my naked body below him. "Do you see how fucking perfect and perky your tits are? What the hell do you even need that thing for?" he asks playfully as his rough palms caress my breasts.

The pad of his thumbs rubs slow circles over my nipples. The delicious sensation has me arching my back off the bed and pressing my breasts further into his palms. Riot takes full advantage of my exposed neck and pulls it between his teeth, sucking lightly before pressing a firm kiss to it.

Desperate for more friction, I lower my head and kiss him hard, wrapping my legs around his hip and pulling him closer. Much, *much* closer.

And, God, does it feel incredible.

His hands have moved to accommodate the change. One rests above my head, his bicep bulging with the added pressure, as the other trails between us until he is spreading me. His tongue dances with mine as his fingers start to unravel me.

Both of my hands come up to cup his face, angling it so I can kiss him even deeper. One of my arms wraps around his neck, keeping him glued to me as his fingers continue to strum me like a guitar.

Never. *Never* have I felt this way. This need for total closeness. It's like I am trying to stitch every available space of my flesh to his. To sew myself to him so thoroughly that we will always be forced to carry each other wherever we go.

Two fingers slide through my slickness and slowly push into me. I moan into Riot's mouth as he finds the spot that has my toes curling where they rest on his beautiful ass.

"God, Sailor, you're so fucking beautiful. I know fate hasn't been kind to you or I, but that's all about to change.

You are a goddess. And it's time for you to be worshipped as such," he affirms as his fingers drag through my slickness.

"I want your essence soaking me, drowning me, because that's what this is, right? The product of your divinity?" He pulls back his hand and licks my arousal off his fingers. "Do you trust me?" he asks. I search his piercing eyes that are heavily-lidded with lust and oh so fucking sexy, already knowing the truth.

I do.

As crazy as that sounds, I really do.

I bite my lip and nod as I lift my hips. His palm grinds against my clit and pubic bone with every stroke of our synced movements. The sounds coming from him, me, and my arousal are only heightening this moment. Up and up we go. Like each clink on the way to the top of a roller coaster... I am about to peak.

He slides off me, sinking further down the mattress. Riot's fingers still continue their iniquitous movements as his other hand shoves my thighs open wider and his mouth finds the core of me coated in a layer of desire. Flattening his tongue, he licks me from entrance to clit, swirling his tongue around the oversensitive bead over and over again.

A swear leaves my lips as I see stars and flashes of our previous lives together. Every ache. Every touch. Every moan and prayer sung from my lips. Every gentle brush of hair off my face as his lips find mine.

My fingers sink into his dark locks, holding on for dear life as he continues his relentless pursuit with his hands and mouth. Quivering thighs clench around him as my hips raise, meeting each thrust of his tongue and fingers and holding him there between them like a vice. I'm so fucking close as he adds a third finger. Deliciously stretching me.

He licks me once.

Twice.

On the third and final swipe, he sucks my clit between his teeth, and I scream out my pleasure.

My rigid body arches off the bed, nearly crushing his poor head as my thighs tremble with my release. "Ryder," I plead. "*Fuuck. Fuck, Ryder*, I can't," I mewl, barely able to get the words to leave my mouth.

"You can, *Little Ember*. And you just did. *Beautifully*. You ignited brighter than I could have ever imagined," he praises before lowering his mouth back down. His muffled chuckles carry over the buzzing in my ears as he lazily continues to lick me. I use my nails to massage his scalp in slow circular motions as I shakily release my thighs and close my eyes. Aftershocks rock my body, sending a delicious shiver up it.

Inhaling a deep breath and then releasing it, he demands, "Don't even think about falling asleep now, Sailor. I just got a taste of you and I'm not nearly finished worshipping you."

I open my eyes on a smile and look down at him. His hair is sticking up in all directions from my finger's ministrations, and it's sexy as hell. In the muted light, I can faintly make out his chin resting on my pubic bone. The slight scratch of his stubble adds to the high I am riding on. His swollen lips glisten with my release, making me blush further.

Is it possible to stay in this bubble and never go back to reality again?

Leaning up on my elbows, I hook my index finger below

his chin. "Then get up here and show me what else you got, Dark Angel."

CHAPTER 29

RIOT

I crawl up her body and spread her thighs to accommodate me, guiding them around my hips. My fingers rake through her hair as I lower myself to claim her soft lips. She runs her tongue along mine, quietly moaning as she tastes herself on me. Those little noises she makes practically disarmed me earlier.

I'm hard as a fucking rock.

The tip of my cock nudges her soaked entrance as I enter her slowly. Inch by fucking mindblowing inch. Warm honey eyes grow wide as I sink deeper, with her sigh skimming against my lips as I become fully seated.

"Ryder," she whimpers. *Are those tears in her eyes? Fuck, did I hurt her?* With pinched brows, I start to pull back, but she grips my ass cheeks in both hands, keeping me put. "I'm okay. I...just... My heart is racing so fast, and I feel like this is some sort of dream, where tomorrow I'll wake up and you'll be gone."

The corner of my lip raises as I stare down at her in awe. *She's so fucking stunning.* I swipe a thumb under her eye where a tear escaped, then collect her hand and place it over my heart.

"Feel that, *Little Ember*? Mine is racing, too. Just like yours." Bringing her trembling hand up, I kiss her knuckles. "Thank you for choosing me. For letting your guard down enough to experience this moment. I'm sure you're thinking about the fact that we practically just met... But tell me why it feels like I have held you like this for an eternity? It's *because I have*. I'm not going anywhere, Sailor. Let me retell our story."

"I wish I could remember," she sighs. Her palm comes up to stroke the stubble on my cheek, and I lean into it.

"You will. Feeling your heartbeat, your skin on mine. On a night where I am protecting you from any threat coming your way...It has already brought flashes of so many incredible memories. Of times like this, when you and I connected like this." I roll my hips for reference, prompting a sweet laugh out of her. I start to move slowly, thrusting into her and making her eyelids flutter. My mouth hovers over hers as I whisper into it, "And it takes my fucking breath away. How much we desired each other. How intimacy always merged our souls in cement instead of tape."

We find our rhythm, her hips rising to meet my thrusts. This isn't how every man imagines fucking his woman—typically, *hard and fast*. Of course I want that—who doesn't? But this moment was designed to be slow and emotional. Our souls are remembering what it feels like to be together in this way.

Her little pants continue to drive me wild. With every stroke, her kisses become more frantic and her legs tighten around me. Sweat beads on both of our chests, slickening our bodies so they glide against each other as my pace quickens. This is the building of a crescendo, the two of us playing our part in perfect harmony.

She's close, as am I. I can feel her walls cinching around my cock. There's a rhythmic flutter before her nails bite into my back. In the spot she loves so much around my shoulder blades. Trying to remove myself from her right now would be like trying to pull your finger out of one of those bamboo finger traps. She's gripping my cock so tightly, I might not be able to pull out of her before I explode.

Fuck. We never talked about birth control, and I haven't seen her take a pill.

I am able to inch back enough to separate our hips, my cock absolutely throbbing, but she slams me back down before crying out. "I'm on the pill, Ryder. Now, *please* fuck me without holding back before I lose my goddamn mind."

I laugh at her bossiness before I capture her lips and fuck her like the animal inside me desires. The creature, never far, is always trying to claw its way out of my flesh. Like the dragon inked into my chest. The old coiled mattress squeaks as I pound into her, adding to the erotic sound of flesh meeting flesh. Little staccato noises leave the back of her throat before she breaks the kiss. Sailor's eyes roll as her body trembles against mine.

"I remember, I remember, I remember," she chants behind closed lids.

She throws her head back in ecstasy as a powerful wave of emotions and pure rapture ignite along my spine, blazing its way up and making my crown tingle.

The spiritual crown, you little hornball, not the other crown... Although that one is also feeling pretty rapturous right about now...

Her pussy clenches down so intensely, stars blast my vision before I explode inside of her. Purple and silver sparkles dance and pulse across the edges of my vision before her perfect face comes back into view. Sailor has the biggest grin on her face as her glossy eyes find mine.

"Wow," her breathless voice says in my head.

"Wow," I say incredulously. "You really are a goddamn savage."

Sailor's feet are in my lap as we lounge on the couch, eating our snacks. After another two rounds of mind-blowing sex, we showered together and came downstairs to replenish our reserves. Her little black satin teddy that she managed to leave behind is riding up her thighs and making me want to ravish her again. She takes another huge bite of her mozzarella string cheese as I peel mine the way they were made to be.

"Why even bother with peeling them? We are adults, Ry. Just bite it!" she giggles, shifting her weight forward and climbing into my lap. She holds out her cheese towards my mouth, raising a dark brow in dare. "Do it. Come on, lose control a little."

"I did lose control. Three times now. And I'd like to do it again, a few more times before dawn." I let out a growl before biting the mozzarella and playfully grazing her finger along with it.

Her mischievous smirk tells me she could get on board

with that idea. *Hell yes.* She taps my cheek reprimandingly before bringing her lips to mine briefly.

"Sorry, all the store had was string cheese." I huff out my irritation. "I planned on grabbing a bottle of bourbon and a variety of the good stuff, but would have been late picking you up from work," I explain while snagging her wrist and stealing the rest of her cheese. "I guess I could have grabbed a bottle before we left."

"I love it. The candy. The string cheese. Probably more so than the fancy cheeses or all that charcuterie crap. I'm pretty simple if you haven't noticed, Ry."

"You are far from simple, *Little Ember*." I smile widely at how adorable she is. Now that her guard is down, it's become addicting to see how go-with-the-flow, relaxed and playful she can be around me.

My hand skims up her thigh, and I drape it over my hips so that she's straddling me. My other hand comes up to cup her face. "Tell me something about you that I might not already know," I demand in a whisper, my eyes locked into her soft gaze.

Sailor giggles lightheartedly. "You don't really know much about me, do you?"

"That's not true. Since the day you left New Orleans, I held onto every scrap of information Cameron would share about you—which was a lot. I know you two had a falling out, but maybe you'll be willing to hear him out. It's been a few weeks now. I don't want you to feel pressured or anything, but I know he's been hurting. He didn't really explain himself very well that night."

She leans back, resting her palms on my chest. "I'll think about it. I'm still angry with him."

"Fair enough," I concede.

"So what do you know about me?" Her top teeth rest along her plush bottom lip as she mindlessly paints little swirls over my bare chest.

"You are an Aries. Born March 31st...which in about..." I trail off and glance down at my black Rolex, then back up to her. "Two hours and twenty-three minutes, you'll be turning 27."

"Wow, and Cameron knew my exact time of birth?" Her nose scrunches up as she purses her lips and narrows her eyes suspiciously. It's fucking adorable and makes me snort out a laugh.

She caught me.

"Well, *technically*, I knew your date of birth because we spent it together way back when. But I did some digging of my own after that. I wanted to compare your birth chart to mine and needed an exact time and place of birth."

She leans down to whisper in my ear. "I'd say that's really fucking stalkery, but the fact that you wanted to learn more about our spiritual life is kind of a turn on."

"That so?" I turn my head and inhale her freshly washed hair. It's tropical and similar to the subtle scent of her perfume. From the looks of the bottle that she also left here before I moved her, it's some combination of coconut and hibiscus.

"Mhm. What else do you know?" she asks as she rests her head on my shoulder and returns back to painting designs onto my skin.

My hand comes up to massage her scalp. Her eyes close as a relaxed smile forms on her face. "Let's see....You love to read, your favorite take-out is Chinese food, you prefer tea over coffee—but in the summer months opt for iced coffee, you have never traveled anywhere except New Orleans and New York, and you hate sports—including watching them. The only reason you went to the football games was to watch Cameron. Your favorite color is green—which is surprising for the amount of black you wear. Oh, and your favorite flower is the Dahlia. Fun fact, did you know that dahlias were gifted to show your love and commitment to another in the Victorian Era?"

She responds with a shake of her head against my shoulder. *No.*

"Did you also know it is a symbol of resilience? That dahlias can thrive in very harsh conditions? Or that it represents a fresh start or rebirth?"

She shakes her head again and stops painting to pull her hair back over her shoulder. There, on the back of her neck, is a small but perfectly detailed Cafe Au Lait Dahlia. *How did I miss this earlier? Or when we were in the shower?* I was so focused on her lips and her stunning eyes while we washed up, I never noticed her tattoo.

The colors are beautiful, a mixture of pinks and creams. Her artist did an incredible job, using shading and her own ivory skin to create the delicate petals.

"I remember now...why I actually got this. It came to me earlier in flashbacks. But when I first decided to get it, I had no clue why. I just knew I needed it. A few days after I came home from New Orleans, I had a couple of extra bucks left on my credit card and decided it must have been a sign for me to get my first tattoo. I figured, why not add a little extra pain to my already painful life?" She shrugs indifferently before continuing.

"The damn flower kept popping up everywhere I went. I first saw it on a sign for perfume at the airport terminal. Then again, on the plane. My seat had a sticker stuck to it with the same flower. A barista drew it on my cup at the cafe in the terminal when I arrived home. Then it kept popping up in my dreams, on Instagram posts, on book covers. Finally, I made my appointment after doing some research on local artists. And honestly, I couldn't be happier. It is beautiful."

I trace the ink with my index finger, eliciting her sweet sigh and a patch of goosebumps springing up in its wake. "If I tell you something, will you freak out?"

"Depends," she says curiously.

"The day I drove you to the airport...I was too much of a chickenshit to give them to you, and I already knew you weren't my biggest fan, so I decided against it... But I had gotten you a bouquet of those exact flowers for your birthday at a little flower shop down the block. When Liv told me it was your birthday, I found myself heading there after my jog. I walked right in and went straight to them. At the time, I had no clue why. Why those? Now..." I trail off, hoping she remembers as well.

A sad smile grows on her face. "You would always get me dahlias. Just because, anniversaries, birthdays. You even planted a garden for me in one vision. Vanessa said we didn't have many past lives actually being together, but in those memories, you and I were happy. I saw hardship and time apart, too; wars and societal factors, but we always found a way to see each other—even if only for a kiss. No matter what, every single time you saw me, you would bring me a dahlia. All different colors. I would dry them out and press them into a book. Next to each one, I would write when you gave it to me. A little diary of you and me."

A tear slips down her cheek, and I notice one is working its way down my own. I had those same visions during my past life regression sessions. I didn't even know she would press them into a book. However, I did know I would always find a way to get her a flower every time we would meet. The times we did get to spend together properly, I would buy bouquets of them for her. One of our cottages was even surrounded by them.

"You're right. We may not know much about each other, or you may know a bit more about me than I do about you in this lifetime. But the more the memories and feelings come back, the more I don't even care about that. My soul recognizes *you*. It did right away, Ryder. I was just too scared and naive to understand it at the time."

I pull her to me and kiss her senseless. Time doesn't exist. Not when our salty tears are blended together and our hearts beat as one.

There's no telling how long we were kissing on that couch, or how long we had been back upstairs getting lost in each other over and over again. I'm currently holding her as she sleeps peacefully in this bed, and nothing but her little snores and the silence of this old home surround us.

That is...until there is a knock on the bedroom door.

CHAPTER 30

RIOT

I grab my Glock off the end table next to my phone that is charging and slip Sailor's arm off my chest. Slowly, I get out of bed and creep toward the door.

I gave specific orders to mine and Diego's men not to enter the home unless it was an emergency. My heart races with adrenaline as I pad towards the door. James wouldn't just knock if he somehow managed to bypass my crew...but you should never underestimate the inner workings of a psychopath.

Turning the knob, I angle the tip of my gun and open it fast, taking aim as the door fully opens.

"Don't shoot!" Cameron raises his hands, his own gun clenched tightly.

I lower my weapon immediately, tucking it into the back of my jeans. My second in command does the same. *Christ. I nearly shot him.*

"The fuck are you doing here?" I whisper-shout, quickly glancing behind me to see if I woke Sailor.

"You weren't answering your phone. I've been calling you," he lowers his voice. Cameron's eyes stray behind me. Possessively, I step into his line of sight, not comfortable with him looking at Sailor as she's basically nude beneath the sheets. She's wearing that skimpy little teddy and matching panties she had on earlier.

"What is it?" I hiss. My concern starts to grow at the reason he's here.

"Your sister hasn't been answering her calls, and security at the house says she never came back after work."

I sigh, knowing she's probably at a bar or some book club thing. "Kael knows how to handle her. I'm sure she's fine. She probably tried to dodge him. The two of them have a very hot and cold dynamic."

"Kael is outside, Ry. You assigned nearly everyone to be here tonight. We have one detail with Vanessa and one with Rose. Carlos is at her apartment, has been there all night waiting. Kael said he hasn't heard from her at all, tried reaching out. He's worried, Ry. And Kael is never worried." Cameron's eyebrows pull together as he frowns, his eyes traveling back over my shoulder.

I rake my fingers through my hair and curse under my breath. "Give me a minute, I'll be right out," I say before closing the door in his face.

Reluctantly, I shuffle back over to the bed and grab my phone. It's off. *The fuck?* I had it charging before we went to bed. Holding down the main button, I power it on and wait for it to prompt me with my Face ID. When it finally powers up, I notice it went through an update. *Fucking updates. No wonder it didn't turn back on.* I toss it back down and start dressing.

When finished, I collect my phone and tuck the comforter tighter around my little ember. She stirs but doesn't wake as I place a kiss on her forehead. I'll be back before she wakes... but just in case, I'll send her a text message letting her know I'm coming back.

Maybe I'll even grab us some breakfast.

I open messages and type it out quickly before going back to check all the missed calls and texts. With one last glance at Sleeping Beauty, I close the door behind me and meet up with Cameron in the living room.

> **CAMERON**
>
> Hey. Rose hasn't been seen since work.

> **CAMERON**
>
> Kael hasn't heard from Rose. Usually by now, she's chewing his ear off about her fictional men. Or about how his tattoos look like a child drew them 😬

> **CAMERON**
>
> Dude, do I send in the troops? You always answer your phone.

> **CAMERON: MISSED CALL.**

> **CAMERON: MISSED CALL.**

> **KAEL**
>
> Hey, Boss. Rosemary isn't answering her phone. She hasn't been seen since she left work. Usually, I take the liberty of tailing her while sticking to the shadows to make sure she arrives safely at her apartment. I'm not her detail tonight. Carlos is. Do you mind if I leave my post here to check on her?

> **KAEL**
>
> Sorry to bother you again, Boss. Something feels off. I know your sister can be a bit unpredictable with her late night plans, but something isn't right. I'll call Cameron.

KAEL

Boss. Are YOU okay? There hasn't been any unusual activity at the house... We just did a perimeter sweep, and all seems well. Do you need assistance??

CAMERON: MISSED CALL.

KAEL: MISSED CALL.

ROSEMARY

Ry. I need you. I was picking up some fun goodies for tomorrow, and I must have fallen and hit my head on the ice. I woke up next to my car. I was going to reach out to Kael, but he'll just be a big bag of dicks about it 💀 I don't need a damn babysitter everywhere I go!! Can you please come get me? I'm listening to music in my car in front of the old Rickety Fence.

ROSEMARY: MISSED CALL.

FUCK. That was two hours ago.

"She hit her head walking back to the car. Slipped on ice. That was two hours ago. Last text said she was in the car listening to music." I tell Cam while pinching the bridge of my nose and releasing a gust of air.

She better fucking be okay. I'll never forgive myself if something happened to her.

"I'll go," Cameron offers.

"No. I'll go. Stay here with Sailor." I grab him by the sweatshirt and tug him towards me until we are nose to nose. "Do *not* upset her. She's not ready to talk yet. You guard her with your fucking life. No one comes into this house but me or you. Got me?"

He visibly gulps. "She was my best friend, Ry. I won't let

264

anything happen to her. You have my word," he vows, his face determined and full of promise.

"Good." I pull him closer and slap his back twice before heading towards the back door.

As I am walking the dimly lit street towards my car, an eerie feeling creeps its way through my body. Like a worm wriggling its way into the soil. My phone rings, and relief fills me when I look down to see it's Rosie.

"Rosemary. Fuck. I'm so sorry. Are you alright?"

"Hello, Son."

My heart drops into my damn stomach hearing the voice on the other end of the line. The voice belonging to a man I haven't heard from since I was an adolescent.

"*Salvatore Black*. Why do you have my sister's phone? What the fuck are you playing at?" Anxiety grips me by the throat, making it sound coarse.

"You have caused quite a few issues for me these last few years. More specifically, these last few weeks. You see, your old man has started up an extremely lucrative business here in the underworld. Or it was, until a certain group of... what do you call yourselves? Your little group of vigilantes? *Demons*. Yes, that's right. You and your *Demons* started to infiltrate, disband, and execute my biggest clients. That's not all, my boy. You have not only interrupted my line of work and fucked with my spotless reputation, but have also gotten yourself involved with my right-hand man's daughter. *Sailor*. Such a unique name. She is quite the beauty. All legs and ivory skin. I can see why you fell for her. She's charming, just like your mother was. A real spitfire, that one. Except feisty women like them... with their need to always know more, always sticking their noses where they don't belong. It gets them killed, Ryder. You wouldn't want that same fate to fall on your sister or Sailor's shoulders, now would you?"

My hands shake as I process all this piece of shit is saying. *He killed my mother?!*

"I don't take well to threats, *Dad*," I say his name through gritted teeth, sarcasm dripping off my words like venom.

"You don't have a choice. Or... I guess you do," he chuckles cryptically.

The fucking ground vibrates as an explosion blows out the windows of Genevive's house, nearly knocking me over. My ears ring and my heart slams against my chest as I'm frozen in shock.

Little Ember.

Flames lick out of the windows and up the side of the house. Part of the fucking roof is blown off. Thick black smoke billows out of it. *NO. NO!* My feet slam across the overgrown grass of Sailor's family home as my father's voice infiltrates my ringing eardrums.

"Go to her, and your sister dies."

I stop in my tracks. *But what fucking choice is this?* I... I don't know what the fuck to do! Every inch of my body is screaming for me to move. To fucking go help Sailor. To get her to safety. I can't lose her. I fucking can't!

My bastard of a father isn't playing games. *Clearly.* He'll kill my sister. I can't let that happen, either. She's my baby sister. My little pink-haired pain in the ass. To never see her smile again or hear her awful singing voice. The organ in my chest beats incessantly against my sternum, and I struggle to catch my breath.

"What the fuck do you want?" I scream as tears begin to prick my eyes at the impossible decision I'm left with.

"Get in your car and meet me at the apartment of the abandoned *Rickety Fence*. Your girl's old place. Tell no one. Bring no one. If one of your men gets word about this, not only will you lose Sailor, you will lose your sister and Vanessa as well. So I suggest you smash your phone and toss the pieces. You are going to get on the right side of the underworld, Ryder. You already have the resources to expand my empire. Your clubs, your connections. I'll even look past your indiscretions. We, father and son, will run the largest arms distribution the underworld has ever seen. Add in Sailor's father, Bruce's, drug dealings that he does through his vessels out in the Atlantic...*Goddamn*. We will live like kings. Well, Bruce and *I* will until you can prove your worth to me. I may need to break you a few times until you become agreeable. Unlike your old man, you have a heart, and that is going to be a real fucking problem."

I open my car door, letting it hold me up as I look out in horror. Bright orange flames roar out of the blown-out windows of Genevive's. Car alarms are going off, and lights are beginning to flick on in the houses close by. Faint and frantic shouts of my men and Diego's can be heard over the crackling and sirens in the distance.

Please, Cam. Please get her out. I can't lose her.

Sailor. I love you. Please, baby. If you hear me, you must know that I love you. One look into your eyes in this life, and I fell for you all over again.

"I'm coming. Don't you touch a hair on their heads," I growl, spittle flying out of my mouth as I fishtail the car.

The tires screech, followed by the sound of my phone being crushed into the blacktop. I press the pedal down until it hits the floor as I race towards Sailor's old apartment.

When I arrive at the bar, I bolt out of the car and race along the side of the building towards the stairs that lead to the apartment. I take them two at a time. As I reach the landing, the door swings open, and I come face to face with my old man.

Same green eyes. Same stature. He's dressed in an all black suit with cuff links that look expensive. *And gaudy.* His greasy salt and pepper hair is slicked back. A thick gold watch with clusters of diamonds rests on the wrist of the hand he has extended my way. Glock poised and aimed at me.

Silencer and all.

My hands tremble with the desire to watch the light leave his eyes. To end this nightmare here and now.

But what about James? Are they connected somehow? What will happen to Sailor if I'm not around?

"Come take a seat, Ryder." He gestures behind him to a single wooden chair.

Not wanting to cause him to do anything impulsive, I do as I'm told.

As I pass him, he tsks. "*Ah. Ah. Ahhh.*" He reaches out, palm opened wide and extended. "Your piece."

I grind my teeth until my jaw clicks and hand him my Glock. The safety is off. Shame it didn't discharge and blow a hole through his fucking chest. *Fuck this prick.* I don't need my gun to kill him. But I won't do anything stupid until I form a plan. Because right now, I know he's serious. *A bomb?* He proved he isn't playing any games.

Christ. *Sailor could be...*

NO. I would know.

I would feel it.

I try my best to focus as I take a seat. Salvatore circles me before he leans against the wall and lights up a cigar, blowing the heavily honey-scented smoke in my face.

"Where is Rosemary?" I seethe.

He inhales deeply, the cherry glowing a cryptic orange as he chuckles to himself. "She's safe. Nice and snuggled in her bed. She'll probably have a bad headache in the morning. Although I'm sure she'll be fine. Your sister has done plenty of recreational drugs. A little blackout, little lapse in her memory won't be a surprise to her. Your guy Carlos received a false location of her whereabouts while my guys brought her home."

He pulls his phone out of his pocket and types a quick message. The sound of it sends echoes bouncing off the walls. "There, he just got an alert that she is home and went to bed after coming home from a party." He smirks, seemingly satisfied with himself.

I want to rip out his fucking tongue and make him eat it for talking about my sister like she's a goddamn junkie. And for having his men put their hands all over her while she's unconscious.

Sick fuck.

"I want proof," I demand.

The light of his phone illuminates his aging face as he clicks away. Too much time spent in the sun makes his skin appear leathery and wrinkled. Salvatore takes another deep drag before blowing the smoke out towards me once more. The room starts to fill up with its sickly sweet scent.

The room spins as I start coughing. There is a heaviness in my chest as my lungs burn. *I can't catch my fucking breath.* My chest heaves as I lean over in my chair. Prickles of pain hit my eyes next as they start to sting like a motherfucker. Then it hits me. This reaction isn't from the goddamn cigar in Sal's hand.

It's my *little ember.*

She's alive. Fuck, she's alive—for now.

I struggle to take a full breath as Sal tilts his phone in my direction. A video of Rose in her bed sleeping soundly plays out in front of me. The time on the video shows it is current.

Thank God. At least she is safe.

I must pass out. For when I come to, Sal is in my face.

"She'll remain left out of this, Ryder. As long as you continue to cooperate. Let Rosemary live her eccentric little life of parties, drugs, books, and questionable men here in Maine. Vanessa will continue to run the parts of your clubs that need attention in your absence. It's just me, you, and Bruce, now."

Bruce, Sailor's father—who clearly is just as fucked up as mine—materializes as if summoned from whatever pit of hell he came from. He casually strolls in with soot covering his shirt.

That fucking bastard. I'll kill him!

He chuckles to himself as Sal offers him a cigar and lighter from his suit pocket. The two of them nod at one another before turning back to me. Sal cracks a sadistic smile as he offers me his version of a celebratory cigar.

"Here's what we need from you..."

CHAPTER 31

SAILOR

Glass shatters around me as I am jostled around in bed. The headboard slams against the wall as my eardrums nearly burst from the explosion that just rocked the whole house. Dizziness has my head swirling; I can't get my bearings straight.

"Ryder?" I scream, reaching around the bed to where he was just lying next to me.

Thick black smoke curls in from under the door and drifts down from the ceiling. The curtains are going up in flames on either side of the bed.

No. This is just another dream.

Breathe, Sailor. It's alright.

Except it's not a dream at all. And it's far from alright. Car alarms are blaring in the distance along with faint shouting.

"Ryder?" I scream again while hopping off the bed. Glass clinks onto the floor as I try my best to step around it. I spin around in a circle, my eyes starting to adjust, the flames brightening the room. "Ryder," I cough harshly as smoke strangles the back of my throat.

My eyes water and sting as the wall to my right goes up in flames. I stumble towards the bed as my nightmare becomes my reality. Tapestry like that of my dream drapes the walls. The beautiful artwork becomes engulfed in flames in the blink of an eye. Tears slip over my cheeks and down my chin as I lower myself to the ground.

A gunshot goes off outside the hall, and my heart rate picks up to a full gallop. *Ryder.* He's out there. I just have to make it to him. With a wave of determination, I crawl my way towards the door. Smoke continues to pour in from beneath it.

Please let me get to him. Please, Please.

A coughing attack keeps me in place before I start to heave. Snot and spit drip down over my lips. I swipe it away with the back of my hand and push on.

"Ryder!" I shout, my voice nothing more than a crackled whisper.

The roof groans and sizzles as the flames cover the entirety of it. A *pop* makes me jump as heat like I have never felt before roasts my back. My fingernails crack as I dig them into the ground, dragging myself towards the door. Silver stars speckle my vision as it wavers in and out.

"You are the flames, Little Ember." Ryder's deep voice reminds me in my mind.

I will not lose him again.

Bloodied from the glass, my knees scrape along the wooden floor as I reach out to grab the doorknob. Nearly there, only an inch further. I'm about to make purchase, when it swings open. Thick black smoke rushes in, followed by a brief wave of fresh air. I inhale deeply, taking in as much as I can.

Cameron squats down and pulls me into him, cradling my head against his chest.

"I've got you, Sai. We need to move. This house is going to collapse any moment," he shouts.

He coughs roughly before pulling me up and guiding me out the door. We stumble along the walls, the hallway blurred in smoke. I can barely see a few inches in front of me.

We managed to get to the first floor, nearly missing a few steps on the way down. The front door is completely blocked off by collapsed sheetrock and wooden framing. It blazes, next to a pile of ash and ember.

Cameron looks towards the kitchen and heads that way. His arm tugs me closer, navigating us around a person face down and bleeding out on the linoleum floor. I do a double-take, pulling back in denial.

"Please tell me that's not Ryder. Please, Cameron, tell me that's not Ryder!" I screech out in hysterics.

Strong arms come around me and lift me, stepping around the person and the blood. Smoke billows around us, and the temperature of the room is unbearable as the flames close in on us. The entrance to the garage is just off the kitchen. Cameron is heading straight toward it. We both cough harshly as he stumbles forward.

Once. Twice.

We both go down.

Cameron is breathing heavily and coughing. I reach for him and try to help him up. There's no moving him. He's panting against the floor.

"Get up, Cam. Come on. The garage is right there," I demand, shaking him.

With the strength of a bull, he shoves me forward into the small room leading to the garage.

"The garage isn't an option. You're going to—" he coughs, laying his head down on the floor and groaning. "That's not Riot. He isn't here. James is dead. I... killed him. He came through that hidden door there. Behind the bookshelf. Those rumors about the..."

Another vicious wave of coughs interrupts him. "The copycat Shanghai Tunnels are true. They lead you to the wharf. To *Mayhem*. That's how he was able to get in. He's been infiltrating *The Demons'* meetings for weeks. *Go*. Get out of here, Sai. Go find Ry. NOW. I'll be right behind you."

Eyes wide and filled with tears that sting, I scramble, trying to get back up and get to him. To drag him with me if I have to. "I'm not leaving you!" I wail into the shroud of smoke.

There's an awful groan and then a massive crack before the ceiling in the kitchen collapses. Dust, smoke, and fire flare my way, blinding me.

I think I scream. Maybe it's all in my head.

Pain erupts through my lungs, and I know this is it. *My time.* They say you know when you're about to die. There's a feeling you get. *Impending doom.* Right now, that feels like a thousand knives slicing through my body.

Fire licks its way towards me, calling my name. *Beckoning me.* I open my heavy lids one last time.

My father is the last thing I see as he pulls me into his arms and enters the dimly lit, dank tunnel behind a bookshelf. The same shelf I've looked at a hundred times. All filled with books I've borrowed from Genevieve.

What. The. Fuck.

"These tunnels are an exact copy of the ones in Oregon. They were once used to kidnap sailors and bring them to boats waiting offshore at the wharf. Ironic that I'm taking *you* through them." A deep chuckle permeates the hazy barrier of my mind. "Sleep well, *Little Sailor*. Don't say your old man never did anything for you. I truly hope we don't cross paths again. But something tells me that won't be true."

A wet washcloth glides over my face, dampening it. The lids of my eyes feel glued, the singed eyelashes trapping them shut. The rhythmic movement of terry cloth continues until my eyes crack open. Dim light filters in, revealing a kind face.

"Easy there, dear," Vanessa soothes gently, her unique violet eyes swirling with concern.

Slowly, I look around until it registers where I am. The basement of *Mystical Mayhem*. The room where Ryder holds court. *The tunnels.* All at once, flashes of what happened come rushing in. A crackled, gut-wrenching sob leaves my lips as I press a hand to my dry lips.

She places a steady hand on my back and rubs small circles around the tender flesh.

"I came here as soon as the vision hit me," she explains.

Tears burn as they spill over my lids and down my cheeks. Every drop feels like a knife slicing down my face. "Cameron. He's...Oh God, Vanessa. He's dead. *He's dead.* And my dad... *my father*... he was there... he brought me here." I sob some more.

Shudders rock my whole frame as she wraps both her arms around me and pulls me into a motherly hug.

"Where is Ryder?" I croak into her shoulder. "Where was he?" I demand, my voice breaking at the end.

"I don't know, sweetheart. I just saw the vision of Cameron helping you escape through this tunnel. There was no man here when I came down. Just you. I always heard rumors of them. The image was clear of where I needed to go, but I never expected to find your little body unconscious and left broken in front of this bookshelf. It must have been hiding the tunnels this whole time, right under Ryder's nose."

"Or he knew," I accuse through clenched teeth. Teeth that are chattering even with the pressure I have placed on them. An uneasy feeling snakes its way around my intestines. I hold back a wave of nausea as I think of what this could mean.

"We will figure it out, Sailor. We need to find my son and get you to the hospital," she says more firmly.

"No. I don't want to go. *Please.* Can you just get Riot here and someone to come check me out? *Please*, Vanessa," I beg, voice hoarse as I pull back to look into her conflicted eyes.

"Alright. Can you stand? I want to at least move you to my office. You can lie on the couch as we wait."

I nod. She helps me stand, guiding me towards the elevator. When we reach it, the sound of the gears grinding alerts us to someone coming down.

My reflection off the stainless steel doors is a ghastly sight. Vanessa steps in front of me protectively as the doors slide open.

Riot stands there looking like the true dark angel he is.

His bloodshot emerald eyes immediately find mine. Horror and pain and *longing* swirl within them before they harden and become cold.

Distant.

"Oh, good. You're alive," he says harshly. A shallow laugh leaves his pursed lips. Almost indifferently. As if Genevive's house didn't just blow up. As if only a few hours before that, we weren't tangled up in the sheets.

Entwined.

Mind, body, and soul.

"Ryder William Black!" Vanessa scolds him, as appalled as I am.

"I don't have time for this right now," Riot grits between clenched teeth, side-stepping both of us and walking over to where the trapped door is leading to the tunnels.

"Ry...Cameron..." My voice wavers, knowing I'll have to be the one to tell him. "He was the one who saved me. He killed James. That bastard was in the house when the explosion happened. Cameron he...he didn't...make it," I screech, another sob leaving me. Riot's back stiffens, all the muscles in his back tense at once.

My feet guide me toward him, so confused by his behavior, but still tethered to him nonetheless. Vanessa supports me as I hobble over towards him. I go to place my palm on his back. To fall into his sturdy arms and break alongside him, but as I do, he spins abruptly towards us. Fear creeps up my spine at how cold he is.

"Vanessa. I need you to get her the fuck out of here," he roars.

I flinch and take a step back into Vanessa. For a brief

second, the muscle of his jaw tics, and his hand shakes as he gently raises it to reach for my face.

"Sailor... I..." I hear in my head. His voice is raw and panicked.

Then he continues aloud. All traces of the man I thought I trusted, *gone.*

"Apparently, I have a funeral to plan. Good news is, James is dead. You don't have to worry about him anymore. Our job here is done. You don't need me anymore." He shrugs like he couldn't care less about what happens to me next.

"I get it, Ry. You need time to process this all. So do I. But we will be okay," I croak out, then cough, bending over at the hip as I struggle to catch my breath.

Short little breaths are the only way air is entering my lungs at all. My vision starts to go again as silver speckles creep in, threatening to take me down.

The floor seems a lot closer than it just was...

His hand clasps my shoulder. "Sailor?" The panic is back. Concern filters through his voice. "Sailor!" he shouts more firmly as anxiety grips his tone.

Ice runs through my veins as my body gives out on me.

Cold. I'm so fucking cold.

The only thing tethering me here, to my body, to any reason left living for, is his warm body pressed against mine. And the feeling of safety in the chaos.

Then we are moving, and I am being shuffled.

Up and up and up we go...

CHAPTER 32

SAILOR

Three days later, we are all standing over the grave dug for my childhood friend. Sniffles and sobs echo out around us as the beautiful wooden casket is lowered into the ground. Silent sobs shake my freezing body. The muscles ache from the events and tension of the last few days.

Rose wraps a steady arm around me as her mother does the same from the other side of me. I am cocooned between two incredible women.

Two women who have done nothing but dote on and support me these last few horrendous days. I've done nothing but cry since I woke up in a hospital bed surrounded by police officers asking me a thousand questions. They believe the explosion was the result of a gas leak from the boiler.

Little do they know, James detonated a bomb that caused a massive explosion.

I won't be telling them that, though.

Even though Riot can barely stand to look at me right now, I couldn't help but protect him and his role in all of this.

As if sensing that I'm thinking about him, his eyes glance

up and connect with mine from across the grave where he stands with Cameron's wife, Stacy, and the young girls he left behind. My chest constricts as I think about the blue-eyed angel sacrificing himself to save me. Guilt and anger crush my lungs even harder. *He had a family. A wife... He shouldn't have even been there!*

I never told Cam I forgave him.

I never told him that, although I was angry and hurt with the way he treated me, I was willing to work on getting back what we once had. That I missed my best friend who made me chocolate chip pancakes and cuddled me in blankets when my dad never came home. That I was proud of the father he had become. So proud. Especially after hearing the beautiful stories told at the wake the last few nights. Seeing the family that raised him meet the family he built.

Another sob escapes me as I hold Riot's gaze. *I miss him, too.* His intense emerald eyes are shining with unshed tears as he holds Stacy to him. She cries as hard as I do. Her hands hold her babies close as they watch their father being lowered into the early spring ground.

Snow starts to fall around us. The chilly flakes tickle my nose. A small smile tugs the corner of my trembling lips. Riot tilts his head slightly, probably wondering how the hell I could be smiling right now.

Well. He lost that right when he completely abandoned me. When I needed *him*, too. When I was hurting. *Grieving.* He's not the only one.

Truth is, Cameron loved snow. Any time even a few flakes would fall, he would drag me and Liv outside and run around like a husky with the zoomies.

Fuck. I miss him.

I should have told him so.

Speaking of my other best friend...Liv, his twin, stands with her parents and boyfriend directly in front of the grave. Their family is huddled together, tossing roses onto the casket as the priest continues his closing prayer.

Liv turns to walk away, dabbing her nose and eyes with a tissue. She reaches out and squeezes my hand as I move forward to join the line forming to pay their final respects. Riot whispers something into Stacy's ear as he pats her back and slowly makes his way towards me.

My heart rate spikes as he gets nearer. Each step is like a goddamn drum. The sound grows louder and louder, pulsing in my ears as he steps closer and closer.

We haven't spoken at all since before he collected my failing body off the floor and brought me up to Vanessa's office. The ambulance met us there. Rosie told me Riot just disappeared after that. Leaving me in the care of Vanessa and the paramedics.

I don't understand. *We were fine.* Ry— *Riot* and I, we...we connected in a way that was ineffable. I finally understood what it meant to be a twin flame. To share my soul with another. To long for someone so intensely. Even when they are right in front of you. To be completely and utterly vulnerable with them. To let them see the parts of you that you hide from the rest of the world.

Sniffling, I step out of Rose and Vanessa's secure embrace. They nod knowingly and step forward together to pay their respects.

My breath hitches as Riot makes his final approach. His smoky palo santo scent coils around me like the embrace I've been craving from him.

He really does look like a dark angel today.

Sharp black suit. Black shirt. Tie. Even his cuff links and watch are black. My mind conjures up those black wings I always seem to envision him with. It makes him appear even more sinister.

He doesn't reach for me. Doesn't exchange pleasantries. Just walks up with me and tosses one rose in as I do the same. We stand there for a moment. A little bubble around us. It feels like a truce of some kind. A break from the chaos and uncertainty surrounding us. I hear him quietly sniffle and then sigh.

"Thank you, brother. For saving *her*," he whispers.

"I'm sorry, Cameron," I add. "I want you to know I forgive you. For it all. And I'm sorry, too. For not hearing you out. I promise you I will watch over your family. I will watch over your little girls. And Stacy, too. *And Riot,*" I whisper that last part.

But he heard me. He always does.

His shoulders stiffen, his spine straightens.

"I don't need you to look out for me, Sailor," he says irritably, walking past me.

I quickly catch up with him, nowhere near done talking to him. He owes me an explanation. At the very least. *Is this it then? The end of whatever we were trying to build.*

As we walk towards the lingering crowd gathered by the limos and line of cars, he looks around before pulling me off to the side. His warm hand briefly squeezes the back of my neck while his thumb skims over my tattoo. A black dahlia is pressed into my shaking palm, its petals soft against my frost-bitten palm.

"I'm leaving tonight, and I'll be gone for a while. Not sure when I'll be back. Take care of yourself, *Little Ember,*" he whispers in my ear, his voice cracking on his nickname for me.

Riot clears his throat and places a chaste kiss on my wet cheek before walking backward. Emerald eyes take me in from head to toe one last time before he enters the limo with Cameron's family.

I swipe angrily at the tears cascading down my face and glance back down at the dahlia in my hand. Its delicate petals are a haunting shade of crimson.

Betrayal.

Black dahlias represent *betrayal.*

THE END.

ACKNOWLEDGMENTS

Writing this book has been a completely different dynamic than The Triskelion Series. The addition of divination practices and magic takes this to a whole new level. For those of you who don't know, I am blessed with the ability to channel spirit. When I was younger, I always chalked it up to coincidence or just being a "Pisces." But as I got older, and really honed in on my abilities—especially after losing many loved ones—I realized I could communicate with them.

During Covid, I really dove into that side of myself that was begging to come out. That was when I had my first *awakening*. I learned Tarot and started a TikTok channel. I was so nervous to channel for others, but soon recognized that I was helping so many people receive beautiful messages. From there, I opened my Etsy page and started doing private readings. Since then, I continue to do so with more confidence and knowledge of the spiritual community and practices than ever before.

Each day, I discover more of my purpose not only in life, but in love, too. Twin flame connections are very special to me, and you'll see that in my writing.

Becoming a writer was the next big step I took on this journey. And that was where The Triskelion Series was born. A story of life, loss, and fated love. This series is all that and more, where we can discover the beautiful world of spirituality, its practices and gifts, and the twin flame mission.

I hope you enjoyed this book and will continue the series. This is only the beginning, and Sailor is just getting started with her abilities.

Now for the big thank yous for my amazing crew—who, without you all, my books would never come to completion:

First and always, my daughter Milena. Mommy loves you so much. Each and every day, you put a smile on my face. Watching you grow has been the best gift I could have ever received. I learned how to slow down and live in the moment with gratitude. In a world of go-go-go, there is nothing better than just appreciating each and every precious moment. I hope that one day (not in the near future) you read these books and never settle for a love that doesn't start a fire in your soul. With a spirit as wild and loving as yours, I hope you find another who complements you and lifts you up. Someone who grows with you, who heals with you, who finds even the smallest, most mundane moments together special. I hope one day you'll understand why I wanted that for us. Lastly, I hope you continue to read and believe in the magic that comes with it. The magic that surrounds us every day. If only we all just took a closer look.

Next up is my amazing cover and interior artist, Emily. You have been with me since my debut! Now here we are, years later, and on my second series. I am so thankful for you and your beautiful mind. You turn my ideas into the most exquisite covers. Life gets crazy for the both of us, yet you somehow manage to always answer my crazy requests, last minute changes, and questions. You are the absolute best!!! This cover slays—as always.

Janice, Amanda, Mariah, and Norell. Thank you for being my eyes and brain when they become too tired and overlook things, or just can't hit the mark. Your review and support of my books mean the world to me! Without you guys, I'd be lost. Thank you, thank you for all the reposts, comments, late night phone calls/texts, and dealing with my plot twists... hehe. You girls are amazing!

Lastly, my thank yous go to my OG crew and my spirit team. You are always showing me the way and encouraging me. Being an author has always been a big dream of mine. Your unwavering support means the world to me. My sisters, my friends, my family, and YOU– thank you so much for always believing in me. For following me on this journey and trusting the process. For falling in love with my characters. For giving me grace and a chance as an indie author. Thank you, thank you. Especially this last year. My personal life was chaos, but you always gave me reasons to keep smiling.

If you loved this book, would you please consider leaving a review? It would mean so much to me!

Until our next adventure, friends.

Luna Everly 🤍

MORE BOOKS BY LUNA EVERLY

The Triskelion Series:

Tomorrow's Never Promised

If Tomorrow Never Comes

A Promise For Tomorrow

ABOUT THE AUTHOR

Luna Everly is an indie romance author who would like to share the fantasyland she has in her mind with the world. This dream world consists of strong, sarcastic men who find themselves grounded by their smart and sassy heroines. Add a bit of suspense, impossible decisions, and amazing besties to these characters' lives--and you've got yourself quite the adventure to go on. Grab the tissues for emotional ups and downs and a fan for some seriously steamy moments.

As a Pisces, Luna often gets lost daydreaming. When she's not lost in thought, she's spending time with her daughter, family, two rescue dogs, and her clingy cats Loki & Sage. Luna enjoys cooking, game nights, getting lost in a good book, self-care bubble baths, and even the occasional marathon of Call of Duty.

You'll never find her far from her cup of coffee--or multiple, for that matter.

Luna Everly is a pen name. She currently resides in New York with her family.

GET SOCIAL

Subscribe to my **newsletter** to stay up to date
on new releases and giveaways.

Follow along with my **blog** to keep up
with me and my wild adventures.

Please consider leaving a review on
Amazon: amazon.com/author/lunaeverly
or
Goodreads: goodreads.com/author/show/30026286

It would mean the world to me! 🥹

authorlunaeverly.com

facebook.com/100088486166891
tiktok.com/@authorlunaeverly
instagram.com/authorlunaeverly

PLAYLISTS

I don't know about you, but I love listening to music while reading and writing. It makes the story even more intense and emotional for me. I hope these songs make you feel those emotions the same way!

Follow Luna Everly on Spotify for music inspiration!
https://open.spotify.com/user/316m6ysvzaqe
zo4wyehkmziwkz5q

The Triskelion Series:

Book 1: Tomorrow's Never Promised
https://open.spotify.com/playlist/
3viN4lg4bjvIJMvtCAxc7U

Book 2: If Tomorrow Never Comes
https://open.spotify.com/playlist/
3l2GbTy9ILBgKJ3ect3a7B

Book 3: A Promise For Tomorrow
https://open.spotify.com/playlist/
21qhQsyuVSET5ZYq74Kgso

The Mystical Mayhem Series:

Book 1: Divination
https://open.spotify.com/playlist/
6QGIO1Top2uof1UngzbıyZ

- If you made it this far. Thank you. Listen to *Can You Hear Me* by UNSECRET & Young Summer — this beautiful song was on repeat for the last two chapters and made me bawl like a baby.
- *How to Save a Life* cover by Ruelle also played a big part in the last few chapters. 🙂
- Of course, *Start A Riot* by Banners is Riot's theme song. I feel like it really helped build the energy of this book.